# DREAMS OF HER OWN

---

## BOOK 3

### REBECCA HEFLIN

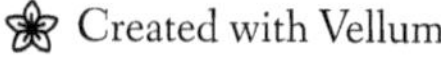 Created with Vellum

# ACKNOWLEDGMENTS

*For my readers.*

Though this is a re-release of DREAMS OF HER OWN, I'd like to, once again, I'd like to thank my ensemble of beta readers: Lynda, Yvonne, Paul, and of course, my hubby, Ron. Your feedback is invaluable.

I also owe a debt of gratitude to Linda Lombardino for her insight into dyslexia and all its facets. Any mistakes in my portrayal of the disorder are purely my own.

# QUOTE

*It's better to be absolutely ridiculous than absolutely boring.*

– Marilyn Monroe

# CHAPTER ONE

If the *Guinness Book of World Records* had a category for the world's most boring life, Millie Stephens knew she would hold the record.

Bundled up in her brown wool coat against the chill of a New York fall, she hurried down the Brooklyn sidewalk to the pharmacy to pick up a prescription for her boss.

As personal assistant for best-selling romance author Darcy Butler-Ryan, Millie kept her calendar, edited her manuscripts, handled her social media, and through her agent, Gloria Madison, scheduled her public appearances, among other duties. Since Darcy had become pregnant, Millie had also taken it upon herself to run errands and generally oversee Darcy's health and well-being.

Thus, the trip to the pharmacy for Darcy's anti-nausea medication.

Millie consulted the day's to-do list to see what other errands were on it. Lists were her life. They provided organization, structure, and a sense of accomplishment. She loved ticking things off her list so much that if she accomplished something that wasn't on the list, she'd write it down just so she could have the pleasure of marking it off.

She had a list for everything. Errands. Tasks. Books to be read. Special dates to remember. If something needed doing, she had a list for it, all appropriately categorized, of course. Shoving her errand list into her coat pocket, she stopped at the corner and waited for the pedestrian signal. As soon as the light changed, she stepped out into the pedestrian crosswalk, anxious to get to the pharmacy and out of the cold. She glanced to her left and froze. A delivery truck barreled down the street as if the red light meant nothing. And as if she truly were invisible.

Fear stole her ability to move and she scrunched her eyes closed hoping death would at least be quick.

Next thing she knew she was yanked from behind and hauled up against a hard object, bands of steel around her waist, her feet dangling in the air.

"Are you okay?" a gruff male voice asked, his breath warm in her ear.

She nodded, unsure if she could do any more than that.

"I'm going to set you back on your feet. Do you think you can stand?"

Nodding again, she realized the hard object at her back was a man's chest, and the steel bands were his arms. She slid down his body and felt the sidewalk beneath her feet. A wave of dizziness washed over her.

"Breathe." Her rescuer turned her to face him, his hands on her shoulders, and she gazed up and into eyes the color of a winter-gray sky, earnest with concern. His already-tousled brown hair ruffled in the wind whipping around the corner, and his chin bore the stubble so many women were fond of.

Millie inhaled deeply, drawing in the scent of something spicy and leathery.

"Better?"

She nodded, still speechless.

"You should always wait after the signal changes before you cross a street. I've got an appointment. You're sure you're okay?"

She nodded.

"Be more careful next time," the stranger in the leather jacket said before he turned to walk away.

Millie managed to put one foot in front of the other for another block before coming to a bus stop and collapsing onto the bench. Her legs shook, her hands quivered, and she struggled to take in a deep breath. All she could think about was how your life was supposed to flash before your eyes when confronted with a near-death experience, and hers . . . didn't. Instead it was like a film projector that had run out of film—a blank screen.

What did that mean?

*It means, Millicent Grace Stephens, that your life has been so boring that the highlight reel is nonexistent.* Her thirtieth birthday was right around the corner, and what had she accomplished with her life?

Not much, *that's* what.

Sure, she had a bachelor's in literature, summa cum laude, with a focus on the Middle Ages from Sarah Lawrence College. She had a job she loved. And she could support herself. Other than that, she might as well have become a nun for all the excitement her life held.

She recalled the hard strength of her rescuer's chest against her back. The rough and tumble look of him. She'd bet her first edition autographed copy of Edith Wharton's *Age of Innocence* that *his* life wasn't boring. That if he had a near-death experience he'd have a highlight reel worthy of an action movie.

Rising on still-wobbly legs, she drew in a long, slow breath then resumed her errand in an I-almost-died daze.

———

The sun warmed Ian's back through his leather jacket as he weaved his motorcycle through the Manhattan traffic. The cold start to the day had given way to brilliant blue skies and crisp fall air with a hint of warmth to come later in the day. But for now, the brisk temperatures called for jacket and gloves.

He'd spent most of the morning out in Westchester, meeting with electricians and plumbers about the mansion he was remodeling. Then out to an architectural salvage company to check out a set of exterior doors for the mansion before looking at a job in Brooklyn, where his day had taken an unexpected turn—that of rescuing a distracted woman from certain death.

Funny, when he'd spotted her standing, petrified, watching the oncoming delivery truck, he'd thought she was an elderly woman in her frumpy clothes and sensible shoes, but when he'd seen her face, he'd been shocked to see a young woman. Pretty face, despite the brown glasses and brown knit hat.

She'd scared ten years off his life. Idiot driver didn't even slow down for the red light. Just barreled right through the intersection almost taking out the poor woman. He sure hoped she was okay, that she wasn't in shock or anything.

Now he was meeting his best friend, Caleb Montgomery, an electrician by trade, who owned an up-and-coming commercial and residential electrical contracting company. Caleb had a potential new client he wanted Ian to meet.

To that end, Ian pulled up at a quaint four-story wood building, squeezed between two multi-story brick buildings. According to Caleb, the Upper East Side house, built in 1866, was one of five remaining wood buildings in the neighborhood. A real historical gem.

Caleb paced along the sidewalk, smartphone to his ear, gesturing with his free hand. Tall and rangy, he seemed more at home in jeans, boots, and flannel shirts. Seeing him in wool slacks, a sweater, and a tweed jacket made Ian itch.

He and Caleb met on a construction job years ago, not long after Ian had acquired his general contractor's license, and his business plan as an historical preservation and renovation contractor had just been a longshot. Caleb too had plans to start his own business, and he'd encouraged Ian to do the same. They'd had each other's backs ever since.

Waiting for his friend to end his call, he checked his voice messages and emails. While not exactly a techie, he appreciated the convenience of smartphones and grudgingly admitted they made his job a lot easier by allowing him to handle problems on the fly. And the text to voice feature was a godsend for him. With no major fires to douse, he locked his phone just as Caleb approached him.

"What's up, man?" Caleb asked.

Ian snorted. "I should ask you that. What's with the get up? You look like a metrosexual."

"Had a meeting with a big client today. Jillie suggested I take it up a notch."

Jillie was Caleb's wife and business manager.

Ian snorted. "Next thing you know you'll be getting a manicure and manscaping."

"Funny. Question is, when are you going to start dressing the part, hotshot?"

"Oh, no. You're not turning me into a metrosexual. I like my jeans, T-shirts, and leather jacket just fine."

Caleb shook his head in mock disappointment before walking with Ian to the front door. "The McKenzies bought the house last month. Just a warning, the previous owner stripped the interior of all its historic features." At Ian's expression, Caleb continued. "I know. Breaks your heart to hear. But the good news is the McKenzies want to restore it to its former glory, which means a new project for you."

"All right. Let's see her."

———

The next day, Millie set aside the manuscript she was editing to gaze out the window at Darcy's tidy backyard. The elm tree stood naked and leafless in the late-November cold.

As workplaces went, working out of Darcy's Park Slope brownstone provided lots of perks, like a cozy office, a garden view, a full kitchen, and all the hot tea she could drink. Picking up the mug at her elbow, she took a sip of Earl Grey and her thoughts turned to her close encounter with death yesterday.

She'd been weighing her options and considering her next steps. Because, really, she needed to get a life.

"I'm ready," she said to the empty room. Ready to step out of the shadows where she'd spent most of her adolescence and all of her adult life. Ready to stop hiding from the world. And from herself.

A change was in order. To that end, she'd created a new list: Millie's Get a Life List or GALL for short. The list had two categories: Goals and Dreams. The categories were separate because to her mind, goals and dreams were two entirely different animals. Goals were realistic and personally achievable, while dreams, well, they were the polar opposite. Just pie-in-the-sky notions she had no hope of ever fulfilling. Like becoming a sex symbol. Not in the cards for her. Ever.

She'd started with the category of Goals.

Reaching into her pocket, she took out the list-in-progress. She considered this list to be a living document, one to be expanded as new opportunities presented themselves. First, finish the historical romance novel she'd been secretly writing off and on for years now.

She frowned. Writing a romance novel somehow felt disloyal to Darcy, even though Darcy wrote contemporary romance. She'd better work through that, otherwise what was the point of writing the novel if she wasn't going to seek its publication.

Number Two in the Goals category: sex. This one made her squirm just looking at it. She had no idea how to go about accomplishing that item, making the possibility so remote she thought about moving it to the Dreams category. Chewing on her lower lip, she wondered if maybe she shouldn't reverse those two. Sex, then completing the romance novel.

She snorted. If she did that, she might never finish the novel. Besides, having sex was key to writing authentic scenes in her novel.

Deciding to leave the order as is—she didn't have to accomplish the items in order, after all—she moved on to the next item. Get drunk. Okay, not a laudable goal, but something she'd never experienced.

As for the Dreams category, it held only two items: find

love and find happiness and not necessarily in that order. Reconsidering, she took her pencil and drew a line through 'happiness,' writing 'contentment' instead. In her experience, happiness was an unattainable elevated emotion, especially for her. But she could settle for contentment.

She stared at the two dreams. They were too vague.

As a consummate list maker, she knew the more specific the item or goal, the greater the chance of accomplishing it. Tapping the pencil against her lips, she pondered that issue a moment. She didn't know what would make her content, so how was she supposed to quantify that on the list?

And as for love, well, she didn't think love was meant for people like her. People who often preferred the company of a good book to that of other people. And who would ever be interested in the likes of her? Making Number Two close to impossible, she realized. Maybe she should change 'love' to 'strong like.' Or, at the very least, 'respect.'

The grandfather clock in the foyer chimed eleven o'clock. "Stop daydreaming and get back to work," she muttered. Stuffing the paper back into her pocket, she'd ponder contentment and love later. Right now, she had some tweets to schedule.

———

Contemplating the mountain of paperwork on his desk, Ian decided in favor of proactive procrastination. Picking up the slip of paper with Darcy Ryan's number on it, he tapped it into his phone.

Gloria had asked him to call Darcy ASAP about a remodeling job, and since he owed Gloria more than he could ever repay, this much he could do. He'd just have to figure out how to juggle it with the other jobs he currently had going.

"Hello?"

"Hi, this is Ian Brand, Gloria said you'd be expecting my call to set up an appointment about a room remodel."

"Yes, Mr. Brand. Let me check the calendar."

*Whoa!* He held the phone away from his ear as if he could actually see who was speaking. The voice on the other end of the call could have been that of a phone sex operator, all husky and full of promise.

"I know it's short notice, but would one o'clock today work?" the Voice asked.

"Sure." He'd squeeze it in, if no other reason than to meet the owner of that voice.

"Do you need the address?"

"No. I have it."

"Fine. See you at one, then."

He ended the call, wondering if The Voice belonged to Darcy. And if her appearance matched her fuck-me voice.

# CHAPTER TWO

Millie hung up the phone and entered the appointment on Darcy's calendar. She refused to use the iPad Darcy had purchased for her last year, preferring to stick with the tried and true Daily Planner. She knew this made her a Luddite, but better a Luddite than a digital addict. Besides, she used technology enough in other aspects of her job.

Finished with the social media posts, she retrieved the draft chapters of Darcy's latest manuscript, *You Had Me at Merlot,* picked up her red pencil, and returned to the edits.

───

After climbing off his Harley, Ian carefully checked the number on the Park Slope brownstone against the number he'd entered into his phone. Confirming the address, he approached the door, rang the bell, and turned around to admire the tidy brownstones lining the street, many decorated for the fall holidays.

He'd always admired the Park Slope neighborhood in

Brooklyn, with its stately Victorian Era brownstones and their limestone carvings and ornate ironwork. And with Prospect Park nearby, it was a great place to raise a family. Much nicer than his own childhood neighborhood.

When the door opened, he turned to see a petite woman, clearly pregnant, her compact belly resembling a soccer ball.

"You must be Ian," she said as she opened the door wider for him to enter. "I'm Darcy. Thanks for coming on such short notice."

Pretty, but definitely not the woman he'd spoken with on the phone. Unlike that husky voice, her voice was bright, cheerful. "Sure."

Ian stepped into the foyer, surveyed the place, pleased to see that the owner had kept the character of the old building in the little details, like the crown molding, hardwood floors, and plaster ceiling medallions. So many renovated brownstones looked more like cold, empty boxes, all signs of their historic architecture stripped in favor of minimalism with its hard lines and cold surfaces. The eclectic mix of contemporary furnishings and antique accents in this one created a perfect balance of home and style.

He also searched for someone who could be The Voice, before turning back to Darcy. "Gloria said you wanted to renovate a room for a nursery."

"Yes. Right this way."

Darcy preceded him up the stairs talking about the previous work she'd done on the place, how long she'd lived there, and her April due date. "I hope you can complete the work by March so I can get the furniture moved in and the room set up." She entered a bedroom furnished with that same combination of current and past.

Ian stepped inside, eyeing the space. "Gloria said to

spare no expense." He turned back to Darcy, "So what did you have in mind?"

"Gloria's far too generous."

Can't argue with that, Ian thought. Beneath Gloria's prickly exterior beat the heart of a fairy godmother, someone who thrived on random acts of kindness.

Stepping over to what should have been a closet, Darcy said, "The previous owner, for reasons that escape me, installed cabinets where the closet used to be, but I'd like the closet back." She then proceeded to share her ideas for the space, while Ian took notes. She had a good eye for details, and he thought the two of them would get along just fine. "I'd like to take this room from baby to toddler and up through high school without any major renovations."

He nodded. "I think I can handle that."

"I'd also like to open this wall for an entrance to the bathroom on the other side, and close off the current hall entrance."

"Show me."

Darcy took him around to the other side.

"We'll need to revamp the bathroom. Relocate the major fixtures," Ian said as he studied the space. If he moved the tub/shower along the far wall, shifted the vanity and toilet a foot or so to the left, it could work.

"Will that be a problem?"

"I don't think so. Do you have blueprints for the home? This would help with my drawings, eliminate any surprises, and consequently, speed up the renovation process."

"Sure. I'll just go get them for you."

Ian stepped back into the bedroom, pulled out a tape measure and began by measuring the room's two windows. Making some notes on his clipboard, he walked over to the cabinets the previous owner had installed. Kneeling on the floor, he opened up a cabinet to see if it had been attached to the wall, or if the cabinets were just a front. Sticking his head inside to look around he heard The Voice, in chastisement mode, right outside the door.

"Why do you keep going up and down the stairs? Tell me what you need and I'll get it for you."

In his haste to see who spoke, he banged his head on the top of the cabinet. "Ow! Shit," he muttered, rubbing his head. Stepping out into the hallway, he didn't see anyone. The Voice had vanished.

"I'm looking for the blueprints," Darcy yelled from downstairs. "Where did I put them?"

Shaking his head, he turned back to the room, measured the square footage then jotted the number down. The sound of footsteps carried up the stairs.

"Mr. Brand, I'd appreciate it if you'd—"

The Voice.

Ian whirled to find another petite woman holding out a roll of blueprints. The same woman he'd saved from becoming New York City roadkill the day before.

Dressed from head-to-toe in brown, her brown hair pulled back into a bun, brown-rimmed eyeglasses framing brown eyes open wide in surprise, she resembled some prim, uptight spinster from a gothic novel. Her baggy brown sweater covered an equally baggy brown dress, but the biggest libido-killer was the brown orthopedic shoes on her feet. They reminded him of the shoes his aging fifth grade teacher had worn. No wonder he'd thought she was old when he'd rescued her.

Suffice it to say, her appearance served as a cold shower to douse the erotic visions her voice had evoked.

"Are you okay?" he asked.

The woman in brown nodded, as speechless as she'd been after her near miss.

"You were saying?" At her continued silence, he prompted, "You'd appreciate it if I didn't . . . what?"

She blinked. "Oh, if you didn't, um, send Dar— I mean, Mrs. Ryan on these errands," she said.

He took the blueprints from her. "I'm sorry. I didn't realize Mrs. Ryan had to go downstairs."

Who was this woman, and what was she to Mrs. Ryan? Were they a couple? he wondered. The woman before him appeared flustered, her chest rising and falling rapidly as if she'd just run up the stairs.

"Are you sure you're okay?"

"I'm fine. Thank you. And thank you . . . for, for saving me," she stammered.

"You're welcome."

She continued to stand there, staring at him.

"Is there something else?" Ian asked, growing uncomfortable.

"N—No. Nothing." She turned toward the stairs, muttering over her shoulder, "Um, Mrs. Ryan will be downstairs waiting for you when you're done."

Right. Still in shock maybe? Either that or she had a speech impediment. Not that he could cast any stones.

He made a few more notes, took some additional measurements, then headed down the stairs. He found Mrs. Ryan in the living room, stretched out on a chaise, reading. No sign of The Voice. She'd so unnerved him that he'd failed to ask her name. "Mrs. Ryan—"

"Please, call me Darcy." She set aside her book.

"Darcy. I'll take a look at the blueprints and should have some plans drawn up for you by the end of next week."

"Oh, but that's Thanksgiving."

"Right. How about next Wednesday, then? Should I give you a call when they're ready?"

"That's terrific! Thanks." Darcy started to rise.

"No, please don't get up." He walked over, shook her hand.

"Thank you, again."

He nodded. "I'll be in touch."

———

Millie hid in the kitchen waiting for Ian to leave and attempted to slow her racing heart. With a population of eight-point-four million people in New York City, she attempted to run a quick calculation of the odds of the contractor for the nursery renovation being the same man who'd rescued her yesterday, but she couldn't get her left brain to function properly. Her right brain seemed to have taken over.

Ian Brand stole her breath, along with her composure. She must have been too overcome by shock yesterday to notice his utter . . . maleness.

She'd never met anyone like him. He looked like a thug in his black leather jacket, dark hair all mussed, his face covered in stubble. Tall, a good foot taller than she, he'd been confident. Imposing. Sexy. Not her usual encounter with the male species.

And he'd also saved her from becoming another pedestrian versus motor vehicle death statistic.

She placed a hand low on her abdomen. Just the thought of him had something warm and tingly curling low in her belly. Another new sensation that started in her scalp and ended in her toes leaving her hyper-sensitized. Her clothes felt scratchy and cumbersome.

She'd never experienced this . . . awareness . . . of a man before.

Of course she'd read about the physical manifestations of attraction—the breathlessness, the racing heart, the sweaty palms—all the result of a flood of norepinephrine to the brain. But she'd never personally experienced them. Until now. Even Kevin Hardy had failed to shake up her insides like this. Add knight-in-shining-armor to the mix, and it was a devastating combination.

She also knew the body and the brain didn't always line up when it came to physical attraction, which explained why so many women made bad relationship choices.

What did it matter, anyway? She'd read the disappointment in his eyes when he'd seen her. She got that a lot.

"Don't be ridiculous," she admonished. "He's a thug." A polite thug, but a thug just the same. Not her type at all.

She snorted at the absolute absurdity of that thought. Her *type*. Who was *she* to have a type?

Millie shook her head then set her attention to preparing Darcy's favorite herbal tea. Placing the teakettle on the stove, she opened the cupboard, taking down the box of lemon-ginger tea. Still holding the box, she sighed, gazing into space. If she was completely honest with herself, she did have a type. At least in her fantasies.

*He's smart, well-read, and loves music and art. He's also kind, quiet, and thoughtful. If he's handsome, that's a bonus, but not a requirement. And above all else, he sees inside her soul and loves what he sees.*

The kettle released a shrill whistle, yanking Millie out of her daydream.

She heard the front door shut just as she'd loaded the tray with the tea and some sliced fruit. As she entered the living room, her favorite shoes squeaking on the hardwood floor, she found Darcy watching The Thug out the window.

Setting the tray down, Millie stood behind her, hands on her hips. "Hmph. Of course he rides a motorcycle." Guilt jabbed her. He'd saved her life after all. Unable to help herself, she, too, watched as he slung a denim-clad leg over the motorcycle before pulling on his helmet, and zipping up his leather jacket. It was a nice leg, too. And of course he had another one to match.

She shivered. How the man could stand riding that death machine in the cold late-November air was completely beyond her.

Darcy snickered. "You have something against Ian?"

Millie started, not realizing Darcy was watching her. Where should she begin? A man like that probably had a different woman every night in some seedy bar in Brownsville. "I can't believe Gloria recommended him. Why would she send a thug over here to remodel a nursery?"

"It's her gift, I guess she can hire whomever she likes," Darcy said. "I like him. He's the perfect bad-boy hero, all yummy edginess and gruff appearance."

Millie rolled her eyes as Darcy settled back on the chaise. "I think you've written too many romance novels." Millie drew a light blanket over her legs, tucking it in over her belly.

Shaking her head, Darcy continued, "Millie, I'm pregnant, not sick."

Millie stood, hands on her hips. "Even so. You don't need to catch cold."

"Ooh!" Darcy grabbed Millie's hand and placed it on her stomach. "He kicked. Feel it?"

She had a habit of doing that now. Any unsuspecting

person could suddenly find his or her hand pressed against Darcy's belly. Millie felt a flutter beneath her palm and her eyes suddenly went damp with emotion. Hard to believe that in a few short months, Darcy would be bringing a baby into the world.

Blinking, she composed herself, but as she turned to go, Darcy held on to her hand. Her eyebrows winged up in surprise. And discomfort. Displays of affection were not high on any of Millie's lists.

"Thank you, Millie." Darcy patted her hand. "For everything. If there's ever anything I can do for you, all you have to do is ask. You know that, right?"

Feeling her chest tighten, she withdrew her hand. "Don't be silly. What would I ever need?"

Hearing the motorcycle roar to life, Millie glanced out the window once more just as Ian pulled out onto the street. Hmm. Maybe she'd add 'death machine ride' to her GALL.

## CHAPTER THREE

Rolling his Harley through the steel roll-up door of his Brooklyn warehouse loft, Ian looked forward to a hot meal and an even hotter shower. He brushed off the light rain that had begun to fall a few blocks from home. No worries, a little water wouldn't hurt the loft's concrete floors.

He and Caleb had purchased the four-story, ten-thousand-plus square foot Williamsburg warehouse near the Navy Yard as an investment. The spacious old building had good bones—he'd checked them out himself—and would provide ample space for subdivided apartments when he and Caleb were ready to start. They'd been working with an architect on a design to renovate the other three floors, along with the basement, which would serve as storage and laundry facilities for the residents.

For the time-being, the ground floor provided him a place to house all of his passions in one place. The space served as his home, office, and workshop, as well as his garage.

Flipping on lights, he debated what he wanted first: hot

food or hot shower. The shower won out, so he climbed the stairs to the loft area he'd built over the last few months in the north corner of the space.

Directly beneath the loft he'd put in an eat-in-kitchen, laundry area, and half bath. The half bath came as an after-thought when he got tired of climbing the stairs every time nature called.

His next downstairs project—a personal library and a killer sound system for his music and audiobooks.

So far, the corner of the loft area held a bedroom, small sitting area, and bathroom. He'd found a twelve-by-nineteen-inch Persian area rug in the house he was remodeling in Westchester County. The owners of the house had discovered it in the attic and were throwing it out. He'd been more than happy to take it off their hands.

Either they didn't know what they had, or, more likely, just didn't care. After some phone calls and a fortuitous meeting with an interior designer in an architectural salvage store, he'd traced it back to the late nineteenth century as a Kashan rug signed by the master-weaver Mohtashem.

He removed his boots and socks and padded across the rug barefoot, enjoying the feel of the plush wool beneath his tired feet.

Other than a bed and an antique wardrobe, the rug was the only other furnishing upstairs, unless you counted the sixty-inch flat screen TV hanging on the exposed brick wall, which contrary to popular opinion, wasn't for sports. No, it was for his favorite shows like *This Old House* or HGTV's *Rehab Addict*. That Nicole Curtis is one hot contractor. Something about a woman with a tool belt and a nail gun.

After stripping, he flipped on the hot water and stepped into the spray. Being in the construction business, an added bonus was access to high end products at builder's prices.

He groaned in pleasure as the body sprayers pounded his aching muscles into submission.

What a day. It had started in Westchester County where he was renovating an early twentieth century mansion on the Hudson River. The trophy wife had ideas for the house that made his head hurt. Then it was back to the City for a meeting with the foreman of a boutique hotel job he'd started just last week in SoHo. After that, he'd headed back to the loft with the best of intentions—tackling the ever-growing mountain of paperwork on his desk.

He poured some shampoo into his hand and lathered his hair. He really needed to hire a personal assistant. Business was good, but not good enough that he could justify that expense. Not yet. His company currently had no full-time employees, other than himself. He had a bookkeeper to wrangle the accounts payable and receivable, and he preferred to contract with subs for everything construction-related, including his job foremen. Those expenses took a good chunk of change.

Aside from his personal carpentry skills, his greatest skillset lay in orchestrating the work, a team of top trades-people who worked well together, and truly love and respected the work that they did. That was how he managed to hire the best in the business. His ability to visualize the space in all its historical glory allowed him to stay true to the period.

His thoughts circled back to his latest job—the nursery renovation. Looked easy enough, barring any unforeseen structural problems with revamping the bathroom. He'd sub out the plumbing work, maybe the electrical—to Caleb, of course—but he'd do the rest, as Gloria had requested. Said she had her reasons.

Gloria had been the first to give him a chance when he'd

started his business. As a new business owner, Ian had taken just about any renovation that had come his way. She'd started him off with one room of her Gramercy Park townhome, a spare bathroom. He must have impressed her because she'd hired him to do the rest of the place. His first major renovation. And, thanks to her, he'd received even more job referrals. Her referrals alone had kept him in work for over a year. And while he could now focus on what he loved most—major historic renovations—he'd taken the Park Slope job because he owed Gloria the favor.

A vision of The Voice appeared. What woman dressed herself head-to-toe in brown? He wondered what her story was. He recalled her petite little frame against him after he'd hauled her out of the street. Much smaller than her clothes implied.

Shutting off the water, he grabbed a towel, and headed for the 'closet,' a battered late nineteenth century wardrobe he'd found in a used furniture store. Once he got around to refinishing it, he'd have a beautiful piece. Until then, it served.

He liked to think he looked beneath the surface of things to see the beauty beneath. Old buildings, ill-used furniture, and his latest completed project, his 1978 Harley SuperGlide. The last bike Harley made called "the Milwaukee vibrator," because of the way it vibrated everything loose while riding. What appeared to be a rusted hunk of metal to most people, he'd painstakingly restored over the course of the last year to reveal the hidden beauty.

Grabbing sweats and a worn T-shirt, he threw them on, then headed down to the kitchen for that hot meal, and the chore his disability made so difficult. Paperwork.

————

A week later, the alarm buzzed, waking Millie from a dream. Ian had pulled the pins from her bun, and was just pressing passionate kisses to her neck, his bad-boy stubble scraping against her skin sending delicious tremors up her spine. She sat up with a start, glancing around her studio apartment.

"Abelard and Heloise!" She hadn't seen the man in a week, and he still starred in her dreams.

She slapped the button on the clock silencing the alarm. The sounds of her upstairs neighbor, stage-name Chelsea Chandler, already practicing her dance routine for some off-off-off-Broadway performance she'd landed echoed off the walls.

"Thank God it isn't tap," Millie muttered as she made her way, all five feet of it, to her kitchen. Putting the kettle on for tea with one hand, she opened the fridge with the other reaching for the cream.

She'd stop by Darcy's favorite bakery and pick up some Morning Glory muffins for breakfast. Darcy didn't exactly rise with the sun. Most mornings Millie arrived before Darcy'd ventured downstairs, but she didn't mind. She enjoyed the quiet time between Josh, Darcy's husband, leaving for his office at the law firm, and Darcy's rising. That would end once the baby came along.

Taking her mug of tea with her, she opened the cubby that served as her closet. Should she wear the brown dress, or the brown skirt and sweater? "Take a walk on the wild side." Closing her eyes, she reached into the back of the closet and grabbed the first thing she touched. "Oh, the brown corduroy dress with the tiny mustard yellow flowers. That's different."

After brushing and flossing her teeth, she twisted her

long brown hair into a bun and secured it with hairpins. "That should do it."

Picking up her copy of *What to Expect When Your Expecting* from the nightstand, she tucked the book into her backpack.

She slid on her brown SAS moccasins, and grabbing her heavy coat prepared to bundle up for her eight block walk to the subway.

———

"Hi, Millie. Bye, Millie," Josh said as he rushed out the front door Millie had just unlocked.

"Bye." Closing the door behind her, she shivered as the warm air inside touched her chilled face. Walking straight to the kitchen she unloaded her bundles. After shucking her coat, hat, scarf and gloves, she headed to what served as her office in the brownstone. Last year, Darcy had remodeled a room on the third floor as her writing space, leaving the one downstairs for Millie's use.

First up, check Darcy's calendar to ensure she didn't need to wake her for any meetings or appointments. Nothing on the schedule until two when she sees . . . *Romeo and Juliet! Ian.* Her hand flitted to her hair of its own volition, as if to check its tidiness.

Embarrassed by the unaccustomed girlie reflex, she cleared her throat and recited the periodic table of elements: "Hydrogen, helium, lithium, beryllium . . ." The calming effect of the recitation steadied her as always.

"I can handle this."

Dragging up a seat at the desk, she glanced over the morning's to-do list. Some social media posts to schedule, the newsletter to draft and send out, a few autographed books to mail out, some phone calls to return, and a list of topics to research for the latest manuscript. Nothing too taxing.

She couldn't say the same about seeing Ian again that afternoon. That might tax her more then she cared to admit.

Absurd.

She wasn't that timid, anxiety-ridden teenage girl anymore. The one who didn't fit in. The one who cared what people thought about her. Not that she fit in now. It just didn't matter anymore. So what if a man like Ian completely dismissed her?

Only it wasn't just men like Ian. It was *all* men. Except for Josh, of course. And Darcy's brother, Brandon, and his life partner, David. But they were gay, so really, did that count? And then there was Nathan, the husband of Darcy's best friend, Laura. They noticed her. Were kind to her.

Darcy and her family always made Millie feel included.

So really, what did she care if men had no interest in her? She had her few friends, she had her books, and she had her job.

Of course, that made achieving Number Two on her list difficult at best. A naughty thought flitted through her brain. She could pay for sex. Cringing, she dismissed the idea. She didn't relish the thought of calling Josh to bail her out of jail for solicitation. And what man would want to have sex with her, no matter the payout?

No. She'd have to come up with another plan. But what?

Her boss stirred above, so Millie headed back to the kitchen to make tea and set out the muffins. Since Darcy woke each day with morning sickness, Millie liked to have a cup of lemon-ginger tea waiting when she staggered into the kitchen.

Darcy stumbled in a little while later, her hair in a messy twist, looking pale. "Boy. Whoever said their pregnancy was a breeze never had morning sickness."

Millie thrust the cup tea into Darcy's hand. "Sit." Covering the muffins for later in the morning when Darcy's appetite usually returned with a vengeance, she made herself a cup of tea and sat with Darcy.

"I heard from Laura last night." Darcy blew on her cup of tea. "She and Nathan will be home next Thursday." She took a careful sip, then sighed with pleasure.

Laura, formerly known as Queen of the Booty Calls, had shocked everyone when she and Nathan got engaged. They'd married the beginning of November on board the *Nave dei Sogni,* the ship on which they'd met, in the middle of the Mediterranean.

Millie had been invited—her first trip abroad—and the experience had whetted her appetite. The museums, the cathedrals, the art, and the history of Italy, she couldn't get enough.

"No broken bones, then?" After their wedding and a week on the ship with their guests, Laura and Nathan had flown off to the Swiss Alps for skiing. She'd rather have headed to the UK, to the Bodleian Library in Oxford, or maybe Trinity College Old Library in Dublin. Or both. If you're going to dream, might as well dream big.

Darcy cautiously sipped her tea. "No, but I'm guessing they left behind some broken beds."

"And on that note, I'm off to work," Millie said. "There are Morning Glory muffins in the basket when you get hungry. Let me know if you need anything."

With Ian Brand on the brain, the question was whether she'd get anything done.

# CHAPTER FOUR

Engrossed in her editing, Millie lost track of time until the doorbell rang. "Darcy and Elizabeth! It's Ian." Setting aside her work, she drew herself up, and just as she reached up to pat her hair, she snatched her hand away.

Already flustered, she opened the door to find him standing on the porch looking all scruffy and confident. And sexy. She envisioned a thought bubble above her head, and in it read 'Holy hot guy, Batman.'

"Oh, hi," Ian said, sounding disappointed. "I have a meeting with Darcy."

When Millie didn't respond, he continued, "Today. At two. Which is . . . now."

"Oh. Right."

"Millie, is that Ian?" Darcy called down from upstairs.

"Yes. But don't come down. He'll come up," Millie responded. Stepping back from the door, Millie let him in. "She'll meet you in the nursery."

"Thanks."

He breezed past her, the scent of his soap or cologne, she didn't know which, mixed with the hint of leather from his jacket, making her almost dizzy, he smelled so good. She had to concentrate on not inhaling like she'd just surfaced from the deep end of the pool, the fact that she couldn't swim making her metaphor a bit absurd.

She watched as he climbed the stairs, fascinated by the way his jacket bunched over the muscles of his back. And then there was the glute area, which his jeans hugged lovingly. Shaking her head at her own fancies, Millie forced herself back to the office to return to her work.

She appreciated beauty, in all its forms. Painting, music, sculpture, and especially the written word. She was just appreciating the beauty of a fine male form, not unlike Michelangelo's *David*. At least that was what she told herself, as she imagined Ian as naked as that famous statue. *Jane and Rochester! Is it hot in here?*

No sooner had she settled back at the desk when Darcy called her to come up.

Heaving a heavy sigh, Millie set the work aside yet again, and climbed the stairs to the second floor. When she entered the room to be renovated, Ian and Darcy were bent over the blueprints laid out on the bed, the only surface in the room large enough to accommodate them.

"Come see the drawings," Darcy said, her face beaming with excitement. She reached out and drew Millie between her and Ian.

Ian glanced up at her, making her knees wobble and her heart stutter. This close, she got a good whiff of him, and he smelled like heaven . . . and leather. The heat of a flush engulfed her face. She'd once read that blood travels at about zero-point-seven miles per hour, meaning her flush took all of point five seconds to manifest itself.

"This is where we'll cut the door to the bathroom," he

was saying, "which will require us to move the shower/bath along this wall."

She tried to pay attention to the schematics, but all she could think about as she watched his fingers slide over the drawings as he pointed out details were how beautiful his hands were. Strong. Square. Capable. Not the pale hands of a man who spent his time in libraries researching dusty old tomes, like her father. But the hands of a man who clearly made his living with them. In other words, not the kind of man with whom she would have anything in common.

———

I an glanced up to gauge Darcy's reaction and instead found himself looking into Millie's face. She gnawed nervously on her bottom lip, drawing his eyes to her mouth. A mouth that featured a rosy, lush bottom lip.

His eyes slid back to her face, where a faint blush had appeared. *Jesus.* Just a look was enough to make her blush?

"I love it," Darcy said. "What do you think, Millie?"

"Um, yes. It's—It will be very functional," Millie stammered.

"Millie, you okay?" Darcy asked. "You look a little flushed. I hope you're not coming down with something."

As Ian gazed at Millie, the flush deepened.

"I'm fine. I, uh, I just remembered, I need to call your publicist." Millie spun on her heel, almost running into the doorjamb before he heard her practically sprint down the stairs.

"Huh," Darcy said as she stepped into the hall to watch her progress. "I wonder what's got into her?"

Besides a whole lot of strange? Ian rolled up the blueprints, securing them with a rubber band. "These are yours."

"Thank you." Darcy took the blueprints from him. "When can you start?"

"You don't want to look them over with . . .?" He wasn't sure what to say. The relationship between Millie and Darcy remained a mystery. Life partner? Housekeeper? Future nanny? Spinster sister?

"My husband? Definitely. But he'll defer to whatever I want," she said with a shrug.

A husband? Well, that solved some of the mystery. Sort of.

"Well, I can start next week." He'd be wrapping up the remodel on the house in Harlem by then.

"Perfect. Why don't I give you a key, so you and your men won't be dependent on me or Millie to let you in?"

He looked into Darcy's trusting eyes and was overwhelmed by what that meant to him. He knew his appearance didn't necessarily engender warm and fuzzy, and while his business had an excellent reputation, he appreciated Darcy's trust in him personally.

Before he could say anything, she continued, clearly seeing something in his eyes. She placed a hand on his arm. "You came with Gloria's seal of approval, and since Gloria doesn't give that approval lightly, it's all I need. Also, I want you to make yourself at home."

"Thank you. And other than the occasional plumber or electrician, there won't be anyone else." At Darcy's surprised expression, he continued, "Gloria's one condition."

———

The following week, Millie unlocked Darcy's front door then bent to pick up the box of books UPS had delivered while she was out running errands. As she entered the townhouse, she was surprised to hear strains of Beethoven pouring down the stairs. The house had been empty when she'd left, and Darcy and Josh were at a prenatal doctor's appointment. Besides, Darcy didn't listen to classical music. And neither did Josh.

After closing the door quietly behind her—why, she didn't know—whoever was in the house wouldn't hear her over the music, she tiptoed over to the hall closet, opened it, and gingerly withdrew a baseball bat from Josh's bag. Heart pounding she climbed the stairs.

Emotion told her not to be the girl in the horror movie who was too stupid to live. Logic told her neither a burglar nor a serial killer would play classical music loud enough for the victim, much less the neighbors, to hear.

Halfway up the stairs, she stopped. Unless that was how he lured his victims to their deaths. And covered up the screams. She gasped, then clamped her hand over her mouth. The Classical Music Killer.

Nonsense. She'd been reading too much Donald Wells.

The music clearly came from the soon-to-be nursery. Drawing the bat over her head, ready to strike any would-be murderer, she stepped into the room to find . . . Ian, covered in sweat and dust, his hair thick with it, a stack of what appeared to be cabinet doors leaned against the far wall. *Cathy and Heathcliff!* He looked beyond sexy. He looked downright edible. But then again, she wasn't a cannibal.

Something must have drawn his attention, because he spun to face her. "Jesus! Give a guy a little warning next time."

She'd never expected to be so physically drawn to a guy who looked like he belonged in the cast of *Westside Story*. Black T-shirt, a thin layer of white dust over it, worn jeans, a hole just below his left knee, thick unruly hair, and a face that hadn't met a razor blade in the last two, maybe three, days.

Before the invention of the razor, people used hammered metal, flint, or sharp shells for shaving. No wonder early man wore beards. But what was his excuse?

A leather tool belt hung low on his hips and on his bare right forearm, a tattoo in Roman script read: *Scientia potentia est*. Knowledge is power.

A tattoo. How cliché. What it said, however, was far from it. Heart still pounding like a jackhammer in her chest, she said the first thing that came to mind, "That's 'Beethoven's Ninth Symphony.'"

---

I an stepped over to the battered, dust-covered boom box he used for construction jobs and reduced the volume. "Sorry. I thought I was alone."

He took in the quick rise and fall of Millie's chest, the Louisville Slugger hanging from her fingers, and felt the corner of his mouth lift. "You planning on using that?"

At Millie's continued catatonia, he stepped over and slipped the bat from her fingers, leaning it against the wall.

"How-How did you get in?" she finally asked.

"Darcy gave me a key."

"Of course she did." Millie glanced around the room.

"I'm pulling out the cabinets today. Tomorrow I'll start on the bathroom fixtures."

She walked over to the boom box sitting on the

makeshift work table constructed of two saw horses and a piece of plywood. Blueprints held open by a hammer and wrench stretched across the table. She turned back to face him, pointing at the boom box, still not speaking.

Funny. When he'd met her before she hadn't appeared to be mentally handicapped. Awkward, yes. Disabled, no. Maybe his original theory had been correct: she had a speech impediment.

"You were listening to Beethoven," she said again.

Feelings from his adolescence bubbled to the surface. The need to defend himself. From his stepfather. His step-brother. The kids at school. Before he could go on the defensive, Millie spoke.

"I love Beethoven's 'Ninth.' Though many feel that his 'Eroica Symphony' was his masterpiece. And of course, when most people hear the name Beethoven, they think of his 'Fifth.'"

Okay, so maybe not mentally handicapped. He also nixed the speech impediment. Ian picked up a cloth, wiped his hands, then joined her at the boom box. "It surprises you that I listen to Beethoven."

"Yes." She took a step back.

"I like music," he said with a shrug.

Millie nodded.

"I'll use my iPod and earbuds instead," he said, as he withdrew the device from his pocket.

"No. It's okay. As I said, I love Beethoven. And Bach. And Chopin."

"Well, I don't want to disturb you." *At whatever it is that you do.*

"Suit yourself. I'll, um, I'll just be going," Millie said, but she still stood rooted to the spot.

"Do you mind if I get back to work? I'm on a tight schedule."

"Hmm? Oh. No. I'll just . . ." She left without finishing her sentence.

Ian shook his head at her odd behavior, then got back to work. She was one strange cookie.

———

"What did the doctor say?" Millie asked when she heard the front door open only moments later.

"Everything is steady as she goes." Darcy hung her coat in the hall closet.

"What about the morning sickness?"

Darcy sighed. "Some women are just lucky—like me—and they have it their entire pregnancy. But, there's still a chance I'll get past it in the last trimester. In the meantime, I'm starved."

"I made a fruit salad. I'll get it for you."

"Millie, you do remember I can cook, right?" Darcy stood, arms akimbo, belly filling her tunic sweater.

"Yes."

"And that I still have two arms and two legs with which I can wait on myself?" Darcy indicated her arms and legs, imitating Pinocchio.

"Yes."

"But?" Darcy lifted a brow.

"But nothing. I'll get the salad."

"Ian's here?"

"Yes, upstairs." Looking far too sexy for his own good. And hers. "I almost brained him with one of Josh's bats."

Darcy gasped, hands on her hips. "Why on earth would you do that?"

"Because I didn't know it was Ian. You didn't tell me he had free reign over the place." As Millie headed for the kitchen, a thud from above startled her. "Cheese and crackers." How was she supposed to have peace of mind with that racket going on? For that matter, how was she supposed to have peace of mind with that man in the house? His very presence gave her the jitters.

She closed her eyes in mortification over her behavior earlier. When she stood next to him, felt the heat rolling off of him, her brain had simply . . . shut down. Like the power grid during a blackout. All synapses ceased.

She just needed to steer clear of him. Like that would be possible over the next several weeks.

Taking a bowl from the cupboard, she turned to the fridge and grabbed the container of fruit salad, placing them both on the counter.

That a man who looked like Ian, who worked in construction, rode a death machine, and had at least one tattoo—that she could see—listened to, and apparently enjoyed, Beethoven shocked her. Putting the two together was like entering one of Asimov's alternate universes.

How had Ian come to appreciate the music? And what else did the man appreciate? She shivered at the possibilities.

# CHAPTER FIVE

"**B**rand," Ian growled as he climbed off his bike, not even looking to see who called. He was dirty, cold, tired, and hungry. A lethal combination.

"Ian? Geez, what crawled up your ass and died?" Caleb returned.

Ian sighed. "Nothing that a hot shower, a soft bed, and a juicy burger couldn't cure."

"Shouldn't you eat *before* you go to bed? I mean, I don't usually eat in bed, especially hamburgers." He snickered.

"What do you want?" Ian set his helmet on the seat and walked over to the interior door.

"I'll buy you that burger."

"What? Jillie kick you out of the house again?" Jillie had a weekly book club where a bunch of women got together, ate desserts, drank wine, and, oh yeah, sometimes got around to discussing books.

Tossing his keys on the desk, he headed for the kitchen.

"Yeah. Shower and meet me at Sea Witch in thirty. That give you enough time to do your hair?"

"Fuck you," he said on a laugh. "What's the emergency?" Opening the fridge, he grabbed a bottle of water, twisted off the cap.

"I've got some news."

"Christ, you're like the town gossip." Ian took a gulp of water, then wiped his mouth.

"Yeah. Well, you'll like this bit of gossip."

Half an hour later, Ian strode into their favorite watering hole and spotted Caleb already at a booth, a beer in his hand.

"Another Sorachi Ace," Caleb called to the bartender.

"You know I don't drink," Ian said has he slid into the booth.

"Not for you." Caleb lifted the bottle he had and drained it.

After ordering his usual, the Sea Witch burger and a root beer, Ian stretched out his legs and directed his attention to Caleb.

"Oh, sure, so now you want to know my news," Caleb said.

"I want my burger, but in the meantime . . ."

Caleb leaned forward conspiratorially. "You remember my buddy Jon, works for the Landmarks Preservation Commission? He said a permit came in to renovate the old Yardley Mansion, one of the few remaining Gilded Age mansions. The new owners want to turn it into a *chichi* inn.

"Okay . . . and this is news, how?"

"Boy, are you grumpy when you're hungry," Caleb said. "This is news because the owners are going to be soliciting RFPs from companies on the very extensive renovations they require . . . renovations that, because of the building's landmark status, will need to conform to the historical style of the era."

His hunger forgotten, Ian sat forward, then cringed.

Another RFP. He'd done dozens of RFPs in the last few years. Check that–Ruby had done dozens of RFPs. He had one in the hopper already for a job that, if he got the bid, would take his business international. But the Yardley job sounded intriguing.

Could he do it? Ian wondered. "When?"

"Jon thinks the RFP will be posted on their website this week or so. Once posted, they'll expect the responses in about a month, so probably after New Year's, I'd say."

Cutting it close to the other job. "And you're interested?"

"Damn right I'm interested, but I can't do this without a general contractor, one with expertise in historical renovations. That's where you come in."

"I made the first cut on that renovation in England, Hawkins Hall."

"Dude! Congratulations!" Caleb lifted his bottle in a toast.

Ian met it with his root beer mug before taking a swig.

"If you get the England job, when would you start?"

"In the spring."

A new waitress delivered their burgers, flashing a come hither look at Ian, which clearly didn't go unnoticed by Caleb, because as soon as she walked away, he said, "She wants you, man. You should go for it."

Ian snorted, then picked up his burger and took an enormous bite. His stomach practically rolled over in pleasure.

"How long has it been since, you know?" Caleb lifted his eyebrows.

"Since what?" Ian asked around a mouthful of juicy red meat.

"You know." Caleb made a crude motion with his hands.

"What are you, like twelve? None of your damn business," Ian returned.

"Too long," Caleb said with a nod, then took a pull from his beer.

"What the hell are you talking about?" Ian stuck a fry in his mouth, eyeing his friend.

Caleb shrugged. "If you'd gotten some recently you wouldn't be so pissy."

"Asshole."

"That jealousy talking 'cuz I'm getting it on a regular basis?" he asked with a grin, setting his beer back on the table.

"Back to this RFP—"

"Nice deflection," Caleb said with a smirk.

"Shut it. So, you're thinking I respond to the RFP, and include Five Boroughs Electrical on the deal as one of the subs."

"Of course."

Ian chewed his burger, washing it down with the root beer. It'd be great working with his friend on this project. If he got the job, he'd have to hire the skilled labor to do it. And subs. Lots of subs. He already had some of the best tradesmen—and women—in New York he worked with on a regular basis. *Getting the cart before the horse, Brand.*

Ian sat back, his hunger finally sated. "All right. Let's see what they're looking for. I don't plan on responding to an RFP if I don't think I can do the job."

"You can do it," Caleb said with enthusiasm.

If only he had Caleb's confidence. He had no doubt he could do the renovation, even with all the other jobs he had in the queue. Completing the RFP? Well, he'd leave that up to Ruby.

———

F riday evening, Millie hurried up the sidewalk to her apartment building, tugging her coat around her as a particularly icy blast threatened to rip it off her.

"Hey, Mousey Millie, got a hot date tonight?" a teenager called from behind her, followed by the guffaws of the other boys with him.

"Yeah, with a vibrator," another one replied, as the others laughed even louder.

Heat flared up her neck and into her face. *Ignore them and keep walking.* She put her head down, the familiar taunts an unwelcome reminder of her painful middle and high school years. "Thugs," she muttered, then began reciting Descartes' rule of signs to herself. *The number of positive real roots of a polynomial is bounded by the number of changes of sign in its coefficients.*

One of them must have said something else because the group's laughter followed her all the way to the building.

Just as she opened the door, her neighbor, Chelsea, breezed past her wearing leggings, sky-high boots, and a barely-there halter top.

"Hi, Millie!" Chelsea said in her breathy voice.

"You do know it's winter, right?" Millie asked, confused by her neighbor's skimpy attire.

"It's okay, my date is waiting with his car."

Millie glanced out to the street and saw a small, shiny car waiting at the curb. "Have fun," Millie muttered.

Chelsea received a few catcalls from the same group of thugs, which elicited a flirtatious giggle. "Thanks, boys!" She sashayed down the sidewalk. "Don't wait up," she added with another titter.

Millie rolled her eyes and stepped into the foyer, stopping to check her mail. Friday evening and Crazy Chelsea had yet another date.

The thugs were right about one thing. *She* didn't have a hot date. Or even a cold one.

Climbing the stairs to her third floor apartment Millie planned out her evening. A microwave dinner and some in-depth research. She unloaded the stack of library books she'd picked up that afternoon. Anticipating Number Two on her list, one of the books in the pile was *The Joy of Sex*.

The key to reaching goals was preparation. The book would also come in handy for her novel's sex scenes, which she'd been putting off. Despite the extensive research, she'd found it difficult to write realistically about an act she'd never experienced. Of course she knew the mechanics—insert Tab A into Slot B—as well as the biochemistry, but she couldn't write the emotion or the physical response with any authenticity. She could always fall back on her extensive vocabulary, but would it ring true?

Her phone rang before she could even remove her coat. "Hello?"

"Millicent. We've done it!" Her mother's voice was uncharacteristically excited. The fact that her mother had even called her came as a surprise. Most of the time she wondered if her parents even remembered her existence.

"Done what?"

"Done what? Millicent, what have your father and I spent our careers trying to prove? Found definitive evidence that the unsigned manuscript is in fact, Hardy's." For as long as she could remember, her parents, college professors specializing in Victorian literature, had been doggedly engaged in proving that a particular unpublished manuscript they'd unearthed in an archive—in the New York Public Library, of all places—had actually been written by Thomas Hardy of *Jude the Obscure* fame.

"That's great." Millie couldn't work up the enthusiasm she should feel for her parents' life's work. They'd paid her very little attention when she was growing up, not out of disdain; they simply forgot about her, they were so focused on their scholarly pursuits. So how could she be anything but indifferent?

"We're drafting our paper on it now for submission to the *English Literary Journal,* so we won't be able to meet you for dinner tomorrow night. You don't mind, do you?"

"No. No, of course not." She was surprised her mother even remembered their monthly dinner date, having spent many an evening alone in a diner or restaurant because her parents had forgotten.

"We'll reschedule soon. Your father's calling me, so I have to run. Thank you for sharing our news."

Did she have a choice? "Sure. Talk to you soon." But her mother was already gone.

## CHAPTER SIX

Monday evening Ian carried two bags of groceries into the Sunset Park apartment building. Ringing the bell, he shifted his burden then reached inside his pocket for the key.

"Ruby," he called as he entered.

"Ian? Is that you?"

*"Yes." Who else would it be?*

"Come on in. I'm just watching reruns of *Murder, She Wrote.*"

Ian strode into the kitchen to set down the bags, then walked into the living room that hadn't changed since he'd first set eyes on it back in sixth grade.

Ruby sat up from her recliner appearing frailer than she had last week. It broke his heart. Yet she refused to let him take her to the doctor.

"Come. Sit. Tell me about your day." She muted the TV.

Before she'd retired ten years earlier, Ruby had been the head librarian at the Sunset Park Branch Public Library. The library had served as a haven for Ian when he was

growing up, keeping him off the streets. And just as important, out of the house and away from his stepfather's version
of discipline—his fists.

He leaned down, pressed his lips to the papery skin of
her cheek. "I brought food. You should eat."

"In a minute."

Here lately her usually robust appetite had been off. "If
I tell you about my day, do you promise to eat some soup
and a grilled cheese?"

"We'll see."

Ian sighed, dropped to the sofa next to the recliner, and
proceeded to describe his day. Nothing exciting, but she
listened with rapt attention.

She and her late husband, Curtis, never had children.
Her one regret, she'd once told him.

He'd apprenticed with her husband, learning the ropes
of construction, renovation, and historical preservation.
Curtis taught him everything he knows. In fact, he owed his
life to Curtis and Ruby. Without his and Ruby's kindness
and direction, he'd likely be on the street, in prison. Or
worse, dead.

Curtis had given him a job when his stepfather kicked
him out of the house at seventeen. And Ruby had given him
a home until he could support himself.

After he'd stumbled into the library with a shiner and a
busted lip, Ruby had introduced him to her husband, who'd
taught Ian self-defense. Hard work on the construction sites
had added bulk to Ian's scrawny frame. Before long, Ian
could stand up to anyone stupid enough to get in his way.
Including his stepfather, which was the reason the asshole
eventually kicked him out of the house. He didn't like his
prey fighting back.

Ian hadn't started the fight, but he hadn't walked away from it either.

When Curtis died, Ian had been surprised to learn that he'd purchased a second life insurance policy, naming Ian as the beneficiary. 'Use this money to start your business,' he'd said in a letter Ruby had given him after the funeral. Ian had been blown away that a man who was not his father would take out an insurance policy just for him. But that was Curtis.

He ended his story with the RFP.

"You'll get it." Ruby nodded. "Don't let the old fears take hold. Remember, divide it into bite-size pieces so it's not so overwhelming." She paused, her eyes a little misty. "Curtis would be so proud of you." She held his gaze, and Ian tried to swallow around the grapefruit-sized lump in his throat. That anyone would be proud of him seemed . . . impossible. He'd been lucky to get through high school, even with Ruby's help.

"Speaking of RFPs"—Ruby pointed to a neat stack of paper on the coffee table—"the one for the Irving house in Westchester is ready."

Washington Irving's house, Sunnyside, needed some preservation work. Easy enough job, to Ian's mind.

Thanks to Ruby's writing skills, he'd garnered numerous jobs over the years. Taking her frail hand in his, a twinge of guilt swept through him. Clearly, she'd grown feeble over the last few months. He shouldn't be asking her to do what amounted to hours and pages of work. Perhaps it was time to look at alternatives.

"Now, how about that soup?" Ian finally asked, slapping his thighs with his hands.

"You're a good boy." Ruby unmuted the TV and went back to her show.

In the kitchen, Ian opened the can of tomato soup, and poured it into a pot on the stove. Then he buttered two slices of bread, sprinkled them with dried Italian herbs, and placed two slices of provolone between them.

Ian heard Ruby shout at the TV, "It was the snooty maître d, you twit!"

He chuckled, shaking his head. She might be physically frail, but her mind was sharp as ever. He popped the sandwich onto the heated griddle, and since Ruby was more likely to eat if he ate with her, made another one for himself.

With Ruby's help and encouragement, Ian had discovered a love of learning he'd never thought possible, spending hours in the library studying philosophy, history, art, and architecture after Ruby showed him the audiobooks that were available free to anyone with a library card. Up until that point, he'd just assumed he was the moron his stepfather had often called him.

He'd discovered classical music when Ruby had played Beethoven's "Ninth Symphony" for him one day. He'd never heard anything so beautiful in his life.

At home he'd be more likely to hear the loud bangs and explosions of action movies, to-the-death video games, and real life action on the streets. Or hear his stepfather yelling and cursing, mostly about him. And at him.

So classical music provided yet another welcome escape.

He placed two bowls of soup on the kitchen table and called for Ruby. He'd had many a meal at this table with her and Curtis. Sometimes the only decent meal he'd had all day. Not because his mother didn't cook, but because he didn't want to go home.

Ruby shuffled into the kitchen. "Smells good."

"Ian's special tomato soup and grilled cheese."

She patted his cheek then slid up a chair. It warmed Ian's soul when she picked up her spoon without any urging from him and began to eat.

Ian took a bite of his sandwich. "I'll take a look at that leaky faucet after dinner."

"And then we can watch *Miss Marple*."

Ian mentally cringed. "You got it."

———

Ian had struggled in school from kindergarten through the sixth grade. By the time he'd hit fourth grade, the school had labeled him both a troublemaker and learning deficient.

His stepfather, Hank, wasn't surprised. His performance in school only confirmed what he already knew—that Ian was stupid. Not that Hank was a rocket scientist. Still, he had no qualms with throwing stones.

After some boys in his school called him a moron, Ian had stood up for himself by punching one of them in the stomach, even if he hadn't stood a snowball's chance in hell of winning. This grew into an all-out brawl, with Ian getting the worst of it. He'd managed to get away and had ducked into the first building he came to, the Sunset Park Public Library.

His lip split and his right eye already swelling, he glanced around for the bathroom where he could clean up a little before going home.

Already a target for his stepfather's cruel jokes, when he came home looking like he'd lost a fight, he'd never hear the end of it from his stepfather or his asshole stepbrother, Clint. Knowing Hank, he'd likely be disciplined for getting in the fight. Any excuse to use the belt. Or his fist.

He turned a corner and ran right into an old woman. At least she'd seemed old to him at the time. Glasses framed her face and brown hair salted with gray was pulled back into a tidy ponytail. She took one look at him and gasped.

"Son, who did this to you?" she asked as she took his chin in her hand.

He snatched out of her grasp. "No one." Fisting his hands in frustration, he turned to the bathroom door.

"Stop right there, young man. Where do you think you're going?"

"Bathroom," he replied, his chin jutting forward in defiance.

"That's the ladies' room."

Ian looked up at the door in front of him and felt the heat of shame rise to his face. He scanned the hallway for another door that could be the men's room.

"The men's room is down there." The woman pointed down a hall.

Ian didn't say anything, just walked in the direction she indicated. Closeting himself in the men's room, he dropped his backpack on the floor before splashing cold water on his face, wincing as it stung the cut on his lip and beneath his eye. His eye already bruised, he knew there'd be no hiding it from Hank. Maybe he could just sleep here tonight. And every night after.

Wetting a paper towel, he pressed it to his face, and slid down the wall, contemplating what he should do. He must have fallen asleep because the next thing he knew someone was shaking him.

"Son, wake up. You can't stay here."

He opened his left eye, the right eye now swollen shut, to see the woman he'd run into earlier stooped in front of him.

"Do you have somewhere to go?"

Ian struggled to stand but didn't answer.

"Here, let me help you." The woman took his arm and hauled him to his feet. "You're going to want to have that eye looked at. Can I call your mom?"

"No."

"Then come with me."

Great. Just what he needed. She was probably going to call the cops. Or worse, family services. He yanked his arm out of her grasp, picked up his backpack and headed out the door.

"Young man, stop."

He can't say why he did, but he obeyed.

"I have a first-aid kit in my office. I can at least put something on that cut before you go home."

Ian turned. "You're not calling the cops?"

"Why would I do that?" She lifted her brow. "Unless you have something you'd like to confess."

"No."

"All right, then."

The woman introduced herself as Ruby Sinclair, head librarian, and asked his name. After dabbing on some ointment and covering the cut below his eye with a Band-Aid, she gave him a cup of hot chocolate and some cookies she had in her desk drawer.

It was the nicest thing anyone had done for him in a long time. Before she met and married Hank, his mother would have kissed away his pain. After marrying Hank, she kept her distance and let him handle everything, while alcohol became her preferred form of escape from a marriage she clearly regretted.

"Now, why don't you tell me what happened?" Mrs. Sinclair asked.

Ian gazed into her kind, warm eyes and felt his own fill with tears. Ashamed, he buried his face in the crook of his arm.

"Nothing wrong with crying, son. Don't let anyone tell you otherwise." She put her arm around his shoulders and gathered him to her, rocking him like a little baby. This made him cry harder. He should be a man. He should refuse her coddling, as Hank called it. But, God, how he'd missed the warmth of a hug. The compassion in the gesture. The motherliness of the touch.

Her kindness that day had affected him so deeply that every chance he got, he'd detour to the Sunset Park Public Library to see the woman who would not only uncover his dyslexia, but would teach him coping mechanisms and strategies that would open up a world of learning. And whose influence would change his life. For the better.

———

"Caleb? Ian. I'm going after the RFP," Ian said into his phone as he paced around his desk at home.

"Awesome! Anything I can do just let me know."

"First, you can meet me at the Mansion for the first walk through. Wednesday, two o'clock."

"I'll be there, man. Glad you decided to give it a go."

"See you Wednesday. Tell Jillie *hi* for me."

After his conversation with Ruby, and remembering the phrase tattooed across his stomach, he'd made up his mind to go for it.

Ruby would help, as she always did.

———

"How's my god-granddaughter?" Gloria asked Darcy as soon as she stepped into the foyer, her glass-in-a-blender voice harsh on the ears. Forty years of smoking did that to a person.

"Or god-grand*son*," Darcy replied. "Fine and dandy." Darcy took Gloria's hand and placed it on her belly. "He, or she, is happy to see you."

Gloria's craggy face softened and her sharp eyes became dreamy, then she harrumphed. "Tell me again why you don't want to know what you're having?"

"Josh and I want it to be a surprise." Darcy made a circular motion over her belly, as if soothing the child.

Millie observed the exchange as she took Gloria's coat and hung it in the closet.

"How's Ian coming along?" Gloria asked, looking up the stairs where the whine of a saw commenced.

"It's going great," Darcy replied. "I can't thank you enough for your gift. It's beyond generous."

"Pfft. What are godmothers for?" Gloria tucked her cashmere gloves into the cavernous tote bag she always carried.

"And Ian is wonderful," Darcy continued.

"He did some work in my townhome a few years ago. I wouldn't let anyone else do it. And he's not bad on the eyes either, aye, Millie?"

Millie felt Gloria's eyes on her and she glanced up in confusion. "I hadn't noticed," she muttered.

Gloria snorted. "Girlie, you'd have to be dead not to notice."

"Millie thinks Ian is a thug," Darcy divulged.

Heat rose in Millie's cheeks. "He's just . . ."

"All man, is what he is. And he's great with his hands. I

bet he knows his way around a woman's body. Could probably teach her a thing or two. Great inspiration for a romantic hero, too. And did you see the size of his feet?" Gloria waggled her thin brows.

"Actually, there's no correlation between a man's shoe size and his penis size. The average Caucasian penis is five point one inches long when erect."

This factoid was met with stunned silence, deepening Millie's flush. "I'll just go serve lunch," she muttered as she headed for the kitchen and her escape route. She pressed cool hands to her heated cheeks. *Just shut up with your random facts, Miss Know-it-All.*

And speaking of know-it-alls, how did Gloria know *things*? Almost as if she could read your mind.

She had no doubt that Ian could teach her a thing or two. In bed and out. He could provide her with the knowledge and experience she needed to finish her novel. And he served as perfect inspiration for Hugh, her rake-turned-hero.

But of course, just like Kevin Hardy, Ian would never give her a second thought. Which didn't matter, because not even for the sake of her Get a Life List, would she ever open herself up to that kind of humiliation again.

# CHAPTER SEVEN

Millie had been a sophomore in high school when Kevin Hardy, a junior transfer, sauntered into her life . . . and into her lonely teenager's heart. He'd come from Southern California, and had the blond surfer hair to prove it. A star quarterback on his former high school football team, he'd come in and taken over for the ailing varsity team.

Tall, muscular, with the beach-boy hair and blue eyes, Kevin caught the eye of every female in the school, and possibly Anthony Rigatelli's eye. Even Millie, who didn't pay much attention to boys, wasn't immune to his smile.

But, awkward at best, she had had no hope of him noticing her, unless being an object of ridicule counted. But two weeks after he'd arrived, he passed her in the cafeteria and smiled at her. And the angels sang.

Then one day, Cassie Olivier of the long blond hair, dazzling teeth, and swimsuit model's body, and one of the most popular girls in school, sat next to Millie in the library and said, "I have a secret."

Unclear why Cassie would share a secret with her, Millie simply said, "That's nice."

"Don't you want to know what it is?"

"Well, if it's a secret should you be telling me?"

"Oh, but this kind of secret needs to be shared."

Sighing, Millie set aside the copy of *Wuthering Heights* she'd been reading and gave Cassie her full attention.

"Kevin Hardy, like, asked about you." She flipped her long blond hair over her shoulder with a flourish.

"Oh." Millie's heart fluttered cautiously in her chest.

"Come on. Aren't you dying to know what he said?"

Did Marie Curie win two Nobel Prizes? But she kept her you-can't-hurt-me-no-matter-what-you-say mask in place. "If you want to tell me." She thought the shoulder shrug was a nice touch.

"He, like, asked who you were, and was all, like, you looked really brainy, and that like, he really dug brainy girls."

In the midst of counting 'likes' Millie's brain skidded to a halt. Wait. What? Could this be true? Could Kevin Hardy be the one to see past her unappealing exterior to the real Millie inside?

Cassie picked up a lock of Millie's hair. "You know, you could be, like, really pretty. A little makeup, some cool clothes. He'd, like, totally go for you." She stood up and glanced in the direction of her friends. "Give it a try. Come to school on Monday ready to impress Kevin, and I'll set it up."

"I don't know . . ." Millie's hopeful heart wanted to trust Cassie, but the survivalist in her remained cautious. "Why would you help me?"

Cassie shook her hair behind her back. "Call me a matchmaker."

Millie hesitated.

"Come on, Millie. Don't you want Kevin to like you?" Cassie prodded.

Suddenly she wanted that more than anything.

Cassie leaned over, grasped Millie's shoulders and looked her in the eye. "You can do it. I'll see you Monday. The cafeteria. At eight, before the first bell."

Millie watched as Cassie sauntered back to her friends, closely examined the way she walked, how she carried herself, her shiny, bouncy hair, and her clothes. Millie sighed. *The Book of Matthew* was wrong. The meek don't inherit the earth. The beautiful do.

*I can do this,* she thought. How hard could it be? After all, she had an IQ of one thirty-five.

She used her hard-earned allowance to purchase the latest fashion magazines and took them home, read them cover-to-cover, studied them like she studied chemistry or philosophy, then began searching through her closet and her mother's for something, anything, she could piece together. Giving up, she hit the thrift store. After that, using a photo of Sarah Michelle Geller–whoever she was–as a guide, she concentrated on makeup, using more of her money at the local Duane Read.

When Monday morning arrived, Millie examined her reflection in the bathroom mirror. She'd brushed her long wavy brown hair and secured it with a headband. After nearly putting out an eye with the mascara wand, she'd managed to get more on her eyelids than her actual lashes. She blinked constantly, feeling as if she'd glued on bristles from her hairbrush, and her lashes scraped against the lenses in her glasses. She'd slathered on sticky, gooey pink lip-gloss, and smeared blush across her cheeks.

Wearing a short denim skirt and a cropped sweater in

bubblegum pink, she'd pulled on tights as an afterthought, uncomfortable with showing so much bare leg. She thought the multi-colored striped tights matched the pink in her sweater. On her feet, she wore a pair of Doc Martens-type boots in bright red. At least her feet wouldn't hurt.

Gnawing on her lip, she wondered if Kevin would like what he saw.

Cassie stood with her friends waving to Millie when she entered the cafeteria. Three of the girls spoke behind their hands and then snickered.

"Millie!" Cassie hauled her to the center of the room. Some of the students were staring at her. "You look awesome! Kevin is going to, like, fall over himself when he sees you. He should be here any minute. Now, stand up straight and smile."

Cassie's Barbie Doll friends, Alicia, Nicole, Megan, and Amber—a.k.a. The Mean Girls—stood off to the side whispering and giggling. A bad feeling settled in her stomach.

"Oh! There he is!" Cassie said. "Kevin! Over here, I have someone who wants to meet you."

Confusion skittered across Kevin's face, but he made his way over to where Millie stood, her knees practically knocking in fear.

"What's up, Cassie?"

By now, Millie had become the center of attention. Her face flamed, the makeup itched, and she fought not to fidget.

Cassie's eyes gleamed. "Kevin, this is Millie Stephens. She's been dying to meet you. Doesn't she look amazing?"

"Yeah, if you like clowns!" one of the other Mean Girls shouted.

Cassie and her friends burst out laughing, along with some of the other kids in the cafeteria. Others just looked away, embarrassed for her.

Millie's stomach knotted as tears filled her eyes, and she bit down on her lip until she tasted blood to hold the sob in.

To his credit, Kevin didn't laugh. In fact, he glowered at Cassie and said, "Cassie, you are such a bitch."

He turned back to Millie with pity in his eyes, but before he could say anything, Millie spun around and ran out the closest door and she didn't stop until she'd hit Yellowstone Park, where she slid down behind a tree and sobbed with all the pain and heartache of a young girl who just didn't fit in. And the truth was, she never would.

Millie didn't know what was worse. Cassie's cruelty, or Kevin's pity.

She vowed she'd never do anything to attract attention to herself again. From that day forward, she'd become the invisible Millie Stephens.

———

The next day, Ian dashed down Darcy's stairs pulling on his jacket as he went. *Damn drill.* The last thing he wanted was to go out into the freezing rain for a drill bit.

"Oh, Ian," Darcy called after him.

Stopping in his tracks, he turned around, "Yes?"

"How about a hot bowl of soup?"

He glanced to the back of the house and out the window at the misty rain swirling around in the icy wind. He hated that kind of rain. The kind that floated through the air finding its way into every gap and crevice between you and your clothes, chilling you to the bone.

"Soup, huh?"

"Yeah, homemade lasagna soup." Darcy flashed him a cheerful grin. She knew she had him, and she'd be right. In fact, she'd had him at soup.

The drill bit could wait. "Smells amazing." Removing his jacket he followed Darcy into the cozy kitchen.

"Have a seat," Darcy said as she chatted away. "I had a burst of energy and a craving for carbs, meat, and cheese. Homemade lasagna soup fit the bill." She ladled heaping spoonfuls of curly lasagna noodles and ground beef in a rich tomato broth into a bowl, making his mouth water and his stomach growl. Then she topped it off with a healthy dose of shredded mozzarella cheese.

She brought the bowl over, set it in front of him, and walked back to the stove to repeat the process. "I love to cook, but ever since I got pregnant I've been sick and the smell of food cooking . . . Well, let's just say it wasn't very appetizing."

After filling another bowl, she stepped into the hallway, "Millie! Come eat." Setting the bowl on the table across from Ian, she circled back to the stove once more. For someone so pregnant, she moved with efficiency.

"Why are you—" Millie stood at the kitchen threshold, mouth slightly agape. Today she was swathed in a thick brown sweater, the too-long sleeves hanging over her hands, her fingertips barely peeking out the end, and some nondescript brown pants.

Come to think of it, it was the first time he'd seen her in anything besides a baggy dress, brown stockings, and brown orthopedic shoes. His gaze drifted lower. Check that, she still wore the orthopedic shoes.

"Come eat while it's hot," Darcy reminded her.

She closed her mouth and took a step forward, her brow furrowed in confusion as she stared at the empty chair across from him. He watched as several emotions crossed her face, indecision, insecurity, then resolve, before she finally decided to take a seat.

Ian shoveled a spoonful of noodles into his mouth, closed his eyes, and released a low hum of pleasure.

"Good, huh?" Darcy asked with a grin.

"Oh yeah."

"I could give you the recipe."

At Ian's skeptical expression, she continued, "It's so easy even Josh can make it. And believe me, if Josh can make it, anyone can." She slurped up a spoonful of noodles herself.

He liked Darcy. Her cheerful energy always left him feeling a little brighter. She was going to make a great mom.

Ian glanced at Millie, who'd yet to take a bite of her meal and looked as if she'd entered a snake pit.

———

Millie watched Ian. When he had released that hum, she'd felt it all the way down to her toes, which had curled up in her shoes.

Notwithstanding her factoid outburst in front of Darcy and Gloria yesterday, she had a sudden compulsion to check out the size of Ian's feet. Letting her napkin slip to the floor, she leaned over to pick it up and surreptitiously inspected Ian's work-boot-clad feet.

"Millie? Why aren't you eating? Aren't you hungry?" Darcy asked.

Millie sat up, replacing her napkin in her lap and casting a glance at Ian.

His eyes sparkled as he mouthed, "Size thirteen."

*Tristan and Isolde!* He'd overheard her conversation with Gloria and Darcy? Heat flooded her face, and with shaking hands, she picked up her glass of water and took a gulp. She longed to hold the cool glass to her hot face.

"Eat up, Millie, before it gets cold," Darcy cajoled again.

Obediently picking up her spoon, she studiously avoided looking across the table at her male lunch companion and took her first bite. It *was* delicious. Especially since she'd forgotten to eat breakfast that morning. She'd been so engrossed in Darcy's latest manuscript, which had included a particularly instructive sex scene, that the next thing she knew Darcy was calling her to lunch.

A wave of chagrin passed over her. She needed to pay more attention to Darcy. She shouldn't have let her cook this lunch. Although she did appear to be feeling better, she thought, eyeing her boss. She had color in her cheeks and a good appetite if the way she was devouring the soup was any indication.

Cutting her gaze back to Ian, she observed his disheveled hair, the day's stubble covering his lean jaw, his gray eyes, and his mouth. Who would have thought a man's mouth could be so . . . sensual. Ian glanced up, caught her staring, and the corner of that sensual mouth tilted up ever-so-slightly.

Prying her eyes off him, she turned to Darcy, "You're feeling better," she blurted out.

"Yes. I'm finally feeling human again," Darcy said, wiping her lips with her napkin.

"Good. Don't forget your interview this afternoon."

"I won't. My publicist scored an interview for me in *Wine Enthusiast Magazine*, since my latest series is set in Sonoma and Napa Valleys around winemaking," she explained to Ian with a gleeful shrug.

Ian nodded, picking up his glass of water and draining it in one gulp.

Millie noticed how his strong hand grasped the glass, and how his Adam's apple moved with every swallow. Fascinated, she had this absurd desire to put her mouth there. Against his warm, unshaven skin . . . Giving herself a mental shake, she passed off her uncharacteristic preoccupation to reading too much about sex, between *The Joy of Sex* and Darcy's scenes. Reciting the Constitution's preamble to herself helped.

Taking a deep breath to clear her mind of these images, she inhaled a noodle. Or a piece of meat. Something. It didn't budge when she attempted to swallow. Gasping for breath, she reached for her water glass, but in her haste, knocked it over. Then the asphyxiation began in earnest. Spots appeared in her vision, just before it began to tunnel. Death by soup. Not the way she wanted to go.

"Millie? You okay? Did it go down the wrong pipe?" Darcy rose with alarm, but Ian was faster. He hauled Millie out of her chair and performed the Heimlich maneuver on her. One squeeze, and out popped a chunk of ground beef, landing right back in her bowl of soup.

Air filled her lungs as mortification filled her soul. She coughed again, her esophagus spasming, and tears ran down her face.

Ian still held her against his lean, hard body. "Better?" His warm breath tickled her ear, his arms two steel bands around her. She longed to stay, yet longed to flee.

She nodded. All she was capable of doing at the moment, as her esophagus continued to spasm.

He finally released her, gently setting her feet back on the floor, then pulled her chair out for her. She shook her head. "Thank you." Her voice came out in a raspy whisper. "Please excuse me."

Then she fled.

———

Hiding in the powder bath, Millie splashed cold water on her face. Why? Why did these things have to happen to her? Wasn't it enough that she wasn't pretty? That she'd never had a boyfriend? Or sex? Did she also have to be a total loser? First the shoe-size factoid, now this.

"Millie, you okay?" Darcy's voice came through the door. "Honey, let me in."

Millie unlocked the door then collapsed onto the toilet seat, while Darcy squeezed past the door to face her.

"There's not enough room in here for both of us," Millie said.

Darcy snorted. "Gee, thanks."

Propping her arm on the sink, Millie buried her face in it, tears threatening.

Darcy rubbed her back. "Aww, honey."

Millie sniffled.

"There's nothing to be embarrassed about. It could happen to anyone."

*Yeah, but why did it have to be me? And why in front of him?* "Has it ever happened to you?"

"Well . . . no."

*Of course not.*

"But, do you remember that blind date I had with, oh, what was his name? Sean? Sven? Anyway, he choked on a piece of steak the size of Texas and the waiter had to perform the Heimlich Maneuver on him. The piece of steak popped out like a cork out of a champagne bottle and landed in another diner's wineglass, setting off a domino effect."

Darcy shook her head. "The force of the expectorated meat knocked the glass of red wine over, the diner jumped from her chair, tipping it over, hitting another diner in the back causing him to lunge forward so that he ended up with his face in the mash potatoes." Darcy shook her head. "Used it in *Her Last First Date*."

"And did you ever go out with him again?"

"No."

"And this is supposed to make me feel better, how?" Millie asked, glancing up at Darcy.

"But that's not why I didn't go out with him again." At Millie's raised eyebrows, Darcy continued with a sigh, "I didn't go out with him again because he smelled like *lutefisk*."

# CHAPTER EIGHT

Unsure what to do, Ian began cleaning off the table, mopping up the spilled water with paper towels he'd found on the kitchen counter.

He hoped Millie was okay. Choking was scary business. Curtis had choked on a hamburger once on the job. Scared the life out of Ian who'd thought he was having a heart attack. Luckily one of the guys knew the Heimlich maneuver and was able to save him. After that, Ian had learned it in case he ever needed it. This was the first time.

Funny thing, after the initial adrenalin rush, he'd again noticed how nicely Millie's petite body fit against his. Beneath those oversized clothes lurked a dainty, but curvy frame. He'd also noticed how she smelled. Nothing floral or musky. Nothing perfumey. Just fresh. Clean.

Darcy toddled back into the kitchen. "Oh, Ian. I can't thank you enough for saving Millie!" She laid her delicate hand on his forearm. Unlike Millie, Darcy never seemed intimidated by him.

"Is she all right?"

"She will be. She's just . . . composing herself." She

turned to pick up the empty bowls, then eyed the wet paper towels in his hands. "And thanks for cleaning up the water."

"Sure."

She set the bowls on the counter. "Hey!" Darcy said to her stomach, making Ian jump. "Watch it, Peanut." Then the next thing Ian knew Darcy had his hand in a death grip and was dragging it toward her soccer ball-sized belly. For a little thing, she sure was strong. "He's frisky today." She grinned up at Ian as she held his hand in place.

"Uh . . ." *Can you say awkward?* "Oh!" Then Ian felt it. A flutter of movement. "Wow." He gazed into Darcy's shining eyes and thought that movement was the most incredible thing he'd ever felt.

"Pretty amazing, huh?"

"Yeah. Yeah it is." And it was. After another moment waiting with no more activity, he withdrew his hand. "I'll, uh, just go get the new drill bit and be back."

"Stay warm," Darcy called after him.

His heart would stay warm thinking about the feel of the little life inside Darcy's belly. His body would stay warm thinking about Millie's body pressed against him.

———

Later that evening, still smarting from the Heimlich debacle, Millie soothed her wounded pride with a cup of tea and a good book. Curling up on her loveseat, she promised herself just one chapter, then she'd pick up her own manuscript and get to work. But first, a little inspiration from Jude Devereaux and *A Knight in Shining Armor.*

In middle school, Millie had resorted to books for companionship, reading everything in her parent's personal library. From Tolstoy to Kant, Darwin to Pythagoras, and

Edith Wharton to Dante. She'd picked up her first romance novel when she was sixteen—the very book she held in her hands—at the Forest Hills Public Library where it had been lying abandoned on a table. And she'd fallen in love. With beautiful heroines and handsome heroes. With happily-ever-afters and the idea that true love could conquer all. Even if she couldn't find love for herself, she could find it in the pages of the books she read.

She'd earned a bachelor's degree in literature with a focus on the Middle Ages from Sarah Lawrence College. But when she'd seen the job listing for a personal assistant to a best-selling romance author, she'd jumped at it, and never looked back.

A half hour and one chapter later, Millie sighed and set aside her dog-eared copy of the novel.

Booting up the second-hand laptop she'd found on eBay, her one concession to technology, she opened up the file for her latest chapter. She might be a Luddite, but she had no desire to draft her manuscript as Jane Austen had—in long hand.

She'd taken a booklet she'd discovered in the library about courtship in Regency England and used each chapter as the basis for her own chapters. While she might be mousey and shy, her heroine, Lady Georgina Spencer, was not, and she broke every rule in the book. Which is how she ends up falling for a rake of the first order.

Last she'd left her heroine, she'd been in a drawing room alone with her rake. First mistake. Then, they'd been caught by society's most notorious gossip. Second mistake.

She'd set a word count goal of eighty-five thousand words, and was well on her way, but for the dreaded sex scenes. Cursing her inexperience, she focused on getting her heroine in as much trouble as possible *sans* sex.

Her mind drifted to Ian and the way his lean hard body felt against hers when he'd held her. That was after the all-too-humiliating chunk of meat popped out of her throat and landed in her bowl of soup.

At least it had been her bowl of soup, and not his. Small favors, and all that.

Closing her eyes, she recalled Ian's sinew and muscle, his breath in her ear, the tight band of his arms around her rib cage. The clean, fresh smell of him. Yes, she could write that authentically enough. But without the choking part.

She didn't want to think about what it would be like when she saw Ian again. Would he bring it up? Or would he pretend it never happened? She hoped for the latter.

That was why sex was so far out of her league. Who wanted to have sex with a woman who couldn't even swallow her food? Who couldn't walk across a street without almost getting run over? Who was an accident looking for a place to happen? No one, *that's* who.

*That's* why her heroine was beautiful, and graceful, if not a little strong-willed. Hardheaded, even.

Putting the day's lunch disaster behind her, she sought to create a disaster for her un-Millie-like heroine instead.

———

The next day, Millie poured a hot bowl of leftover soup for Darcy and placed it on a serving tray next to hers, while Darcy set the table. "I hope I don't keep eating like this after Peanut is born. I'll be bigger than Grand Central if I do."

"You should gain one to five pounds in your first trimester and about one pound a week after that."

"How'd you know that?" Darcy asked.

Millie shrugged. "I read it somewhere." She'd actually done some research, concerned over Darcy's continued morning sickness.

"Watch out for that—"

Before Darcy got her sentence out, Millie's foot slipped on something wet and soft. The next thing she knew, the tray tipped backward, spilling the hot soup down the front of her. Gasping as the hot liquid soaked into her sweater and hit her skin, she dropped the tray to the counter with a clatter and grabbed her sweater to pull it away from her body, burning her hands in the process.

"Oh!" Darcy grabbed the hem of the sweater and jerked it over Millie's head and off, dropping it onto the floor, leaving Millie standing in nothing but her bra and her noodle-splattered skirt.

"Are you okay?" Darcy asked. "Did you get burned?"

Millie just shook her head, peering down at the red splotches on her stomach. "No. I'm okay."

Darcy plucked a towel off the rack and ran it under cool water and began blotting Millie's stomach, making her squeal.

Just then, Ian rounded the corner and barreled into the kitchen. "Dar—"

Millie yelped, turning her back on him while trying to cover herself, mortified that he should see her like that.

"Sorry. What happened?"

She glanced over her shoulder to see he had turned his back, then she reached around and snatched the wet kitchen towel out of Darcy's hands and held it up in front of her chest. Why she didn't know, since she had her back to Ian.

"Millie spilled a bowl of hot soup," Darcy volunteered. "I yanked her sweater off."

*Great.* First, he'd snatched her from the jaws of death on the street, then she'd nearly choked to death in front of him. Now this. What other lame, embarrassing things could Ian witness? She shuddered to think.

*That's it.* She and soup would never cross paths again.

"Quick thinking." Ian nodded. "Anything I can do?"

"No!" Millie exclaimed.

"No," Darcy added more calmly. "Thank you." Taking an apron out of a drawer, she threw it around Millie's shoulders. "Let's get you out of the rest of your clothes and into something clean and dry."

Millie couldn't help but think she'd just heard Darcy's mothering voice. At least what she imagined a mothering voice sounded like, since she'd never heard it from her own mother.

On the way out of the kitchen, Millie sneaked another look over her shoulder. Ian still had his back to her, hands shoved into his jeans pockets.

Upstairs in her bedroom, Darcy took out a pair of pre-pregnancy jeans and a soft turtleneck sweater in navy blue. "Here. You can wear these." She stepped back as if assessing Millie's size and nodded. "They should fit," she said, laying the clothes on the bed.

"Thanks," Millie muttered, still embarrassed over her display.

"Aw." Darcy gave her a brief hug. "Could've happened to anyone."

"Yeah. And did it ever happen to you?"

"Well, no. But that doesn't mean it couldn't."

Millie grimaced.

"I'll just leave you to change," Darcy said as she headed for the door. "If you want, you can throw your clothes in the wash."

"Can you tell me when Ian leaves? I think I'll just stay here until he does." Millie eyed the clothes on the bed, certain they were too small.

"He won't say anything. For all his rough appearance, he's quite the gentleman." Darcy sighed. "He turned his back immediately."

*Right. Probably because he couldn't bear to look at me.*

———

The visual Ian got as he'd rounded the corner into the kitchen wouldn't leave his brain. Millie, standing there in nothing but a white bra and brown skirt, her breasts filling the cups to a pleasing capacity. Her gently curving hips visible without the bulky sweater.

She had a sweet little body beneath all those brown clothes.

Then he recalled the red splotches across her bare midriff. *Don't be such a dick,* he thought as he scrubbed his hands over his face. He shouldn't be thinking about her body and how much he'd like to touch it. She could have been burned.

He'd been coming to tell Darcy she could check out the newly installed bookcase he'd built. Seeing what was left of what appeared to be the lasagna soup on the floor, he grabbed a roll of paper towels and began mopping up the mess. Darcy didn't need to be on her hands and knees, that was for sure. He didn't miss the fact that this was the second time Millie and soup had crossed paths and she'd come out the loser.

"You don't need to do that," Darcy said from the doorway.

Ian stood. "It's no problem. Is Millie burned?"

"No. She'll be fine. I think I got her sweater off before the soup could soak in." Darcy wet a handful of paper towels, which Ian took from her and continued to clean up. "Seems you're always cleaning up around here."

"Yeah, a jack-of-all-trades, I guess." Ian worked in silence a few minutes, as Darcy pulled out the trashcan for the soiled paper towels. Recalling her kindness to Millie, he glanced up at her, "If you don't mind me saying so, you'll make a great mom."

Darcy hesitated a moment then gazed down at him. "No. I don't mind at all. And thank you."

"That should do it," he said as he rose.

"By the way, what were you coming to tell me?" Darcy asked, her head tilted.

"The new bookcase is finished if you want to take a look."

"Ooh! Definitely."

———

Millie gingerly opened the bedroom door. She'd heard Darcy and Ian talking in the nursery earlier, but it had been quiet the last twenty minutes. No bangs, no thuds, so Ian must have left. She climbed a few stairs to the third floor where Darcy's office was and called out, "Is he gone for the day?"

"No," Ian said from behind her, making her yelp. "He's still here."

She froze, closing her eyes, feeling yet another flush creep up her neck. Will she ever stop embarrassing herself in front of him?

"Darcy, however, is not here."

This snapped her out of her mortification, and she spun to face him. "Where'd she go?"

"She mentioned something about Red Velvet Cake and Aunt Butchies."

"Cheese and crackers! I forgot!" Running down the stairs, she remembered to grab her coat before heading out.

"Where are you going?" Ian called.

"To catch up to her." She slammed the door in her haste.

Millie practically ran down the sidewalk, buttoning her coat as she went. *How could she have forgotten?* Darcy had a luncheon tomorrow to benefit the Readers for Life Literacy Program, and several women who'd bid on and won lunch with the best-selling author were coming. She'd ordered the cake just yesterday, and with all the humiliation hullabaloo, she'd forgotten to pick it up.

Ian needed to finish his job and leave her in peace. Ever since he'd started working in the house, she couldn't keep her mind on her own work. Or, apparently, eat or prepare soup without endangering her own health and well-being. And it was all his fault with his well-worn jeans, tool belt that pulled those jeans precariously low on his hips revealing the band of his underwear—blue today—and his size thirteen feet.

He made her nervous and all too aware of his presence. He didn't even need to be in the same room with her, and she could feel him. Except just now when she'd needed to most. She closed her eyes again in mortification at her latest humiliation.

And nearly ran into a street sign.

*Note to self: Don't close your eyes while running down a sidewalk.*

Who was she kidding? She didn't need Ian to make her

a klutz. She'd done just fine on her own the twenty-nine years prior to meeting him. Like the time she'd been reading *The Kadin* and tripped over a skateboard in the middle of the walkway. In her defense, it had been a *very* juicy part. She'd since forsaken reading and walking at the same time. Or at her high school graduation when she'd walked up to receive her diploma and almost did a face plant on the stage. To this day, she had no idea what she'd tripped over.

No. Ian couldn't take all the blame for her mishaps. But his shoulders were more than broad enough to carry some of them.

---

I an shook his head. Millie was a strange one. But he couldn't help but notice her body in what were obviously Darcy's jeans and sweater. She looked good in something besides brown. The curve of her breasts, a trim waist. And her ass. Well, it was worth seeing, especially in those snug jeans and fitted sweater. Who would've thought she hid such treasures?

He also couldn't help but notice how she took care of Darcy. Granted she got paid for it. Well, most of it anyway. But she clearly went above and beyond, preparing lunch, picking up muffins every morning on her way there, fussing over Darcy's stair-climbing. He doubted any other author's assistants, which he'd recently learned from Darcy was her job, took their occupation that seriously.

He'd just picked up the sander when his phone buzzed with an incoming call. He frowned at the number—Maimonides Medical Center—then got a sick feeling.

"This is Ian."

"Mr. Brand?"

"Yes."

"This is Dr. Ackerman from Maimonides Medical Center. Mrs. Ruby Sinclair has you listed as her next of kin."

His knees went weak and he dropped the sander to the worktable with a thud. "Yes?"

"She's being admitted for acute respiratory distress. We'll need your permission to put her on a ventilator."

He thought about a conversation he'd had with Ruby a couple of years ago—no life-prolonging procedures.

"A ventilator?" Ian struggled to get the word out. "Is this permanent?"

"No," Dr. Ackerman said. "We think she'll recover some lung function. We just need to get her stabilized."

"Then, yes. Put her on the ventilator. I'm on my way."

# CHAPTER NINE

Millie carried the cake as she and Darcy made their way back to the brownstone. She'd caught up to Darcy just as she'd entered the bakery and withstood Darcy's lament about being a grown woman, needing exercise and being perfectly capable of picking up a cake by herself.

When they rounded the corner at Darcy's street, Millie noticed Ian's motorcycle was gone and felt a mixture of relief and disappointment.

After opening the door, Millie headed for the kitchen with the cake, and spotted Darcy's phone on the foyer table. "You left your phone."

"I wondered where that was. I'm getting so forgetful these days. Baby brain, I guess." She picked up the phone and frowned.

"What is it?"

"A text from Ian. He said something came up and he had to leave. He doesn't know if he'll be here tomorrow, but he'll let me know." Pocketing her phone, she ambled over to the closet to hang up her coat. "Maybe something with that renovation in the Upper East Side."

"How do you know what he's working on?" Millie asked in confusion.

Darcy shrugged. "I talk to him. You should try it sometime."

*Talk* to him? About what? She couldn't think what she would have in common with someone like Ian. Someone whose idea of reading was probably *Construction Today*. Someone who probably attracted women by the dozens. Beautiful, sexy women. Women who didn't let soup get the better of them.

"Did you know he renovates historic buildings? I think that's fascinating." Darcy paused in the process of hanging up her coat. "Hmm. I wonder how he'd feel about me picking his brain for a character. Anyhoo, what else do we need to do for the lunch tomorrow?"

"If you want to autograph a stack of books, I'll bring them down."

"Sounds good."

Millie climbed the stairs to the third floor, passing the room under renovation, and thought about what Darcy had said. Maybe she'd try striking up a conversation with Ian. Surely she could think of *something* to say. *That is,* if she could keep her brain functioning around him long enough.

―――――

Ian approached the bed where a frail Ruby lie, a ventilator tube protruding from her mouth, the hissing of the machine breathing for her loud in the room. Other machines beeped and flashed. An IV bag hung by the bed, dripping something into her arm.

The nurse had said she was sedated, but Ian pulled up the visitor's chair and took her thin hand in his, his thumb stroking its papery surface.

*Dammit.* Tears stung his eyes and clogged his throat. This woman, who was more mother to him than his own mother, was all he had left in this world.

Sure, he had Caleb, but Caleb had a wife, and in seven short months, would have a child. Ian and Ruby were more than friends, they were family. He'd been there five years ago when Curtis had died of complications following a stroke. She'd been there when, well, every day since that day Ian had first hid in the public library.

After his mom died of cirrhosis, a by-product of her alcoholism, he had no family left. He certainly didn't count his stepfather or stepbrother family. The death of his mother gave him the perfect excuse to permanently remove himself from their cruelty.

If she'd been his teacher and his friend, Ruby had also become his surrogate mother after his own mother's death. What was he supposed to do without her?

"I'm sorry to disturb you, but I'm Dr. Gupta, Mrs. Sinclair's oncologist."

Ian stood and turned to see an attractive woman with an East Indian lilt, a stethoscope draped around her neck. "Oncologist?" he asked in confusion.

"Ah." Dr. Gupta wore a chagrined expression on her face. "She hadn't told you."

"Told me what?" Ian rubbed a hand over the brick that had found its way into his stomach.

"I suspected as much." She took a deep breath. "Mr. Brand, Mrs. Sinclair has stage four lung cancer," she said, her voice soft and full of compassion.

Ian sank back in the chair. Cancer? Why hadn't Ruby

told him? That would more than explain her frailty and lack of appetite. "How did you know my name?"

"Ruby talks about you all the time." Dr. Gupta smiled warmly.

He absorbed that a moment. "When did she find out?"

"We diagnosed it about a year ago."

Scrubbing a hand over his face, he said, "A year ago. But she, nor her late husband, ever smoked."

"One in five women diagnosed with lung cancer never smoked."

"And surgery?"

"The tumors were inoperable, so we began chemotherapy and she responded well, but . . ."

"But?"

"Therapies can lose efficacy after a time."

"So this is it? This is how it ends?" His stomach ached, and his heart thudded heavily in his chest as he turned to gaze at Ruby.

"Not yet. We haven't given up. There are other therapies. There's also a clinical trial she may qualify for. This is a setback to be sure, but antibiotics should get the pneumonia in hand."

"Pneumonia?"

"It can be a complication of the cancer, but it's very treatable. The ventilator is just to provide a bridge until the lung function has improved."

"Can I stay here?" he asked, never taking his eyes off Ruby.

"Not while she's in ICU. But once she moves to a regular room, you're welcome to stay with her."

Ian nodded.

"I'll be back to check on her tomorrow morning. I'll call if there is any change."

"Thank you."

Ian sat in the dimly lit room, surrounded by the beeps, blips, and hisses of the medical equipment, staring out the window at the snow that had begun to fall.

"You can't leave me. Not now. Not yet," he said to Ruby. Laying his head on the bed, he placed her hand beneath his cheek and held on for dear life.

———

That Friday evening, Millie helped as Darcy put the finishing touches on the table setting. Darcy's best friend Laura and her husband Nathan were coming for dinner.

"You shouldn't be going to all this trouble," Millie chided. "You'll wear yourself out."

"Come on, Millie. I put a roast in the oven, I'm tossing a salad, and I've got a cake from Aunt Butchies. It's no trouble."

Millie harrumphed.

"And the invitation still stands if you'd like to join us."

"And listen to Josh and Laura taunt each other all night? No thanks."

"Actually, Laura's mellowed a little since she got married," Darcy said, her head tilted as if that had just dawned on her.

Millie snorted.

"I think Nathan's Southern Gentleman demeanor has rubbed off."

"I'll believe it when I see it." Millie folded a napkin, tucked it next to the plate.

"Then stay and see it." Darcy lifted her brows in challenge. "Don't you want to hear about their honeymoon?"

Millie heaved the sigh of the put-upon. She'd planned to go home and delve into the chapter 'Main Courses,' in *The Joy of Sex*. But, the way Laura liked to brag, *er*, over-share about her sex life, she might learn more if she stayed. "Fine. I'll stay."

"Good."

Josh strode into the dining room, messenger bag draped across his body. Law firm partner and creator and head of the firm's new mediation division, Josh hadn't let success go to his head. No briefcase and designer suits for him. "What's good?" He placed his hands at Darcy's waist and pressed a kiss to her belly.

"Millie's staying for dinner."

"That *is* good." He glanced at Millie and gave her a welcoming smile.

It warmed Millie's heart to see Darcy and Josh, together at last. It took Darcy long enough to recognize that her best friend was also her soul mate.

"What time are Laura and Nathan coming over?"

"In about an hour."

"Good. Gives me time for a shower." He kissed Darcy again. "Smells delicious! I'll be back."

Darcy watched Josh exit the room, a dreamy look on her face, as the oven timer buzzed.

"Darcy?"

"Hmm?"

"The timer's going off."

"Right."

An hour later Darcy and Josh opened the door to Laura and Nathan.

"Morgan le Fay." Josh greeted Laura with a nod.

"Gargamel," Laura returned.

"Some things never change," Millie muttered as she took Laura and Nathan's coats.

"How are an apple and a lawyer alike?" Laura asked.

"They both look good hanging from a tree," Millie replied, and received the evil eye from Laura for spoiling the punchline.

"Millie, you look good enough to eat," Nathan said in his Southern drawl, as he touched his lips to her cheek.

Millie knew he was lying, but she gave him points for trying. She could understand how a man-eater like Laura fell for him. He had more charm than Rhett Butler.

As the men headed into the living room, Laura turned to Darcy, eyeballing her belly. "You're not going to do the hand-grabbing thing, are you?"

"I might."

"Can I at least have a drink before we get intimate?"

Darcy snorted and led the way to the kitchen with Laura and Millie in tow.

Pouring a glass of wine for Laura, Darcy said, "God, I miss wine."

"That alone is enough reason not to get pregnant," Laura said as she offered a toast to Darcy's baby bump.

"Don't you want children?" Darcy asked Laura.

Millie read the look on Laura's face, and waited for the quip, but then her expression changed. "You know, I never thought I'd want kids, what with the whole pregnancy thing, childbirth—" she shivered "—diapers, and spit up, but I really think Nathan would be a great dad. I wouldn't want to deprive him of that." She finished with a rare dreamy look on her face. Then she took a sip of wine, and shook it off. "Wow. What was that? You really need to keep your baby hormones to yourself."

Darcy snorted. "Come on, admit it, you'd love a little Nathan running around."

Laura shrugged. "Maybe." She jabbed a finger at Darcy. "But don't start planning a shower or picking out baby names. I've got a few things to accomplish before I go down the motherhood road."

If she lived to be a hundred, Millie never thought she'd hear Laura even consider children. Maybe Darcy was right, marriage to Nathan had mellowed her.

"Like becoming the most powerful woman in advertising."

Or not.

Laura eyed Millie over the rim of her glass. "I see you're still dressing like a hobbit."

Millie drew herself up. "Better than Vampirella." Not that she really thought Laura was trashy. In fact, she thought she always looked sexy, in a polished sort of way. But she'd rather admit she was still a virgin than tell Laura that.

"One of these days, Millie." Laura wagged her finger at her.

Millie rolled her eyes. Laura's threat of the dreaded makeover had lost most of its bite over the years.

"Shall we eat?" Darcy chimed in.

Halfway into dinner, talk turned to the nursery renovations, and Millie's ears perked up.

"How's the nursery coming along?" Laura asked, tucking a strand of her perfectly straight blond hair behind her ear with a perfectly manicured hand.

"It's been going well, but it's at a standstill at the moment."

"Oh, why's that?" Nathan asked, as he sliced his roast beef.

"Ian, the contractor, has a good friend who's very ill and in the hospital," Darcy supplied.

Millie wondered where Ian had been, but had refused to ask and raise eyebrows at her interest in someone she supposedly disliked. She wondered who was ill.

"Which reminds me, Josh, Ian wanted some legal advice on estates. I told him to talk to you," Darcy added.

"Sure. Just tell him to give me a call."

Estates? Was Ian's friend that ill?

"Now, tell us about the rest of your honeymoon," Darcy prodded. "How was Zermatt?"

"Fabulous!" Nathan said, then took a sip of wine. "We saw Prince Albert and Princess Charlene of Monaco. And then there was the great food, delectable wines, and incredible skiing."

"And don't forget the outstanding sex," Laura added matter-of-factly.

Josh choked on his wine.

Darcy covered a laugh.

And Nathan grinned. "That's my girl."

No, marriage to Nathan hadn't mellowed Laura at all.

———

"Ian, have a seat," Josh said after welcoming him into the house.

Ian liked Josh. Their interactions had thus far been brief, but he recognized his warmth and sincerity.

"How is your friend?" Josh asked as he took a seat in a wingback chair.

"She's out of ICU at least." Ian sat on the sofa, scrubbing a hand through his hair. He was physically and mentally exhausted. Spending nights at the hospital with

Ruby, running home, showering, and heading off to the jobs that couldn't wait. He really appreciated Josh and Darcy's understanding.

"Well, that's good news, right?"

"Yes." Ian hesitated. "I'm really sorry about the delay in the renovation."

"Stop." Josh waved, forestalling the rest of Ian's apology. "You're where you need to be. The nursery will get done. Now, what can I do for you?"

"When Ruby leaves the hospital she's going to need to be in a rehab facility for a week or so before she goes home. The insurance issues, the bills, well, they're a little over-whelming at the moment. After three days in ICU, I'm not sure how she can afford it, and at this point I'm not sure where to turn." Ian had tried reading her secondary insur-ance policy—the backup to Medicare—but even without the dyslexia, he might as well have been reading Greek.

"I'm happy to help. I can take a look at her policy and see what's covered and the facility should be able to give you a good estimate of what her out-of-pocket might be."

"I'd appreciate that." Ian took the papers out of his backpack and handed them to Josh.

"Ian, I hesitate to bring this up, but does Ruby have an estate plan? Does she have an advanced directive, a durable power of attorney?"

"Yes. I know she has a will, and I'm her medical deci-sion-maker and I have durable power of attorney over her affairs."

"Good." Josh nodded. "That's one less worry."

"When the time comes," Ian continued, his throat tight, "would you . . . handle the estate?"

"It's that bad, then?"

"Stage four lung cancer."

"I see." Josh hung his head, and then lifted it to look Ian in the eye. "Ian, I'll do whatever I can to help."

"I appreciate it. I'd better get back to the hospital. I'm meeting with the oncologist about a clinical trial."

———

Millie hadn't intended to eavesdrop, but her office sat right off the living room, so she'd heard every word. She wondered who Ruby was. Not Ian's mother, since Josh referred to her as a friend. His girlfriend? Or an ex-wife?

Clearly, it was someone who meant a lot to him.

So, that's where he'd been the last few days.

She set aside the manuscript and gazed out the window at the snow-covered ground. It would be Christmas soon. A bad time of year to be sick. And a bad time of year to lose a loved one. Not that she'd ever experienced that kind of loss.

That a tough guy like Ian could show so much caring and compassion gave her a new perspective on him. A twinge of guilt poked her. Not for eavesdropping, but for doing to Ian what people did to her: judging a book by its cover.

There was clearly more to Ian Brand than met the eye.

# CHAPTER TEN

Climbing the stairs to the third floor, Millie hoped to avoid an Ian encounter. She'd managed to stay out of his airspace since he'd returned to the job, which in turn meant she'd avoided embarrassing herself in front of him. Telling herself not to look, she tiptoed past the room where he was working.

*Hamlet and Ophelia!* Not only had she looked, but she'd stopped.

Spotting his open backpack sitting on the worktable with a book inside, and unable to help herself, she stepped into the room and found it empty. Curiosity drew her to the backpack like a force field. Whatever the book was, it was a weighty tome. Probably some construction manual.

She peered into the backpack and gasped. Immanuel Kant's *Three Critiques*! What the—? Then she spotted an audiobook CD case of the same work.

"Can I help you?"

"Gah!" Millie jumped like she'd been electrocuted, and her heart pounded like a jackhammer in her chest. She spun to find Ian leaning against the doorjamb, arms crossed over his chest, that tool belt around his hips. How did such a big guy, who wore work boots and a clanking tool belt sneak up on her? His tousled hair softened the scowl currently gracing his face.

"I'm sorry. I saw your book . . ." She trailed off, pointing lamely in the direction of his backpack.

"Do you often go through another's belongings?" Ian asked as he pushed off the doorjamb.

"I— No." Seeking a change of subject, she said, "I'm sorry about your friend." God, how she wished she could hit rewind. She hadn't meant to say anything.

Ian's scowl deepened. "How do you know about my friend?"

"I, uh, I overheard your conversation with Josh." Before he could respond she thought another subject change was in order. "Kant's *Three Critiques* are considered by some as his most influential works primarily because they are so accessible."

He lifted a brow. "So you've read them."

"I've read all of Kant's works. His *Grounding for the Metaphysics of Morals* is my personal favorite."

"I see." He stepped close. Not quite in her space, but only a breath away, and her heart jolted into double time. "This is my first experience with his critiques, but I'm a fan of his *Observations on the Feeling of the Beautiful and Sublime.*"

Stunned, Millie didn't know what to say. That hammer-wielding, death-machine-riding, tattoo-sporting Ian Brand read Kant took her completely by surprise. First Beethoven, now Kant. What else did he have up his sleeve?

She jerked to attention when he raised his hand toward her, and she stepped back.

"You, uh, you have something sticking out of your sweater."

Turning her head she followed his gaze in the direction of her shoulder. Then closed her eyes. Oh, for the love of Shakespeare, could she just once, *just once*, have an encounter with him that didn't end in her looking like a fool? Was it too much to ask? Apparently so.

Before she could act, he'd reached out and tugged on the offending dryer sheet. As he did, his hand brushed her neck, and the warmth sent a shiver through her. He gently tugged the dryer sheet out of her sweater, the scent of Bounce Outdoor Fresh filling the space around them.

She should be mortified, but instead, she could only stand completely still, not even breathing, hoping the moment would never end. He'd yet to step back, and heat, testosterone, and pheromones radiated from his body leaving her weak. His mouth was inches from her hair, and if she didn't know better, she'd swear he'd just inhaled.

———

Ian inhaled Millie's fresh, clean scent—Bounce?—so different from the heavy, spicy scent so many women preferred. He felt the warmth from her body, even though they weren't touching, and inexplicably wanted to lean down and take her mouth with his. Her tongue flicked nervously across her bottom lip. The one he wanted to sink his teeth into. How this awkward, brainy, woman appealed to him, he couldn't say. But appealed to him, she did. Even if she did snoop. And eavesdrop.

The realization hit him like a sledgehammer. He wanted her.

Her breath became shallow and her pupils dilated.

Clearly, he appealed to her too. It might have been a while, but he hadn't forgotten how a woman reacted when she was attracted to him.

So close. Just another inch and he could put his tongue on the sweet spot below her ear. "Millie," he whispered, and bent to do just that.

"Millie, where are you?" Darcy called before walking past the door.

He and Millie parted like the Red Sea.

"Oh! There you are." Darcy narrowed her eyes, her gaze alternating between the two of them. "What's up?"

"Nothing," they said in unison.

"That's funny," Darcy said, "because it feels like something."

*Jesus.* Hell yeah, it felt like something, all right. "Millie just had, a, er, dryer sheet . . ." Ian finished lamely.

"I see." Darcy didn't appear convinced. "Millie, Gloria emailed me the ARC for *Lawyers in Love,* so you can forward it on to the reviewer at *USA Today.*"

Millie nodded. "I'll do that right away."

"Thanks." Darcy started to leave then stopped short. "Oh, while I'm here, I need a million-dollar word for charmed."

"Ensnared," Millie blurted.

"Transfixed," Ian offered.

"Transfixed. I like it. Thanks, Ian," she said over her shoulder as she left the room, giving Millie a knowing look.

Millie stared at him, mouth open. Clearly, she thought him just another Neanderthal construction worker. Not that he could blame her. That's what he would think of himself if he were in her position. Either that, or she was trying to recover from her boss interrupting an almost-kiss.

What the hell had he been thinking? *He* hadn't. His dick had.

Her brow furrowed and she glanced away, a faint flush coloring her cheeks. "You listen to Beethoven and you read Kant."

Well, 'read' might be a bit of a stretch. "Yes. Is that a problem?"

Her flush deepened as she paced the room, running her hand over the smooth wood of the bookshelves he'd built and installed. "No. It just seems so . . . incongruous." She stopped, then looked up at him biting her lip.

He yearned to bite that lip, too. Her comment should have been insulting, but it wasn't. He understood why she would see him that way. After all, that's the image he cultivated.

"So, why are you in construction?"

Ian shrugged. "Because I like uncovering and preserving the beauty in an old building. And I like seeing the results of my labors." This was the longest, most coherent conversation he'd had with her thus far.

She nodded. "I can see that. There is something to be said for preserving history. I suppose like art and literature, buildings deserve to be treasured too." The silence stretched, and she appeared to be finished with her end of the conversation. "And you like philosophy," she blurted.

"Yes."

She nodded once more. "I'm sorry I invaded your privacy." Before she walked out, she stopped short at the door. "Have you read Descartes?" she asked without turning around.

"*His Meditations on First Philosophy or his Principles of Philosophy?*"

This time she turned in his direction. "Both?"

"Yes."

"*And his Discourse on the Method?*"

Ian lifted the sleeve of his flannel shirt to reveal the tattoo around his bicep: '*Cogito ergo sum.*'

"Okay, then." And she left.

Ian tugged his shirtsleeve back down and shook his head at the mystery that was Millie.

———

Millie rushed headlong down the stairs to the relative refuge of her office. She needed to process this new information about Ian.

Her heart pounded in her chest, and it had little to do with the exertion of her descent.

"I think therefore I am," she muttered, recalling Ian's tattoo.

First, she finds Kant in his backpack.

Next, she might be completely inexperienced but she could have sworn he was going to kiss her. That is, until Darcy interrupted. She didn't know whether to be thankful or resentful.

Then, she learns that he not only reads Descartes, but has one of his most famous quotes tattooed on his bicep.

And what a bicep it was. Her mouth had gone dry when he'd flexed it.

Nothing about Ian Brand fit.

From his appearance, she'd be afraid of running into him in a dark alley. Then, Beethoven, Kant, Descartes . . . and tattoos that weren't the usual skull and cross bones, daggers or serpents.

What was Ian's story?

Opening the laptop on the desk, it dawned on her that

she'd just had a conversation with him. And she'd been reasonably coherent and articulate. Smiling, she pulled up Darcy's email account to send the ARC to the *USA Today* reviewer.

Then she reached into her pocket, picked up her pencil, and wrote: 'Coherent conversation with a sexy man.'

"Check."

———

Ian sank into his desk chair hoping the strains of Bach's "Cello Suite Number One in G" would release the tension behind his eyes. Even if he hadn't walked through Yardley Mansion, Ian knew he could perform the renovation work. He glanced up at the computer screen where the PDF of the RFI and its instructions taunted him with its jumble of letters. With Ruby ill, he'd have to tackle this beast himself.

The owners had changed tack, and preceded the RFP with a Request for Information or RFI, which had a two-week turn-around time.

But *twenty* pages of instructions for a ten-page RFI. "Shit." He scrubbed his hands through his hair. What the hell was he thinking?

With the dyseidetic, or visual form of dyslexia, Ian had a difficult time with whole word recognition and spelling. The letters 'b' and 'd' and 'p' and 'q' got mixed up with one another, and he had difficulty associating the sounds with the letters. It was better now than when we was in middle school or even high school. Ruby's techniques, like listening to audiobooks while reading along improved his word recognition, pronunciation, and visualization skills. Use of open-source font for dyslexics helped too.

His handwriting was practically illegible, so he typed everything. Autocorrect, though not always perfect, helped immeasurably, and the proliferation of email and text messaging were a godsend for him, as was the voice to text software program on his computer. And the bookkeeper he'd hired when he'd started his business seven years ago made sure his invoices were correct and his bills were paid.

But who the hell was going to help him with this? The RFI would help narrow down the pool of vendors eligible to submit the RFP. Ian knew it was important to take great care in responding to the RFI because it would be used to develop the final RFP, possibly influencing the solicitation in his favor.

He groaned. He couldn't even tackle a ten-page RFI. He'd have about as much chance of completing what could be a five hundred page RFP as a he had of getting through a New York winter without snow. His dyslexia was the one secret he kept from Caleb, otherwise he'd ask for his help. He snorted. No. No, he wouldn't, because he didn't ask for help from anyone but Ruby.

Closing his eyes, he remembered Ruby's admonition—one bite at a time. So, he started with the first question and focused only on that.

———

The next day, Ian stood scratching his head at the wiring he'd uncovered in the bathroom remodel. *WTF?* Darcy had been lucky the house hadn't burned down. Probably because this bathroom didn't get much use.

Well, it would now, and this had to be fixed. Unfortunately, it was out of his wheelhouse. Fortunately, he had a friend whose wheelhouse it fit squarely in.

Taking out his phone, he gave Caleb a call.

"Montgomery."

"Got a bit of an electrical clusterfuck. You have some time to come by the Ryan job in Park Slope and lend me a hand?"

"A clusterfuck, huh? You sure it's not a SNAFU? Or maybe it's FUBAR."

"You free later, or not?"

Caleb snorted on the other end of the phone. "Want me to send out an APB?"

"What for?"

"Your sense of humor. It seems to be missing."

"Never mind." Ian started to hang up.

"I'll be there in thirty."

Ian ended the call wondering how Caleb managed such a successful business with a jokester personality like his. Jillie, of course.

Forty-five minutes later, Ian heard Millie talking to Caleb, telling him where to find Ian. Caleb's heavy work boots clomped up the stairs. Apparently he'd abandoned the metrosexual look. At least for the day.

"What's with the woman in brown?" he asked without preamble.

Ignoring the question, Ian glanced at his watch. "You stop for a coffee break on the way over?" Ian cringed at his own grumpiness. Between the stress of the RFI, Ruby's illness, and his current jobs, his patience was so thin, it was practically nonexistent.

"Traffic," Caleb muttered. "What we got?"

Ian took him into the bathroom and indicated the spaghetti tangle of wiring.

Caleb let out a whistle. "That, my friend, is definitely a clusterfuck."

"Can you fix it without rewiring the whole house?"

"How's the wiring in the nursery?"

"Kosher."

Caleb poked around and got a shock for his trouble. "Fuck!" He shook his finger. "Yeah. I'll get my stuff."

# CHAPTER ELEVEN

Tiptoeing past the bathroom where Ian and his friend, Caleb, were working, Millie paused in the hallway and heard Caleb ask Ian, "How's Ruby?"

"She's at the rehab facility another few days, and then I think I can take her home."

"That's rough, man. I'm sorry. You let me know if Jillian and I can do anything to help."

"Yep."

"Are you almost finished with the RFI?" Caleb continued.

"Haven't started it," came Ian's gruff reply.

"What? Why the hell not? It's due in, what, a week?"

"Yeah. I'll get to it. Get off my back about it."

Just guessing, Millie thought an RFI was a request for information, probably similar to a pre-grant submission. Wonder what Ian's going after? And what's it to his friend?

She could probably knock out an RFI in a couple of hours. In high school she'd helped her parents with their grant submissions, and in college she'd taken a job as a grants assistant in the chemistry department.

"Ian, this job could be huge for your business. Don't you want it?" Caleb continued.

"I said I'd get to it. With Ruby ill I haven't exactly been sitting around eating bonbons. Jesus, when did you become such a nag? Now can we please finish *this* job?"

"I'm sorry, man. You've got your hands full, and I know the timing sucks, but Ruby would want you to focus on this."

"Fine," Ian growled.

Millie continued up the stairs to Darcy's office. If the RFI is so important to Ian's business, he'd better get on it. It should be top priority on his to-do list. Right behind taking care of his sick friend, of course.

Speaking of lists, she could cross off 'edit manuscript.' She set the marked up pages on Darcy's desk with a sense of satisfaction in a job well done.

A few hours later, Millie had completed another task on her list: Darcy's latest research questions. She looked out the window and realized it was dark. Darcy, and Josh, always insisted that she leave before dark. While Park Slope was relatively safe, they didn't like her walking to the subway alone at night. Never mind that she had to walk eight blocks from the Bedford Avenue stop in Williamsburg to her apartment.

Well, couldn't be helped. Josh and Darcy were at the law firm's holiday party, so she'd just have to brave it on her own.

Straightening her desk in anticipation of Monday morning, she heard Ian's footsteps upstairs. He'd put in a long day too. Putting on her coat, scarf, hat, and mittens, she headed for the front door. She picked up her backpack just as Ian got to the bottom of the stairs.

He looked tired, and there was a smudge on his left

cheek. Should she tell him? She wouldn't want to walk around with a smudge on her cheek. Not that anyone would notice. "You, uh"—she waggled her finger at his face—"have a smudge on your cheek."

He scrubbed at his cheek, missing it. "Did I get it?"

"No. Let me." She stepped up to him and brushed gently at the spot. "There." Her hand felt as if she'd just touched a warm blanket.

"Thanks. You just leaving?" he asked as he zipped up his leather jacket.

"Yes. Lost track of time."

"How will you get home?"

"The subway." She shrugged on her backpack.

"You're not walking there alone?"

"Since the subway won't come to me, I'll have to go to it."

His expression grim, he remained silent a moment. "No. I'll give you a ride home."

"On your death machine?"

"My what?"

"Your motorcycle."

The corner of his mouth tipped up. A rare sight, one that made her belly tingle and her knees wobble.

"It's not a death machine."

"If you say so. But almost five thousand people die each year riding a motorcycle."

"Yeah, and hundreds of people are mugged each year in New York City. I promise to get you home safely."

Well, here was her chance to mark 'death machine ride' off her GALL. "All right."

She locked up the house and followed Ian out to the street. He slung his leg over the bike and handed her the helmet.

"What about you? Helmets are required. You'll get a ticket."

"I'll risk it." He snapped the strap under her chin.

The helmet engulfed her, making it difficult to see. "But what if we're in a wreck? You could be injured."

Ian released a throaty chuckle that she felt all the way down to her toes. "My head's too hard."

She'd never heard him laugh. She liked it. "But—"

"Get on the bike."

Eying the bike, she was uncertain how exactly to climb on.

"Just throw your leg over."

*Hmm. Easy for him to say.* She approached the bike, the realization dawning on her that she would be straddling not only the bike, but . . . him. *Sampson and Delilah!*

"Come on, Millie. I'm not getting any younger here. And it's cold."

She took a deep breath and slung her leg up and over and tried to sit at the far end of the seat, away from Ian.

He twisted around, eying her. "You're going to have to hold on if you don't want to find yourself sitting in the middle of the street."

"Right." She swallowed, then scooted closer to him.

"Wrap your arms around my waist and hold tight."

The bike roared to life, and it was like sitting astride a fire-breathing beast. The vibration shook her to her core. They hadn't even pulled away from the curb and she was breathless with exhilaration.

"And lean into the turns."

"Lean into the turns," she repeated. "Got it." She pressed her chest to his back. Heat radiated off him, warming the front of her. She'd never been this physically close to a man before. Unless you counted rush hour on the Brooklyn-Queens Crosstown.

"You ready?" Without waiting for a response, he took off.

*Mother of Hamlet, it was cold.* She squeezed her eyes shut and finally gave in, pressing her head against his back, using his broad shoulders as a windbreak.

She didn't know what stole her breath more. Being up against the solid wall of Ian's back, or riding this snarling beast of a motorcycle. Ian. Definitely Ian.

She spread her fingers across a lean stomach, undoubtedly solid muscle. Her legs enveloped his harder ones —*much* harder ones—so that she felt every flex of his muscles as he weaved the bike through the multitude of taxis and city busses. Very aware of her breasts against his back, she wondered if he felt them too.

They stopped at a traffic light. Ian twisted around. "Where do you live?"

Oh yeah. That would help. She told him her address and he gave her a funny look. The light changed and he took off again.

This time she forced herself to keep her eyes open, to watch the shops and restaurants, the pedestrians and the cars fly by. She finally understood the fascination with motorcycles. The freedom. The sheer exhilaration.

All too soon they double parked in front of her apartment building and he shut off the bike. "Careful climbing off."

Her legs shook as she stood up and unsnapped the helmet. "Thank you." She shivered without the heat of Ian's body.

He took the helmet from her and pulled it on. "And you

didn't die," he said, the corner of his mouth lifting as he snapped the strap.

*"No. I didn't." In fact, I lived!*

"I'll wait for you to get inside. Goodnight, Millie. Have a nice weekend."

"You, too." Reluctant to leave him, she forced her feet in the direction of her building. As she opened the door, the motorcycle roared again as he hit the gas.

Adrenaline still pumping through her, she knew sleep would be a long time in coming tonight.

———

Stretched out on his bed, a re-run of *This Old House* on the TV, Ian couldn't get Millie off his mind. The feel of her against him, her arms wrapped around his waist, the way her breathing hitched when she'd climbed on the bike. She'd looked adorable in his helmet, the way it fell over her eyes. And if he could trust the light from the streetlamp, her cheeks had been flushed when she'd climbed off the bike and removed the helmet. Whether from cold or exhilaration, he didn't know.

He'd felt so protective of her. As he'd watched her head up the sidewalk to her apartment, he'd wondered what her life was like. Did she have any friends outside of Darcy? Did she have a boyfriend? A spark of jealousy struck him out of the blue.

Why should he care? Even if he was interested in her, he didn't have time. He had a friend who needed him and a business to grow. And speaking of his business, now that Ruby was comfortable at home, he vowed he'd spend the entire weekend working on the RFI if that was what it took, but come Sunday evening, it would be finished. With the deadline looming, it was high time he shit or got off the pot.

And if he finished it early on Sunday, he'd reward himself with a little work on the shelves for his office/library. He'd landed some beautiful Brazilian walnut on closeout that would make a stunning addition to the loft.

Satisfied with his plan, he clicked off the TV and rolled over on his side. As he drifted off, he could swear he felt Millie pressed against his back, warm and trusting.

———

"Millie, be careful. Josh can put the star on the tree when he gets home," Darcy warned.

Millie teetered on the top step of the stepladder, determined to finish the Christmas tree. They still had the banister, fireplace mantel, and front stoop to decorate. *The New York Times Magazine* was doing a feature on Christmas with Best-Selling author Darcy Butler-Ryan, and the photographer would be at the house tomorrow.

That, and she loved decorating with Darcy. She had so many pretty things. Things that meant something special to her. Like the *Pride and Prejudice*-themed ornaments her mother had given her for her first Christmas away from home. And the New York Yankees' ornament that Josh gave her the year they met.

Millie's parents barely acknowledged Christmas. Even over the school break, they were buried in their research. The only gifts she'd received growing up came from her maternal aunt who lived in California, and they were usually items like Barbie dolls and My Little Pony. She appreciated her aunt's thoughtfulness, and while her cousins, Amy and Mindy, probably enjoyed them, the gifts were a complete mystery to her. She'd much rather have received books. Or a chemistry set. Even an ant farm.

Millie didn't put up a tree. Her apartment was far too small. But coming to Darcy's every day, she got to see and enjoy this one.

"Hi, ladies. Need some help?" Ian's voice melted over Millie like hot butter, and her foot slipped as if she'd stepped in the slick stuff.

"Oh!" Millie gasped.

"Millie!" Darcy cried.

It all happened so fast. With all her weight balanced on that front foot, Millie was going down. She just hoped she didn't take the tree with her. Or send it toppling onto Darcy. She flailed about hoping to somehow right herself.

"Gotcha!" Ian's hands slipped around her waist, as she fell into him. He managed to keep them both upright, avoiding the tree, and consequently, disaster. She placed her hands on his shoulders as he slid her down his body, until her feet touched the floor.

*Cheese and crackers!* She'd done it again. Made an utter fool of herself in front of Ian. The heat of mortification burned her skin, as she muttered, "Thank you."

"Oh, Ian! Thank heavens you were here," Darcy said as she placed her hands on Millie's shoulders.

"No harm done," Ian replied as he looked into Millie's eyes. Her heart stuttered in her chest. Great! *That's* all she needed—to have a heart attack in front of him. But then he'd have to perform mouth-to-mouth. Her gaze darted to his lips. *Hmm.*

He dropped his hands from her waist and set her away from him, leaving her disappointed. "Can I help?"

"That'd be great," Darcy said. "Millie was just trying to place the star on the tree."

Ian bent down to pick up the ornament that Millie had dropped in her scramble to stay upright.

Without the need for the stepladder, Ian reached up and set it on top of the tree. "How's that?"

"Turn it just a little to the left," Darcy instructed. "Perfect. Thank you!"

"What else can I do?"

"Could you help hang the garland across the top of the door? Millie can tell you how, while I, uh, run to the little girl's room. Peanut's tap dancing on my bladder."

Millie cringed at Darcy's penchant for oversharing. "Sure."

After opening a plastic bin, Millie took out a garland of greenery, pinecones, and holly berries and led the way to the front door. Ian picked up the stepladder and followed.

Opening the door to a cold blast of air, Ian asked, "Don't you want a coat?"

She shrugged. "We won't be out there long." Then she eyed his short-sleeve T-shirt. "What about you?"

"I'll be fine. Like you said, we won't be out there long."

"There should be nails along the doorframe from previous years. Just center the garland over the door and loop it behind the nails," Millie instructed.

"I think I can handle that." After placing the stepladder on the stoop, he took the garland from her hand. "Hold on to the ladder."

Millie stepped up behind the ladder to steady it, and looking up, got an eyeful of Ian Brand's butt, and what a butt is was! *Friar Tuck!* She had this unholy urge to bite it. Or pinch it. Something. Anything. She couldn't help it. It just filled his jeans so nicely.

She recalled the feel of his hard body between her

thighs as she rode behind him on his death machine, and the lack of a coat suddenly didn't matter.

"Tell me if that's centered," Ian said, breaking into her lewd thoughts.

"I'll have to let go of the ladder."

"Fine."

She stepped back and almost fell backward off the step. *Get a grip, Silly Millie.* Quickly eying the garland for symmetry, she took a little longer to enjoy Ian. Arms over his head, muscles rippling beneath his snug T-shirt, and that butt. The one she'd wanted to bite a few seconds ago. Feelings of lust shot through her leaving her breathless and dizzy. She finally understood the meaning of 'climb him like a tree.'

"How's it look?"

"Oh! Fine. It's fine." The thought bubble above her head said, 'Oh so fine.'

Ian tucked the garland behind the nails, securing it, and Millie took up her position again, holding the ladder and trying not to ogle Ian's butt. Lost cause, that.

No tool belt today. She'd begun to have fantasies about Ian and that tool belt. Like Ian in nothing but that tool belt.

The memory of his hands at her waist as he caught her. The feel of his body against hers as she slid down it, all hard and lean. She wanted to press her cold hands to her hot face and neck, as an unfamiliar ache settled between her thighs.

"That ought to do it."

Yes, Millie thought, that ought to do it.

## CHAPTER TWELVE

L ater that evening, Ian perched against his bike and
watched as Millie stepped out of her apartment
building, pulling her coat around her against the December
chill. Smiling to himself, he shook his head at her
awkwardness.

Yet, he recalled with some degree of lust, the feel of her
body as she'd slid down his.

She was one big accident waiting to happen. He
wondered how on earth she'd come this far in life without
serious injury. For all he knew, maybe she hadn't.

Before she got too far down the sidewalk, three
teenagers sidled up next to her, clearly a little too close for
Millie's comfort. And his.

"Hey, Mousey Millie. What's up? Got a hot date
tonight?" the apparent leader asked, causing the others to
laugh.

Millie put her head down and kept walking.

*Ah, hell.* Nothing he hated more than bullies. He
pushed off his bike and stepped out of the shadows. "As a
matter of fact, she does. With me."

The three thugs looked up with a start, as did Millie.

Ian approached them, noting the smart-ass grins on their faces.

"Really?" the punk-ass leader asked, his expression dubious.

"Really." Ian wrapped his arm around Millie's waist, gathering her in close, and then stepped into the ringleader's space, staring him down. "And if you call her Mousey Millie again, you better hope I'm not around to hear it."

"Dude," the leader said, hands in the air, "we were just joking. We didn't mean any harm, did we, Millie?" He reached out to touch her like they were best buds, then thought better of it.

Ian looked down into Millie's surprised face. "You ready to go, babe?"

She just nodded.

"Good." He put his arm around her and headed in the direction of his bike.

"Dude must have a thing for the homely," the leader muttered.

"Shut up, man," one of the others ground out.

Ian turned, putting Millie behind him, and strode up to the now-quaking dumbasses. "You were saying?"

"Um, nothing, man," one of the other idiots muttered.

Ian leaned in. "Beat it. I don't want to see so much as your shadow when we get back. Understand?"

They nodded in unison.

"Now get!" They turned tail and ran.

"Punk ass kids." Ian strode back to Millie, gathered her close. "They do that often?" He felt her nod against his chest, where the anger simmered. "Next time tell them to go fuck themselves."

Millie laughed, and his heart swelled at the sound. "And where are you going after dark alone?"

Pushing back, she eyed him with a frown. "Drugstore. I have a headache and I'm out of aspirin. What are you doing here? And why did you tell those boys that we have a date?"

*Why was he here?* He didn't know, but now that he was . . . "I live nearby and stopped for dinner at," he looked around, "the diner over there," he said, pointing across the street. "You eaten yet?"

"No."

"Good. Have dinner with me?"

"I– Really?" Her frown turned to confusion, as color flooded her cheeks.

"Sure."

"O-Okay."

"See there, now you have a date."

———

Millie slid into the booth across from Ian, still totally confused by not only his appearance outside her apartment building, but also his offer of dinner.

She'd never been on a date, if that's what this was. Most likely it was Ian just being nice, or worse, feeling sorry for her.

The waitress, who always looked like she'd stepped out of an episode of *Happy Days*, brought menus over. She glanced up at Ian to see that he hadn't picked up the menu, but rather surveyed the other diners. Millie didn't need to read the menu either since she ordered takeout from the diner about once a week, but she was thankful to have a reason not to talk until she could get her nerves under control.

All too soon that excuse fled when the waitress returned to take their order.

Millie ordered her usual, the roast turkey and mashed potatoes.

"How's the meatloaf?" Ian asked.

The waitress leaned over and muttered, "Nothing to write home about. If I were you I'd order the beef stew."

"Fine. And just water to drink."

"How long have those idiots been taunting you like that?" Ian asked as soon as the waitress left to put in their orders.

Millie didn't want to talk about it. "It's nothing. Can we just talk about something else?"

Ian lifted a brow but changed the subject. "Thought you had a headache?"

"I do."

"Order a soda, that always helps me if I can't get my hands on an aspirin."

Millie nodded.

As Ian flagged down the waitress again, Millie took a moment to appreciate the virility that was Ian. He wore his usual leather jacket, but he'd unzipped it to reveal a black T-shirt. His hair was disheveled from his motorcycle helmet, and curled around his jacket collar. She wondered if it would feel silky to the touch. In sharp contrast, his face bore a couple days' growth.

As he turned back to her he rubbed his hand across his chin, and the scraping sound sent chills skittering across her skin. His gray eyes gazed into hers, and she remembered each human eyeball weighs about an ounce.

"Millie?"

"Hmm?"

"You okay?"

"Yes, why?"

"Because I asked you a question and you didn't respond." A half-smile tugged at the corners of his mouth.

"Oh." Heat slid up her neck and into her face. "I'm sorry, what was the question?"

"Have you lived in Williamsburg long?" His eyes held hers and she swallowed.

"About six years. I moved here from Forest Hills."

"Forrest Hills?"

"My parents have a house." The waitress returned with her soda, so she took a sip to relieve her parched throat.

"What do your parents do?"

"They're literature professors at Barnard College."

"That's impressive." His eyebrows winged up.

"I guess. What about your parents?"

Ian spun his glass of ice water on the table and for a minute she thought he wasn't going to answer. "My mom died nine years ago, and my dad died when I was five."

"I'm sorry." Her heart ached for him.

"It is what it is," he said, a sad smile ghosting across his features.

"How is your friend?"

He looked up with a start, then said, "She's hanging in there. She's home now."

"That must be a relief. To both of you."

The waitress slid two plates onto the table. "Let me know if there's anything else I can get you. Like an antacid," she said with a smirk before she left.

The corner of Ian's mouth lifted in response to her remark, and Millie noticed the dimple in his cheek for the first time. She liked how it softened the hard lines of his face.

As he dug into his beef stew, Millie poked around her

brain for something to say. "Did you finish Kant's critiques?"

"Last week," he said around a mouthful of food. "It was enlightening."

"How so?"

As he shared his thoughts on Kant, Millie found herself relaxing and nodding along to his comments. If someone had told her she'd be sitting in a diner across from a tattooed construction worker discussing the finer points of Kant's categorical imperative, she'd have scoffed at them. If they'd told her she'd be on a date with said tattooed construction worker she'd have questioned their sanity.

———

"Can I get you two anything else?" the waitress asked as she cleared the table. "We have some apple pie that isn't half bad."

Ian looked across at Millie, who shrugged. "Sure. A slice of pie and two forks." He watched the waitress walk away and leaned over the table to whisper, "Waitress of the year, she's not."

Millie giggled. Not a high, sparkling sound, but a rich, mellifluous one. Sexy, like her voice, and it sent heat straight to his groin. He wondered if anyone had ever told her she'd make a great phone sex operator.

He'd felt like a creep stalking her tonight, but he was glad he did. Not only did he run off those jerks, he'd really enjoyed his impromptu dinner with her. Of course over the last few weeks he'd discovered her intelligence, but tonight he got a glimpse of the woman beneath all that brown.

A feeling of affection settled over him. He genuinely liked Millie Stephens. Enjoyed her company.

Maybe he should ask her if she'd like to see the public libraries exhibition on New York architecture he'd been itching to see.

The pie arrived and he and Millie dove in. It wasn't bad. In fact, it was pretty good. He glanced up at Millie to see if she was enjoying it, and noticed a crumb at the corner of her mouth. Where he'd like to press his lips. Instead, he reached across the table with his napkin and brushed it off. The blush that crept into her cheeks made him ache. A blush of shame, not just embarrassment.

"Thank you." She gazed down in her embarrassment.

"Millie, look at me."

She lifted her gaze to his, a frown creasing her forehead.

Taking her hand in his, he rubbed his thumb across it. "Everyone does something from time-to-time that's embarrassing. A little misstep, some spinach between their teeth. It's nothing to be ashamed of. Hell, I once hit my thumb with a hammer in front of a bunch of seasoned carpenters. They never let me forget it, but I survived."

Her voice barely above a whisper, she said, "But I always seem to make a fool of myself in front of you."

"Well, I'll see if I can return the favor sometime and nail my thumb with the hammer."

She smiled. "I wouldn't want you to do that. But maybe you could trip or come to Darcy's with your shirt on inside out sometime."

He blinked. Her smile actually dazzled him, all the more because it was so rare. "I'll see what I can do."

"Thank you."

"All right. I'll pay the check, then see you home."

———

M illie floated home. Even the frigid night air couldn't dampen the warmth she felt after her dinner with Ian. Her first date. She nearly let out a girly squeal, but checked herself.

Ian walked next to her, close enough for her to feel his heat, but not touching her. "Are you cold?"

She shook her head. Because, truth was, she wasn't.

They arrived at the door to her building and her stomach quivered. She wondered if he'd kiss her goodnight. *Of course not, Silly Millie.*

"I had a nice time," he was saying as she gazed up at his mouth, wondering how it would taste.

"So did I." Did he catch her staring?

"Don't let those assholes bother you again."

"I won't."

"Goodnight, Millie."

"Goodnight, Ian. And thank you for dinner." She tamped down her disappointment as she watched him saunter down the sidewalk to his motorcycle. The roar of the engine punctuated the night as she turned to let herself in. *Sweet dreams, Ian.* She hoped for the same.

---

T he next morning, Ian listened to Chopin on his iPod as he sanded the window seat he'd built for the nursery. The bookshelves underneath would hold books from *Curious George* right up to *Catcher in the Rye.* Or *Pride and Prejudice* if Darcy had a girl.

Zoning out on the music, he thought about Millie. He hadn't seen her today, and he wondered where she was. Probably running errands for Darcy.

All weekend he'd found himself thinking about her. Wondering what she was doing. Wondering if she ever got lonely.

He'd had a nice time with her the previous evening. In fact, he'd had more than a nice time. The evening had been a pleasant break from his worries over Ruby, the RFI, and the England job. Millie had made him forget all of that, if only for a short time.

And he'd enjoyed discussing Kant with her, before moving on to discussions of their favorite books. He'd learned they had many favorites in common. Like Pat Frank's *Alas Babylon* and Dickens' *David Copperfield*. But he'd also learned she had a soft spot for romance novels, which made sense, given her employment.

There was so much more to Millie than meets the eye, and he of all people should be ashamed for assuming otherwise.

He'd like to get to know her better. If nothing else, they could meet over coffee and discuss books. He stopped sanding. But if he were honest with himself, he would admit he was attracted to her. He felt a kinship to her. She wore her mantle of brown just like he wore his mantle of tough. It protected against the hurt. It cocooned them so that no one could get close. And if no one could get close, no one could hurt you.

Then there was the physical attraction. The overwhelming desire to kiss her goodnight. The zing he'd felt when he'd taken her hand last night. The way her voice turned his mind to baser thoughts. The feel of her body pressed close to him on the bike. And yet she covered it all in a sea of brown.

He wondered what in Millie's life had so damaged her,

and if there was any hope of getting behind the mantle of brown to the real woman beneath.

Millie jumped at the thud from above, followed by a muffled curse. A few seconds later she heard Ian's booted feet clamoring down the stairs.

She stepped out of the kitchen to find him holding a towel around his hand, blood running down his wrist.

"Ian! What happened?"

"I sliced my hand on a piece of metal flashing. I've got a first-aid kit in my truck."

"Here, we've got a first-aid kit in the cabinet." Ian followed her into the kitchen. She reached up, opened the cabinet next to the refrigerator, and took down the small box. "Let me see it."

Pulling his hand over the sink, she unwrapped the towel. Opening his palm, she saw a two-inch cut running from his pinky to his thumb. "It doesn't appear to be deep. I don't think it needs stitches."

Turning on the tap, she held his palm under the running water. "Let it run for a minute." She dug around in the box, took out a large Band-Aid, antibiotic ointment, some antiseptic, and a piece of gauze.

Gently patting his hand dry, she lifted the antiseptic. "This may sting a bit." She doused the cut liberally.

Ian sucked in a breath. "Shit."

"I'm sorry." Lifting his hand to her mouth, she blew gently on the cut.

# CHAPTER THIRTEEN

S*on-of-a-bitch.* His gaze shot to Millie's lips as her breath reached the palm of his hand. He expected the blood from the cut to simply dry up given all the blood in his body had headed to parts farther south.

He stood in Darcy's kitchen, his hand bleeding like a stuck pig and stinging like a mother, and his thoughts had suddenly shifted to Millie's mouth. And how he'd like to put that mouth to better use.

"Better?"

"Hmm?"

"You're hand? Has the stinging eased?"

"Yeah." But something else had flared. He stared into her warm brown eyes, darker with her pupils dilated, and had an overwhelming urge to kiss her.

"Good." A blush tinged her cheeks as she turned her attention to the Band-Aid and the ointment. She slathered ointment on the cut, then carefully placed the bandage over it, the light touch of her delicate hands setting off a fantasy of what those hands would feel like dancing along his bare chest, sliding down to a part of him that desperately needed her attention. And he didn't mean his hand.

*Damn.* "Millie?"

Her wide-eyed gaze lifted to his.

Thinking better about what he'd planned to say, he said instead, "Thank you."

A soft smile touched her lips and she tucked a stray strand of hair behind her ear. "You're welcome."

Then he got the hell out of Dodge.

———

That afternoon, a crazy idea insinuated itself into Millie's brain and wouldn't let go. An idea that would allow her to check off Number Two on her list, while helping Ian out, based on the idiom, *I'll scratch your back if you'll scratch mine.*

She could have sworn there was something between them in the kitchen earlier when she'd bandaged his cut. She'd sure felt it. And she thought he had too.

From everything she'd read, his dilated pupils and shallow breath indicated arousal. And then there was the slight bulge beneath his fly.

Question was whether she had the guts to actually make the offer, and to see it through. She took out her ever-present Get a Life List and stared at it. Stepping over to her desk she picked up a pencil and added: 'Be assertive.' After considering it, she erased 'assertive' and changed it to 'bold.' Satisfied, she'd wait until the opportunity presented itself.

A couple of hours later, the opportunity presented itself, much sooner than she had expected. First, Laura came by to see Darcy, so the two of them were in the kitchen, occupied.

Then Ian came downstairs, jacket in his good hand, looking as if he was heading out. Making the offer at the end of the day, she'd not only give him time to think about it, she could perhaps postpone the inevitable rejection.

*Be bold. Then she added, Be positive.*

Taking a deep calming breath, Millie closed her eyes, then set her jaw and called his name. "Ian? Can I talk to you?"

He entered the office, pulling on his jacket, his brow creased, no doubt in confusion over her request. "Sure."

*Antony and Cleopatra!* What was she thinking? Her hand drifted to her stomach to calm the swarm of butterflies that had taken up residence there.

"Um, how's your hand?"

He glanced down. "Fine. Thanks."

She nodded. "Good," she said then stood there like a mute.

"Well, I have to get going," Ian said, zipping up his jacket.

"How is the RFI coming?"

Ian's brow shot up. "How do you know about the RFI?"

"I, uh, overhead you and your friend talking about it the other day."

"Jesus. Is there anything you don't hear?"

She shrugged. "Occupational hazard when you work in someone else's home."

"Right. It's done." His answer didn't sound convincing.

"Oh." *Mother of invention!* Now what? "Well, if you're selected for the RFP. I could help, if . . ." She ran out of breath. His eyes were on her face, and she couldn't bear it. Closing her own, she took a deep breath, "I'd like to make you an offer. I'll help you with the RFP . . . if you'll have sex with me."

She kept her eyes closed as silence engulfed her. Not even the sound of his breathing. Then she felt him close. Too close. Her eyes flew open and she gazed into Ian's stormy face.

"What the hell are you talking about?"

She cringed. "I, uh, I thought we could help one another out." Her mouth had gone dry, and she'd lost the ability to breathe.

An expression skittered across his face. Anger? Dismay? Disgust?

"Did you, now?" He stepped up to her, still within the boundaries of his own personal space. Barely. His eyes held hers, his a dark stormy gray, then he looked her up and down as if considering.

"Well, how do you feel about cunnilingus?" he asked, as he stepped outside his personal space and into hers, backing her up to the bookcase in the office, the shelf digging into her mid back.

Remembering how to breathe, she filled her lungs with a gasp. "What woman wouldn't enjoy it?" she said, trying to sound nonchalant.

He snorted. "Do you even know what it is?"

"Of course I know what it is. I'm not stupid."

"No. You're most definitely not stupid. Inexperienced, maybe. Stupid, no."

Before she could sputter a response, he stepped further into her personal space, leaving mere inches between them. "How about fellatio?"

"Um, sure. Sex is give and take, isn't it?"

"No. Not always. Sometimes it's all take." He skimmed a finger along her cheekbone. Stepping in a little closer, he asked, "How about if I put my hand here?" He placed his uninjured hand over her breast. "And my mouth here?" He pressed his tongue to the spot below her ear.

The air backed up in her lungs, her knees wobbled, and a heaviness settled between her legs. How could she be both afraid and aroused? No. Not afraid. Intimidated. This Ian was different. Dark. Yet unbearably sexy. But not frightening.

"I—"

The phone on the desk rang, once, twice.

"I—I have to get that." Unsure he would move or that she would be able to budge him, she pressed her hands to his chest—his really, really hard chest—and he stepped aside, a smirk on his face.

"Saved by the bell, sweet Millie?"

———

Ian scrubbed his hand through his hair and strode into the living room. What the fuck was that all about? Damn, but he was pissed. Pissed that she would offer herself like that. And pissed at himself for backing her into a corner. Literally.

He'd meant to scare her. Warn her to stay away from him. Instead, he'd scared himself. The feel of her firm breast in his hand, the warm skin below her ear against his lips, had shot heat straight to his groin. Beneath those ridiculous clothes was a woman's body, as he'd been discovering over the last few weeks.

He remembered her little panting breaths. The way her pulse beat like a hummingbird's in her throat. The fire in her eyes when she believed he'd thought her stupid.

And what he thought were dull brown eyes, proved to

be far from it. Those eyes glinted with golden sparks, lending them depth and warmth.

What the hell had he been thinking? He didn't intimidate women. He didn't back them into bookcases and put his hands on them. At least not without their permission.

What the hell had *she* been thinking? Offering herself to him like an object up for barter. Did she do that with other men? Did she think that was the only way they'd have sex with her?

And the sad thing was, he'd wanted to take her up on her offer. Right then and there, she'd turned him on with her fuck-me voice, and her little pants when he'd put his hands on her. After the encounter in the kitchen, his senses were on heightened alert.

Caleb was right. He needed to get laid. And soon.

Trouble was no one appealed to him. Except Millie in her brown schlumpy clothes and her too tidy bun.

He should check on her, but his inclination was to let it go. Maybe she wouldn't bring it up again. Forget it ever happened. He didn't want to hurt her, but he didn't make deals with women for sex. Even if he did find her appealing. And the image of her naked and writhing beneath him made him hard enough to pound nails.

He strode toward the front door without a backward glance.

———

Millie watched as Ian left without so much as a goodbye. Angry, defeated and beyond aroused, she headed for the kitchen where Laura and Darcy were talking about the upcoming baby shower. She'd vowed she would never put herself out there again. Never open herself up for ridicule. But she had. And look what happened.

At least there wasn't a cafeteria of witnesses this time.

Reaching out, she grabbed the glass of wine from Laura's hand and took a gulp.

"Help yourself," Laura said dryly as she took another glass from the cabinet and filled it with the red wine.

"Millie!" Darcy said. "You don't drink."

"Seems like a good time to start," Millie retorted.

Laura snorted, lifted her glass in a toast and said, "*In vino, veritas*, then."

Millie winced and took another slug. God, she hoped not! She'd be taking that little encounter with Ian to her grave. She only hoped he did the same. The wine spread a pleasant warmth down her throat and into her chest. Tasted pretty good, too. Like plums, and maybe some dark cherries.

"Careful there, lightweight," Laura said with a smirk. "You're supposed to savor wine, not drown your sorrows in it. That's what tequila's for."

And why shouldn't she drown her sorrows in it? She needed to drown them in something. Feeling a little floaty, Millie tossed back the remaining contents of the glass, and tried to slam the glass down on the countertop, but missed it altogether. The fact that she'd skipped lunch only added to the effects of the wine on her motor skills.

The room had lost all its edges, blending into soft lines and colors. From some distant place, she heard Laura snicker.

"Millie? Are you okay?" Darcy grasped her shoulders and stared into her eyes.

"Yes. No." Millie couldn't decide what she was. "Why?"

"Because you were weaving back and forth, and frankly it was making me seasick."

Laura stepped up, stuck her hand in Millie's face. "How many fingers am I holding up?"

Millie tried to swat her hand out of the way, but missed. Twice. Dang Laura and her fast reflexes.

"She's toasted," Laura said, a smirk on her supermodel face.

"Ladies." Josh walked in with Nathan on his heels. "You ready for dinner?"

"Hi ya, Josh. Nathan." Millie thought she handled that pretty well considering the moving floor beneath her feet.

"Millie, what's wrong?" Josh asked.

A funny noise came out of her mouth, a cross between a snort and a *pfft*. *What's wrong?* Where should she start?

"Are you drunk?" Josh raised an eyebrow at Millie, then turned to Laura. "You let Millie get drunk?"

"Me? Why is it my fault?"

"You brought the wine."

"How many has she had anyway?" Nathan asked, peering into her eyes.

"One glass," someone said.

"One!" Nathan chuckled and shook his head.

*Why is everyone talking about her as if she's not there?* Oh right. *Because that's how she wants it. She wants to be invisible.* No, wait. Not anymore. Not since that delivery truck almost pancaked her. Not since Ian saved her from certain death. And held her against that hard body of his. That chick-magnet body. That body that had pushed her against the bookcase in the living room while he talked dirty to her. She shivered at the memory.

"Clearly, Millie is a cheap date," Laura said.

Darcy, Laura, Nathan, and Josh all began speaking at

once, bickering over something. *Whatever.* At least they weren't all staring at her like a bug under a microscope anymore.

Remembering the recent addition to her list, she took the phone from the cradle, and dialed Ian's cell, determined to give him a piece of her mind.

"Brand," Ian answered, his voice gruff.

"Listen here, you, you . . . thug. You think you can get me all hot and bothered and just leave?"

"Millie?" came Ian's surprised voice. Just that sexy rasp had her nerves a-tingle. At least she thought it was her nerves. Could be she just needed to pee.

"Dang right, I mean, *damn* right, it's Millie."

"Millie! Who are you talking to?" Darcy asked with a laugh.

"You think you're God's gift. Well, I'm here to burst that burble, er, babble, er, oh, you know what I mean."

"Give me the phone, Millie." Josh held out his hand, and she put her back to him.

"You think you're so hot. Well, you are. Wait, that's not what I meant to say. Brain cramp." She lifted her hand to her head and massaged her muddled brain.

"Come on, Millie, friends don't let friends dial drunk." Josh finally pried the receiver out of her hand. "This is Josh. Who is this?" He paused a moment. "Ian?"

Darcy's hand flew to her throat, while Laura snickered.

"I like this Millie," Laura said. "She should drink more often. Better than the Stick-Up-Her-Ass-Millie."

Deflated, Millie slid down the wall until her butt hit the floor.

"Yeah, Millie had a tad over her limit. Sorry about that. Yeah, Nathan and I will see her home. No worries."

No worries. *Pfft.* There were worries aplenty. But the

topper—the *numero uno*—was how she'd ever look Ian Brand in the eye again.

———

Millie woke the next morning to the sound of sirens outside her window. Sitting up, she grabbed her head, afraid if she let go it might roll of her shoulders and across the floor. "Oh, God."

Then she remembered. "Ugh. I guess I can cross getting drunk off my list." At this point she was wondering why she'd ever put it on her list in the first place. "What was I thinking?"

Looking down, she realized she still wore the clothes she had on yesterday, and . . . she smacked her lips, her mouth tasted like she'd been licking the bottom of her shoe.

She rose from the bed and even the few steps it took to get to her kitchen might as well have been the last few steps to the summit of Mt. Everest.

Visions of being carried into her apartment flashed across her brain like lightning in a summer storm. But by whom? Mortified, she slid to the floor, her legs exhausted from their hike. Laying her head back against the cabinet, she closed her eyes, and wondered what else she'd done while under the influence.

# CHAPTER FOURTEEN

After letting herself in, Millie tiptoed across Darcy's foyer. Later than usual, and dealing with a headache of massive proportions, she headed straight for the kitchen and the strong cup of tea she hadn't had the energy to make at home.

Darcy had just put the kettle on. "Morning, sunshine."

Millie groaned. "You're up early and feeling chipper."

"I'm not up early, you're just late. And I'm finally over my morning sickness, at least I think I am."

"Sorry I'm late," Millie muttered, embarrassed by her tardiness and unprofessionalism.

"How are you feeling?" Darcy asked as she took cups out of the cupboard.

"Like someone forgot to bury me. Why did you let me drink so much?" She sank into a chair at the kitchen table, unable to do even the slightest thing to help Darcy make the tea.

Darcy barked out a laugh. At Millie's wince, Darcy said, "Sorry." Lowering her voice, she continued, "How many glasses do you think you had?"

"I don't know. A few."

"A few? Millie, you had one." She held up her index finger for emphasis. "One glass of wine."

"One?" Sighing, she put her head in her hands. "I really am a cheap date."

"One of these days you're going to have to tell me what brought that on." Darcy took the kettle off just before the whistle.

Not. In. This. Lifetime. "How did I get home?"

"Nathan and Josh drove you home in Laura's car."

Perfect. It wasn't enough that she'd humiliated herself in front of one man. No. She had to go and humiliate herself in front of two more.

*That's it.* She would erase sex from her list. And alcohol. Because she was going to join a convent. Or an all-female commune. That way she would never humiliate herself in front of a man again.

"Drink this. Good strong English Breakfast Tea." Darcy ran her hand across Millie's back, soothing her, as she placed the cup of tea in front of her. Breathing in the steam, Millie's headache receded a millimeter. "I'll get you some aspirin."

"Did I do anything . . . stupid last night?"

"Depends on your definition of 'stupid.'" Darcy sat the bottle of aspirin in front of Millie and then sat across from her, a cup of tea in her hand.

Millie groaned. Maybe she could find work elsewhere. She'd make a good assistant for just about anyone. "What did I do?"

"You called Ian on his cell phone and said something about being bothered and leaving."

Millie lowered her forehead to the table's cool surface. That settles it. *I have to find a new job.*

"You want to tell me what's going on between you and Ian?"

Millie jerked her head up and instantly regretted it. Holding her head in both hands, she said, "Nothing. There's absolutely nothing going on between me and Ian." And wasn't that just the problem?

———

Ian had an unpleasant task to complete that morning. Rejecting Millie's offer, as if his treatment of her weren't enough. Ruby had taught him that if you get the unpleasant tasks done first thing, then you put them behind you and get on with your day. Problem was, he'd yet to lay eyes on Millie.

Darcy had said something about errands, so he'd have to put it off until she returned.

He thought about her inebriated phone call. She didn't strike him as someone who imbibed. And, he knew the type. Very well. First his stepfather, then his mother to escape the hell of her marriage.

What the hell had possessed Millie to make a deal with him for sex and then get toasted and drunk dial him? Baffled, he turned his attention to installing the Winnie the Pooh outlet plates in the bathroom, now that the painting was completed. Tomorrow he would paint the closet doors and plantation shutters for the nursery.

The job was coming along nicely, on schedule despite Ruby's illness. Too bad he couldn't say the same for the Hawkins Hall RFP. This job was probably the most important of his career, and he'd have to tackle it without Ruby's help. He realized now that he'd used her for a crutch for far too long. Now he may just pay the price by losing this bid.

At the end of the day, Ian pulled on his jacket and gloves, prepared for a particularly frigid ride home. A hot shower awaited him, and a beef stew he'd thrown together using the bachelor's best friend, a slow cooker. Last week he'd made a kick-ass, smokin' hot pot of chili that sustained him a few nights.

Millie had managed to elude him all day, so he still had that business hanging over his head. Going downstairs, he ran into the devil of which he spoke. *Here goes nothing.*

"Millie? You got a minute?"

She looked up at him like a deer caught in headlights.

*Well, shit.*

She nodded, biting her lip.

"About last night—"

"Forget it," Millie muttered, her face aflame.

"Which part am I supposed to forget? The part where you offered a deal for sex? Or the part where you drunk dialed me?"

"Both. Just forget both." She tried to step around him, but he blocked her.

"Millie, listen to me." He kept his distance to avoid making her any more uncomfortable. "I appreciate your . . . offer, but I don't barter for sex." She stared down at her feet. "And you shouldn't either. Jesus, Millie, I hope you don't make a habit of that with the men you meet."

Her gaze shot to his face, her mouth defiant, her eyes glittering. Good. He liked her better that way. Not cowed and embarrassed.

"No. I don't. I just thought . . ."

"Well, don't think like that." At her continued silence, he sighed. "Look, can I give you a ride home?"

"No. I, uh, a friend is picking me up."

He nodded. *So she has other friends besides Darcy.*

*That's good.* "You're not going out drinking, are you? Do I need to shut off my phone?"

Her mouth twitched like she wanted to smile. "No."

"Good. See you Monday."

———

When did she get so good at lying? Millie wondered, as she walked the seven blocks to the subway. She didn't have a friend picking her up. She'd take the subway home just like every other night, eat her microwave dinner, and curl up with a book. Or her manuscript. Alone.

"Be bold," she muttered, drawing unwelcome attention from Darcy's neighbor as he waited for his dog to do his business. *Great plan. And look where that got me.* Humiliated. Again.

Ian had been kind, but he'd made it perfectly clear he had no intention of having sex with her. And not only that, that he had no *desire* to either.

She'd clearly misjudged the kitchen encounter. More likely, she'd just imagined it. Wishful thinking, and all that.

Burrowing deeper into her coat, she stopped a minute to admire the corner brownstone with its holiday light display. The cheerfulness of the scene only made her loneliness keener. She looked back down Darcy's street at the Christmas trees or Menorah's in the front windows, and she thought about the families who lived there. Families who were likely sitting down to dinner together, or maybe curling up on the sofa to watch a sappy holiday movie.

The holiday season had never felt so lonely. Sighing, she continued her commute to the subway and the empty apartment waiting for her, her invisibility weighing on her like a lead cloak.

S aturday afternoon, Ian drove his truck into the loft's indoor parking space. He'd spent the morning taking care of Ruby. First, buying groceries, then preparing lunch, and finally sitting with her while she watched *Inspector Lewis*. She continued to hold her own, and her mind remained sharp as ever, but he knew it was only a matter of time. The doctor said the chemo wasn't working, and she hadn't qualified for the clinical trial.

Life was so goddamned unfair. Never smoked a day in her life and fighting lung cancer. And losing.

After a hot shower to shake off the cold, and some left-over stew, he sat down to tackle the Hawkins Hall RFP. Why he'd ever thrown his name in he'd never know.

Only two pages into the instructions and he struggled. He thought about Millie's offer. Wondered how easy it would be for her to put together a professional proposal. And wondered what it would be like to feel her skin against his. Hear her breathy moans.

Shaking his head, he picked up the instructions again. It had been far too long since he'd had sex. He'd been too busy. That, and he just hadn't met anyone lately who'd flipped his switch. The memory of Millie's body pressed against his resurfaced. Until Millie.

What was it about the dowdy, brainy, klutzy, sometimes socially awkward woman that intrigued him? Taking a pull on his soda, he closed his eyes and listed her attributes. Smart, kind to a fault, efficient, warm . . . sexy. His eyes flew open. Sexy? Where had that come from?

From the feel of her in his arms, in his hands. From the taste of her skin. Her scent. That mouth. That voice. Hell, her voice alone could make a dead man come.

He tossed the fifty pages of instructions down on the desk in exasperation. Maybe he'd been too hasty in rejecting her offer. Right now, seemed like a win-win.

———

A couple of days later, waiting at the bottom of the stairs for Darcy, Millie buttoned up her coat, then took her gloves out of the pocket. Although born and raised in New York, she'd never quite gotten used to the cold.

With Christmas a few days away, she and Darcy were headed out for some last minute shopping. Darcy insisted she get out in the fresh air and get some exercise, despite Millie's assurances that she could handle the shopping on her own.

At least the outing would remove her from Ian's presence.

"Hey, Ian, we're going out for a couple of hours. See you when we return," Darcy said to the devil himself.

"See ya, Darcy."

Pulling on her gloves, Darcy started down the stairs. A few steps from the bottom, her foot slipped out from under her. She teetered on the edge, just missing the railing with her outstretched hand.

Millie watched in horror as Darcy slid down the stairs, feet first, her arms around her belly as if to protect it. Her momentum carried her to the bottom of the stairs, where her head hit with a sickening thud against the bottom tread.

# CHAPTER FIFTEEN

A scream tore from Millie's throat as she scrambled over to Darcy, motionless on the floor.

Ian's booted feet thundered down the stairs. "Holy shit!"

Millie felt the pulse in Darcy's neck. Slow, but steady.

Ian ran into the living room, snatched a throw off the sofa, and draped it over Darcy. "I'll call 911."

Millie placed her hand over Darcy's belly and felt a flutter of movement. "Thank God." Tears stung her eyes. *Please. Please be all right.*

"They're on their way," Ian said a couple of minutes later, as he knelt over Darcy gently feeling her legs and arms for breaks. "The baby?"

"Moving around."

He nodded, his expression grim. "What happened?"

"Her foot slipped and she-she hit her head." Millie tried to still her shaking. "I need to call Josh."

"Go. I'll stay with her."

"Don't-Don't let her move if she comes to."

He nodded again, and took over her spot holding Darcy's hand.

The sound of sirens drew closer as she told a frantic Josh what had happened. Hanging up, Millie squeezed her eyes shut, but after seeing Darcy's fall like a replay in her head, she opened them again and moved back into the foyer.

"Josh will meet us at the hospital." She strode over to the front door as the ambulance arrived and the paramedics jumped out.

"We'll follow the ambulance on my motorcycle," Ian said.

Ian brought coffee to a worried Josh, then took a seat a polite distance away from the family.

Years spent without a visit to the hospital, now twice in less than a month.

Darcy's friends and family packed the waiting room. Her friend Laura, Darcy's parents, sister, and brother. Gloria. Even a woman he gathered was Darcy's editor. Laura held Josh's hand, while Darcy's mom spoke softly to him on the other side. He looked like a man facing a firing squad.

Millie sat next to a well-dressed guy named Nathan, who he thought might be Laura's husband, her hand in his. Like Josh, she wore a mask of shock and disbelief.

A tight-knit group. Darcy was well-loved. And, clearly, so was Millie. He'd watched as everyone who entered gave her a hug. Now Nathan draped an arm around her shoulder and pulled her in for an embrace, before rising and walking out of the waiting room.

Ian got up and took the seat Nathan had vacated. "You okay? Can I get you anything? Some tea?" He'd noticed Millie always either had cup of tea in her hand, or one within easy reach at Darcy's.

She shook her head, and a tear drop splattered on her hand.

His heart squeezed, and he took her hand in both of his. "Hey. She's going to be fine."

Millie nodded.

"You love her, don't you?" he asked, his voice soft.

"She's my best friend," she replied, her voice barely above a whisper. She sniffed. "She was the first person who seemed to really *want* to spend time with me. The first person who paid me any attention." She covered her mouth with her free hand, stifling a sob. "And she wants this baby so much." The last barely audible as she squeezed her eyes shut.

Ian closed his eyes at the pain in Millie's voice. Wrapping his arm around her, he gathered her close, then found himself pressing a kiss to her hair. At the touch, Millie melted against him.

"Mr. Ryan." A woman wearing scrubs, a white coat, and a stethoscope stood in the doorway.

Josh shot to his feet, then stood rooted to the spot. The doctor entered the room clearly realizing she would need to go to Josh.

"I'm Dr. Kincade."

"Doctor, you can tell everyone," Josh said, his voice gruff with pain and worry. "They're all family."

"Well, then. Mrs. Ryan and the baby are going to be fine."

Josh ran his hands over his face, and a collective sigh of relief swept through the room, as hugs were shared.

"She has a mild concussion and some contusions, but no broken bones. We're going to keep her overnight for observation, and she'll be off her feet for a couple of days, but the baby is fine, and I don't see any reason why she can't carry it to term."

"Can I see her?" Josh asked.

"Yes. And she's also asking for Millie?" The doctor surveyed the room.

Millie glanced at Ian, then stepped forward. "I'm Millie."

"I'll be here when you're done. I can take you home," Ian assured her.

———

Darkness had fallen by the time Millie and Ian arrived at her apartment. Still numb from the frightening events of the afternoon, Millie struggled to climb off the bike.

"Hold on." Ian's gruff voice penetrated her haze.

He climbed off and turned to her, lifting her off the bike as if she weighed nothing. Taking the helmet off her head, he said, "If you're going to keep riding my motorcycle, we're going to have to get you a helmet."

*Did she just hear him correctly? He was going to get her a helmet so she could ride with him? She gave herself a mental headshake. No, her brain was just playing tricks on her.*

"Come on. Let's get you inside." He guided her down the sidewalk to her building. Stopping in front of the door, he ran his hand down her back, soothing her, then gathered her against his warmth. "You did good today," he murmured against her hair. "You stayed calm and handled the situation. Darcy's very lucky to have you."

"I'm so glad she and the baby are okay." Mille pushed away enough to look up into his eyes, which had turned a dark gray. His gaze drifted to her mouth and she knew to the depths of her soul he was going to kiss her, and God she hoped so. Then again, she'd been wrong before.

He tipped his head, stopping just shy of her lips. "This okay?" he asked, his voice breathless and raspy.

That raspiness grated against nerve endings she never knew she had. She nodded.

His warm mouth brushed hers so tenderly, like a butterfly landing on a flower. Then his tongue parted her lips, seeking entry. More than willing, she complied, letting him show her how. Sensations flooded her. An amalgam of emotions. Exhilaration, fear, lust, and tenderness.

After the adrenalin rush this afternoon, and now this, she felt faint. She clung to him, her fingers digging into the leather of his jacket, desperate to remain standing. And conscious. She didn't want to forget a nanosecond of this kiss.

His tongue swirled against hers, a dance he was comfortable leading. He changed the angle, deepening the kiss until she thought she might slither to the ground in a boneless heap.

Her fingers found their way to his hair, sliding through the silky locks. A moan escaped. Hers or his?

Withdrawing, he slid his mouth along the line of her jaw to the spot just below her ear. She shivered at his breath in her ear, and she felt it run along her spine to settle in her belly with a slow, simmering warmth. "Millie, I've wanted to kiss you here."

Excitement raced through her. He'd wanted to kiss her? Ian Brand had wanted to kiss *her? Then why had he rejected her offer?*

He backed her up against the building's brick wall and skimmed his hands up her neck, cupping her face.

Thrusting his body against hers, Millie could feel his erection. Her eyes flew open. He *wanted* her?

"Does this . . . Does this mean you're accepting my offer?" Millie asked, her voice husky.

Confusion skittered across Ian's face. "Offer?"

Heat flooded her. He'd forgotten her offer.

———

Ian grasped her shoulders and took a step back. "Is that the only reason you think I would want to have sex with you?" Truth was, her offer was the furthest thing from his mind. He didn't give a good goddamn about the offer.

He placed his finger under her chin, lifting it up so he could see her face. Her eyes were still downcast, and a lovely flush colored her cheeks, but he hated seeing her so ashamed.

"Millie? Is that what you think? That a man would only have sex with you if you promised something in return?"

She nodded.

"Why? Why would you think that?"

She finally lifted her eyes to his. "Look at me."

His chest tightened at her whispered response. "I am." He lowered his mouth to hers, sucking that full bottom lip in between his teeth. She tasted so damn good. Like sweetness, with a dash of heat. His hands slid to her hips, slender beneath her coat and the layers of bulky clothes, and pressed her against his erection. Lifting his head, he said, "Do you think the offer to help me with paperwork gave me this?"

She shook her head.

"No. Remembering how you looked standing in the kitchen in nothing but your bra and skirt gave me this. The feel of your breast in my hand the other day. Imagining you without all these clothes. Tasting your lips, your skin. That's what gave me this." Millie's eyes were round as an owl's, her sexy little mouth open in disbelief. "Millie, I'd like it if you invited me up."

———

At her nod, Ian took her hand and waited for her to unlock the front door. Her legs quivered so bad, she wasn't sure she could make it up the stairs without falling.

On the second floor landing, Chelsea came flying around the corner, killer heels clicking on the floor. "Oh hi, Millie." Then she spotted Ian. "Oh!" She smoothed her hair. "Hi!"

Ian simply nodded and guided Millie up the next flight of stairs.

"Have fun!" Chelsea called up.

Millie wanted to peel off her too-warm coat as the heat of embarrassment combined with the heat of lust elevated her body temperature. *Just let me get him to my apartment before he comes to his senses and realizes he has an appointment.*

*With a psychologist.*

To have his head examined.

For wanting to have sex with her.

At the door to her apartment, she stopped, fumbled with the keys, before dropping them with a loud clatter to the floor.

"Here." Ian bent over and retrieved the keys. "Which one?"

Millie pointed out the key and Ian unlocked the door, allowing her to enter first, before handing the keys back to her. She left the lights off on purpose, but he flicked them on.

As soon as he'd closed the door, he pulled her around and pressed her against the door.

Millie's heart raced, as if trying to clamber out of her chest. God. What if he *was* a serial killer?

He braced his hands on either side of her head, caging her in. But no, she remembered the tenderness he'd shown Darcy after she fell. She recalled his arms around her at the hospital, his lips in her hair.

Latching onto her wrists, he raised them over her head. She dropped the keys. Again. Leaning his whole body into hers, he captured her mouth with his. Maybe he was into BDSM, she thought, as he plundered her, still holding her hands above her head. She didn't care. Whatever he was into, he could get into it with her.

He released her hands and quickly unbuttoned her coat, tugging it from her shoulders, before dropping it onto the floor. She closed her eyes. Couldn't they just have sex like they did in the Victorian era? Fully clothed?

His hands were gliding down her body, finding the hem of her sweater, pulling it up and over her head, leaving her in her white cotton camisole and bra, and her brown wool pants. She opened her eyes wide in surprise.

She could barely draw in a breath as his eyes, heavy-lidded and sleepy, roamed her body. He reached up and took the pins from her hair, then ran his fingers through it to untwist the bun and spread it around her shoulders.

"My God, Millie. Look at you," he breathed, then kissed the top of her breast.

If her knees hadn't been locked, she'd have slipped to the floor.

Kissing her other breast, he worked on the button and zipper of her pants.

"The lights," she gasped, as her hips thrust into his hands with a mind of their own.

"What about them?" he murmured, dragging his lips and tongue across the tops of her breasts, his hands working her pants down her hips to her legs, then letting them fall to the floor.

"Shouldn't we . . . shouldn't we turn them off?"

"No. I want to see you."

He trailed his lips down her abdomen, sending shivers along her spine. Reaching the bottom of her camisole, he lifted it, revealing bare skin. When he bent and pressed his mouth to her navel, she threw her head back against the door with a *thunk* and moaned. And when his mouth drifted lower still, she knotted her hands in his hair, both longing for, and dreading where he was headed.

Embarrassed by her sensible white cotton panties, she closed her eyes, hoping to avoid his disappointed expression. Men preferred Victoria's Secret models in lace and silk, not frumpy bookworms in white cotton.

Instead, he pressed his face between her legs, and she cried out.

"Sweet Millie." His warm breath tickled her upper thighs, flooding her body with heat, and a hunger for anything he was willing to give.

# CHAPTER SIXTEEN

God, she was sweet, Ian thought. He'd never been with a woman who exuded such innocence, yet harbored such passion. Kneeling, he removed her pants, socks, and shoes, and then he stood and stepped back to appreciate her. She hid her beautiful little body so well. No one would ever know what treasures lay buried beneath the brown wool surface.

Lifting his gaze to her face, he saw her eyes squeezed shut. "Millie. Look at me. Open your eyes and look at me."

"I can't." Her head was back, her open fingers spread against the door at her hips.

"Why not?"

"Because I'm afraid of what I'll see."

"Lust? Desire?"

"Disappointment."

His chest tightened again. How could she be a disappointment? And what asshole said she was? "Millie." Stepping closer, he took her hand and placed it over his screaming erection.

She gasped, and her eyes flew open.

Yes, it had been a while, but that wasn't the only reason. "Does that feel like a man disappointed?"

She shook her head, then her eyes drifted to her hand on his crotch, and damned if she didn't blush again.

"Come here." He grasped her wrist and led her to the bed in her tidy apartment. "Sit." He lowered her to the bed and made quick work of his jacket, shirt, and boots. Wearing nothing but his jeans and a hard on, he knelt in front of her and opening her legs, reached around to tug her to him. "Do you need these?" he asked, indicating her glasses.

She shook her head.

"Good. I'd hate to break them."

She inhaled sharply her eyes wide.

He carefully removed her glasses, placing them on the shelf by her bed. Lifting the camisole over her head, he tossed it behind him.

Her smooth, creamy skin looked luminous in the soft lighting from the bedside lamp. He tugged her bra straps down her arms, then reached behind to unsnap it. Her beautiful bare breasts, taut rosy nipples, begged for his mouth.

"Beautiful." Lathing her nipple with his tongue, he reveled in the way she arched into him, as her fingers curled into his hair. Showing the same attention to her other breast, he glided his hands down to her slender waist, felt the erratic movement from her panting breath.

He wanted to take it slow, but her moans were pushing him close to the edge. Slipping his hands into her panties, he tugged them down, kneeling back so he could remove them, and his breath caught at her natural beauty. No spray tan, no bikini wax. Just Millie. Breathtakingly honest, stunningly genuine.

His gaze traveled up her body to her face, where her

eyes were closed, her mouth swollen from his kisses, and her hair tumbled all around her. Tightening the leash on his desire, he parted her legs.

Millie found herself adrift. Lost in sensations, both new and overwhelming, all building, tightening, focused on her core. A spring so tightly coiled that it must surely break under the pressure.

His calloused hands grazed her thighs, spreading her before him. She clenched the comforter beneath her, biting down on her lip, the desire to open herself to him warring with the instinct to close herself off, to hide from his prying eyes.

Already on sensory overload, she nearly came unglued when he put his mouth on her. One stroke of his tongue sent her into orbit, as the tightly coiled spring finally released. He continued to bathe her with his tongue, sending shockwave after shockwave through her. When the shudders receded, she lay staring at the ceiling in absolute wonder, certain no other orgasm in the history of human sexuality could have ever been as powerful as that earth-shattering experience.

Ian pressed soft kisses to the inside of her thighs, murmuring tender words that washed over her like spring rain. His stubble grazed her skin and the spring began to coil low in her belly once more.

He rose, then shucked his jeans and boxers. When his erection sprang free she nearly gasped. Rising up onto her elbows, she couldn't tear her gaze from him. While she'd never seen a naked man in the flesh, she knew this man was perfectly made. All hard muscle and sinew, smooth skin and powerful thighs. Michelangelo's *David,* only hot flesh rather than cold stone. A *frisson* of desire coursed through her. She spied another tattoo, this one across his lower abdomen. And five inches? Try more like seven.

She watched in rapt fascination as he ripped open a packet and rolled on a condom.

Crawling up her body, lowering her to the bed as he went, he positioned himself between her legs.

———

Hissing in a breath when his throbbing erection made contact with her warm thigh, Ian knew this wouldn't last long. He'd make it up to her the next round.

He pushed into her, gratified by her indrawn breath.

Sweet Jesus, she was tight! Gritting his teeth, he held back a moment before pushing deeper.

He lifted up on his elbows, brushing the hair out her face. "Am I hurting you? How long has it been, babe?"

"No." She bit her lower lip, her eyes wary, but she didn't answer his other question.

"Millie?"

She thrust her hips up, crying out, her eyes wide in shock.

*Ho-ly hell.* "Be still, Millie," he said as he gripped her hips, holding her to him. Then he kissed her temple. "Let your body adjust to me." Sweat covered him as he held himself in check. Torture. Pure torture.

He pressed his mouth to hers, coaxing it open for him, and as his tongue tangled with hers, he began to move. Slow, easy strokes until she relaxed and her hips kept rhythm with his.

Pure sensation took over. Overcome by the snug feel of her. Overcome by the surprise that lit her face. She clamped on to his ass with her hands, wrapped her legs around his waist, and thrust upward again, and he quickened the pace.

"Oh, God, Millie."

Her cries grew more fevered with each thrust, his tight rein slipping with each counter thrust. His name escaping her lips proved his undoing, and he poured himself into her, stunned by the all-consuming release.

———

Ian collapsed on top of her, his breathing raspy and labored. The same could be said for her.

*So this is what post-coital bliss felt like.* Her mind drifted as her body melted into a boneless heap into the bed. Her arms slid off Ian's back, as if too weak to be lifted. Sex with Ian had definitely not been all take. He'd given until she'd been dizzy with need. And fulfillment.

Overcome by emotion, her rational brain told her what she was feeling was simply oxytocin flooding her body, intensifying the connection to Ian. She'd read all about it. But nothing she'd read had prepared her for this . . . complete and total loss of control. This pure and unadulterated pleasure.

She had no comparison, but she could measure, and he definitely wasn't average. Still, after the initial pinch of pain, her body had expanded to accommodate him.

"You okay?" Ian asked from where his face was buried in her hair.

"Yes. You?"

He nodded, and rolled off her and over to her side, then gathered her close, and propping his head on his hand he gazed into her eyes. "More than." His mouth lifted at the corner, and she wanted to kiss it.

Heat flooded her face as modesty returned with a vengeance. He'd just had his hands, his mouth, and . . . other parts on . . . or in . . . her body. How could she look at him again?

"Millie, you've never had sex before."

It was a statement, not a question. She rolled over, facing away from him, and curled into a ball, attempting to cover her face, as well as the rest of her body. "No."

She heard him mutter something under his breath, then his arms wrapped around her waist and he tugged her back against his warm, hard stomach, his legs bent around hers, spooning. "Did I . . . did I pressure you?"

She shook her head.

"Did I hurt you?"

Another shake of her head.

"How is it that you haven't had sex before now? And why now?"

She shrugged. "No one's been interested."

"I call bullshit on that," he muttered.

For some reason, his vociferous response made her smile.

"Maybe *you* hadn't found someone who interested *you*. Did you ever think of that? And why now? Why me?"

Oh, God. How was she supposed to answer that? She thought he was the sexiest man she'd ever seen? She wanted to see him in nothing but his tool belt? She liked him? She . . . what? Needed to cross sex off her list?

*Be bold.* She twisted to face him. "I like you. And . . . you're nice to me," she whispered.

"So, you had sex with me because I'm nice to you."

"Well that . . ." Thinking of what Gloria had said about Ian being able to show a girl a thing or two, she continued, ". . . and I figured you would know what you were doing."

He chuckled, a deep rumble in his chest. "If your moans and cries were any indication, I guess that's true."

Mortification swept over her again and she covered her face with her hands.

"Millie, enjoying sex is nothing to be ashamed of. In fact, *I'd* be ashamed if you hadn't enjoyed it."

She giggled, relieved by his statement.

He pulled her in tight against him. "Thank you."

*Thank you? He's thanking me? "For what?"*

"For giving me the honor of being your first." His lips brushed her temple.

Her eyes filled at the sincerity in his voice. Oh, God. Warning bells clanged in her head. If there was anyone she might fall in love with, it was Ian Brand. And there was no doubt in her mind that the feeling wouldn't be reciprocated.

———

Ian woke with a warm, naked woman by his side. Cracking open an eye, he saw the room was still dark, streetlight cast a faint glow through the slats in the blinds. Gingerly, trying not to wake Millie, he rolled over and found his jeans on the floor. Digging his phone out of his pocket, he checked the time. Two-twenty A.M. He needed to head out. He had an early meeting with a plumber in Westchester. Even so, the thought of stepping out into the frigid night held little appeal, especially when Millie sighed and snuggled closer.

Debating about whether to wake her and say goodbye, or just leave, he decided on the former. She didn't need the first guy she'd ever slept with sneaking out in the dead of night without so much as a goodbye.

Rising, he stepped into his boxers and jeans, found his

shirt and jacket, and threw them on. Sitting on the bed, he put on his socks and boots, then twisted around to gaze at Millie.

She slept on her side, facing him, her dark hair swirling around her. The blanket had slipped off her shoulder, exposing the top of her creamy breasts. He shook his head. Who would have thought those baggy, bulky clothes she wore hid such femininity and sexiness?

He leaned over and placed his hand on her shoulder, "Millie."

She opened her eyes, gasped, and sat up in bed, holding the blankets to her chest like a shield. Then recognition flooded her face.

"Sorry." He stroked her cheek where a pillowcase crease marred her beautiful skin. "I didn't mean to scare you. I have to go. I have an early meeting."

She rubbed her eyes, nodding. Not, "Please don't go," or "Why can't you stay?" Just a nod. *Hmm.* He wasn't sure how he felt about that.

"I'll see you tomorrow at Darcy's?" Ian asked.

"After I go to the hospital," she muttered, her husky voice thick with sleep.

"Right." He'd almost forgotten how they'd ended up here in Millie's apartment in the first place. He pressed a kiss to her delectable mouth. A mouth that learned quickly, he thought as he recalled round three. Round two, he'd shown her what else his mouth could do. "Lock the door after me."

"Goodnight, Ian."

Why did that voice make him want to stay?

# CHAPTER SEVENTEEN

S tretching, Millie peeled open an eye to see bright sunshine spilling in through her blinds. *Cheese and crackers!* She glanced at the clock. Eight-o-nine. She'd forgotten to set the alarm.

Did she dream last night? Or did Ian Brand really take her to bed and do delicious things to her very willing body until the wee hours of the morning? Lifting the sheets to reveal her nakedness, she realized it was no dream. She was a tramp. A slut. A trollop. A big grin split her face as she resisted a fist pump.

Then the soreness got her attention. Nothing bad, just a heaviness between her legs, and a twinge of her little-used inner thigh muscles.

She remembered Ian leaving, the way he'd caressed her cheek and kissed her goodbye. Oh, the things they had done! The heights he'd taken her to! She had no regrets.

Rising, she blushed at her own nakedness. She always slept in a nightgown. Feeling wicked, she smiled to herself as she padded barefoot into the bathroom. She spotted a trail of her clothes from the front door to her bed.

Hugging herself she stood in front of her bathroom mirror searching for any change in her appearance. She felt so different, how could she possibly look the same? Recalling Ian's moans, the way he'd growled her name, when she . . . when he . . . God, she'd felt empowered. She'd done that to him. Silly Millie Stephens had made a man like Ian Brand lose control.

Her hair swirled around her, a tangled mess. Her lips were swollen, and she had stubble burn down her neck, across her breasts . . . and inner thighs. But the change she noticed more than anything else was the broad grin she couldn't seem to wipe off her face.

Then she remembered Darcy. Her motionless body lying at the bottom of the stairs, and her joy turned to disgust. How could she be so happy when her pregnant best friend was lying in a hospital bed with a concussion?

Yanking a towel off the rack, she covered her nakedness and hit the shower.

An hour later, she stepped off the elevators at New York Methodist Hospital and turned left. Finding Darcy's room, she heard Laura's laughter.

"Can I come in?" Millie asked as she pushed open the door.

Darcy sat up in bed, her round belly covered with a sheet, a smile on her face. "Of course!"

"How are you feeling?"

"A little sore, and a mild headache—"

"She's got a lump the size of a golf ball on the back of her head," Laura interjected, frowning in a rare show of emotion.

"I'm fine, Millie."

Relieved, Millie's eyes stung with tears. Blinking them back, she gazed around the room. The pullout couch was littered with bedding, a rumpled pillow at one end. Laura sat in a chair next to the bed, her ever-present smartphone in one hand, a coffee cup in the other. No Josh.

"He went downstairs to get some breakfast," Darcy volunteered. "They're springing me from the joint after my doctor sees me this morning." Darcy held out her hand for Millie. "I can't thank you and Ian enough."

Millie took Darcy's hand, but at the mention of Ian's name, her face heated.

Laura glanced up, narrowed her eyes at Millie, and said, "You had sex," her tone accusatory.

"Did not," Millie blurted.

"Did to," Laura returned.

"Laura's Super Sex Sensor never lies." Darcy studied Millie's face. "Trust me."

Warmth flooded Millie's cheeks. Why, oh why, did Laura have to be visiting? "You don't know what you're talking about."

"Oh no, missy." She wagged her finger in Millie's face. "Laura Danforth Armstrong Maxwell always knows what she's talking about when it comes to sex."

Millie rolled her eyes. "You know what they say about people who use illeism."

Laura's eyes closed to slits. "No. And what is illeism?"

"Referring to yourself in the third person. And it shows conceit and an overblown sense of greatness. Or a dissociative disorder."

"Pfft." Laura waved her hand in the air. "Nice attempt at deflection, but it didn't work." Wagging her finger in Millie's face again, she continued, "You had sex and don't try denying it."

"Well, if it isn't three of my favorite women," Josh said, walking into the room.

Millie mentally groaned, wondering if he'd heard Laura's last comment. He looked exhausted, but relieved, and no trace of shock over the conversation about Millie's newly discovered sex life.

"The nurse is preparing your discharge papers," he said as he approached the bed and kissed Darcy's forehead.

"Good. I'm ready to get home to my own bed."

Relieved to see Darcy doing so well, Millie said her goodbyes, both to escape Laura's Super Sex Sensor and to prepare the house for Darcy's return. First stop, Aunt Butchies.

———

The house stood silent and empty when Ian unlocked the door. He thought about Darcy and hoped she'd be home soon. It might be best if he took a few days away from the job when she returned so she could have peace and quiet. Nothing like trying to recover from a concussion while someone hammered nails and ran a table saw.

Guessing Millie was still at the hospital, he climbed the stairs with a little spring in his step and went straight to work.

After he'd gotten home from Millie's and crawled into his big cold bed, loneliness had settled over him. He didn't usually stay the night with women, so why he felt so different with Millie he couldn't say.

Switching on his iPod, he stuck his earbuds in his ears as the strains of Vivaldi's *Four Seasons* began.

Prying open the can of sunny yellow paint Darcy had picked out for the nursery, he recalled how Millie's breath hitched when he traced her jaw with his lips, how his name sounded in her husky fuck-me voice, how her skin tasted under his tongue, and how she looked when he'd left her. All bedhead and drowsy.

He poured paint into the tray then dipped the roller in. As he worked the paint onto the wall, he thought yellow was the perfect color for a boy or a girl. The Winnie the Pooh theme Darcy had planned for the room would also work for either gender.

His thoughts circled back to Millie and the fact that she'd been a virgin. How was that even possible in the twenty-first century? It was refreshing. And that she had bestowed that gift on him tugged at his heart.

But.

He needed to tread carefully. Millie wasn't a one-night stand, or even a one-week stand. She deserved a man who could give her a home, a relationship, kids. Something he wasn't capable of giving to her or anyone else, for a variety of reasons, but primarily because he couldn't enter the relationship with the secret hanging over his head. And he couldn't bring himself to tell anyone and see the disdain, or worse, the pity, in their eyes.

He was about as close to Ruby as he was to anyone. Even Caleb. He'd been close with Curtis, too. But of those three people, only Ruby and Curtis new about his dyslexia.

He rubbed his hand over the ache in his chest. Ruby was holding her own, and while she wasn't losing any more weight, she hadn't put on any either. It tore him apart to see her so frail. And it pissed him off that there wasn't a damn thing he could do about it. He couldn't stop the cancer, and he couldn't slow it down. All he could do was make her comfortable, be with her, and cherish the time they had left.

Maybe that philosophy would work with Millie. *Cherish the time they had together, and don't think about the future.* Not even in Asimov's alternate universe would that work.

———

Was it wrong to want to lick him like a Popsicle? Millie wondered as she watched Ian work the paint roller along the wall. The muscles contracted and expanded in his back. His arms flexed and unflexed, the tattoo on his bicep peeking out from under his sleeve.

To think she'd been pressed against that naked body last night. Memories flooded her brain. Him kneeling in front of her, his lips on her stomach. Him balanced above her as he drove into her. She laid her cold hands against her over-heated face. *Anastasia and Christian!* She'd become a nymphomaniac.

She hadn't even checked sex off her list. Maybe because having sex with Ian meant more than just an item on a to-do list.

Unsure how to act around him, she turned to go before she had to face him in the light of day. But before she could make her escape, Ian twisted to dip the roller back in the paint and caught a glimpse of her.

Her face flamed at being caught staring at him. He drew the earbuds out of his ears and stuffed them into his jeans pocket. "Millie. Hi." A soft smile lifted the corner of his mouth. He rarely smiled, but when he did, her heart soared.

Then a frown creased his brow as he took a step toward her. "How are you feeling?"

"Good. Really good. Great." *Stop stammering.*

He grinned and her knees threatened to buckle. "How's Darcy?"

"She's fine. She'll be home later today, but she's on bedrest for the next two days."

He nodded. "I'll either take off a few days or work on the quieter aspects of the job"—he indicated the wall behind him—"liking painting."

She wanted to tell him how much last night meant to her, but she didn't want to come off needy and desperate, even if that's what she was. How did women do this? She should take a few courses from Laura. "Well, I won't keep you. I have a long to-do list in preparation for Darcy's return." She turned to go.

"Millie?"

She stopped, but didn't look at him.

"I enjoyed last night."

A broad grin swept across her face. "Me, too." She beat a hasty retreat before she could do anything to embarrass herself, but she practically floated down the stairs.

# CHAPTER EIGHTEEN

The following day, Millie carried a tray up to Darcy's bedroom. No soup this time, but a hearty beef stew. Maybe she could escape unscathed.

Darcy set aside her Kindle when Millie walked in. "Ooh! That's smells good. I'm starving!"

Her words, and the fact that she hadn't lost her appetite, warmed Millie's heart.

Millie placed the bed tray across Darcy's legs, below her belly, and draped the napkin across what was left of her lap. "Just let me know when you're finished and I'll come back for the tray." She turned to go.

"Wait. Come sit." Darcy patted the other side of the bed next to her.

Wondering what this could be about, Millie rested a hip on the mattress while Darcy took a bite of stew. "Mmm. Delicious!"

Millie waited patiently as Darcy swallowed.

"So, Laura's Super Sex Sensor was right yesterday," she started, eyeing Millie's face.

A flush crept up her throat, spread over her face, all the

way to her hairline. Why did she suddenly feel like a sixteen-year-old who'd been caught making out with her boyfriend? Only she and Ian had done more than make out. Way more.

"And I think Ian is the likely suspect."

*Suspect?*

Before she could say anything, Darcy continued. "I've seen how you look at him. And quite frankly, how he looks at you. Like you're the tastiest dish he's ever seen."

Millie's flush bloomed into a full-on hot flash.

"I think it's great." Darcy laid her hand over Millie's. "I just want you to be careful. You're not the one-night-stand type, and, as much as I like Ian, I'm not sure he's the white-picket-fence type."

Mortified at first, Millie began to see that Darcy's heart was in the right place, but she didn't want Darcy worrying about her. She had other more important things to concern herself with. Like recovering from a concussion. "I appreciate your concern, but I'm fine. I have no expectations where Ian is concerned." In fact, she had no expectations where *any* men were concerned. They just didn't fall for women like her.

Darcy held her gaze. "Well, if you want to talk about it, I'm here." Taking another bite of her stew, she rolled her eyes in pleasure. "Now," she said around a mouthful, "what are your plans for Christmas?"

Millie shrugged. She had none. But she didn't want to horn in on Josh and Darcy's first Christmas as a married couple. "I'll probably spend it at my parents."

Darcy lifted a brow. "I thought your parents didn't do Christmas."

"They don't," Millie prevaricated. "I'll just spend the day there."

"Well, if you change your mind, my family's coming here, since I can't go to them. You're welcome, too."

"Thank you." Millie left it at that. She didn't expect to go to her parents. She would settle in with a good book, maybe work on her manuscript. Write her first authentic sex scene, she thought with glee, and dine on leftover roast turkey and mashed potatoes from the diner.

———

Ian entered the kitchen in search of coffee. And, truth be told, Millie. Instead, he found Josh working at the kitchen table. "I'm sorry, I didn't know you were here," Ian said as he left the room.

"You're not disturbing me." Josh ran two hands through his hair, looking a little frazzled. No surprise there, after the last two days. He rose and walked over to the coffeemaker, poured himself a cup and invited Ian to do the same.

"I, uh, I'm glad you're here," Josh said, discomfort written all over his face. "Have a seat." He indicated the chair across from his.

Ian frowned, wondering what this was all about. A problem with his work? "What can I do for you?" Might as well clear the air.

"Well, you see," Josh hedged, "Darcy asked me to speak to you. And when your pregnant wife, who is filled with raging hormones and recovering from a concussion, asks you to do something, you do it." The corner of his mouth lifted. "No questions asked."

"Shoot." Ian looked Josh in the eye. If this *was* about his work, he wanted to know so he could fix it. He had a reputation to protect.

"It's about Millie."

Ian felt his brows wing up. *Millie?*

"Darcy thinks you two are a . . . thing."

"I see." He should be pissed that Josh sat him down to talk to him like a father would the horny teenager dating his daughter, but Josh's actions spoke volumes about how much Millie meant to Darcy. And to him.

"And, I'm not just speaking for Darcy here. Millie is a good and loyal friend to Darcy, but I think of her as the baby sister I never had. And I wouldn't want to see my sister hurt."

Ian waited for Josh to continue.

"I know you're both adults, but Millie has lived a, shall we say, sheltered life, and may be more vulnerable than most women her age. So, I'd appreciate it if you would keep that in mind. I'd hate to have to kick your ass," he finished with a warm smile, but his eyes held the truth of that statement. He wouldn't hesitate to protect Millie.

Ian nodded. He didn't want to hurt Millie either. "Understood. I'd hate for you to have to kick my ass, too."

"So, we're good then?" Josh asked as his hands slapped the table.

"We're good."

---

L ater that evening, after several hours trying to make sense of the RFP instructions, Ian had had enough. His stomach growled, and with nothing in the fridge, he'd have to go out. But the thought of eating dinner out alone depressed him. Caleb and Jillie had gone to Buffalo for Christmas, and Ruby was likely asleep by now.

He wondered about Millie. Would she be home alone?

He'd promised himself he'd leave her alone. Not lead her on. But truth be told, he missed her company.

What the hell. It was only a burger.

Taking a chance, he called up her number on his cell phone and tapped the call option.

"Hello?"

He smiled at the sexy, throaty voice on the other end. "Millie, hi, it's Ian."

"Ian? Is everything okay?" she replied, her voice anxious.

He realized he'd never called her before. No wonder she sounded worried.

"It's fine. I'm going to grab some dinner. Care to join me?" Crickets. "Millie?"

"Oh. Yes. Sure."

"Great. I'll pick you up in twenty minutes. That enough time?"

"Uh, sure."

"See you in a few."

Ian's face split into a big grin.

Thirty minutes later, after picking up Millie, Ian pulled up in front of Sea Witch. Helping her from the truck, he ushered her into the warmth of the pub.

Finding a booth in the corner, he slid in across from her. Dressed in her usual brown, her hair in a bun, her cheeks pink from the cold, she surveyed the room, taking in the large oval fish tank on one wall and the bold mural on another.

He'd never brought a woman here. It had always been his and Caleb's place. "This is my favorite burger joint," he offered.

Millie nodded as the waitress came over to take their drink orders and drop off menus.

"Hi there, Ian. Haven't seen you in a while."

"Hi, Kendra. Been pretty busy."

"You're usual?"

"Yeah."

"And for you?" Kendra turned to Millie.

"I'll have what he's having."

Kendra lifted a brow, then shrugged. "I'll get your orders in."

———

Millie watched with great interest as Kendra walked over to a computer to punch in their order, wondering if she and Ian had a . . . relationship.

"Kendra's a single mom, working here and putting herself through school," Ian volunteered. The corner of his mouth twitched. "And, no. We've never dated."

She couldn't say why, but relief swept over her. Not that it was any of her business who Ian had dated, or was currently dating for that matter. They'd only had sex, right? Ian had never promised or even alluded to anything more than that. Look at her, being all Laura-esque. "She's pretty," Millie murmured, finally shucking her coat and gloves.

Feeling Ian's eyes on her, she asked, "What?"

"For a native New Yorker, you don't seem to handle the cold very well."

"No. Winter is not my favorite time of year."

"I like the spring and fall. Great time to have a motorcycle."

"Ian, why did you ask me to dinner?"

Clearly surprised by her forthrightness, he paused. "Because I consider you a friend. And I like your company."

She glanced down at the table, then couldn't suppress

the smile that played around the corners of her mouth as she reached up to tuck a loose strand of hair behind her ear. "Thank you."

"And I think you like mine."

She gazed down at the table again, before nodding. "Yes. I do," she whispered, tempering her excitement.

Recalling his conversation with Josh, he added, "But let's keep things light, okay? No promises, no commitments."

Her hopes took a bit of a hit. But what had she expected?

He tilted his head sideways to get her attention. When she looked up and nodded, he said, "Good. We're on the same page, then." Picking up his root beer, he threw out what was clearly intended to be a conversation starter, "So, what book are you currently reading?" He took a swig of his drink.

*Masters and Johnson*! As if the flush in her cheeks weren't enough, she felt her face go up in flames at Ian's innocent question. She couldn't tell him she was alternating between *The Joy of Sex* and the *Kama Sutra*. She'd been especially interested since she and Ian had . . . Well, since she'd had sex. She went with the other book she'd been reading. "*What to Expect When You're Expecting.*"

Ian blanched, choking on his root beer.

Appalled at what he must be thinking, she stammered, "Oh. No. I mean, I'm not. It's for Darcy."

"Good to know," he said, nodding, as his eyes watered.

"What about you? What are you reading?"

"*How We Die.*"

"Oh." Sorry she asked, Millie searched for a change of subject, then decided to be direct. "So, your friend, Ruby, she's not doing well?"

He spun his glass in a circle on the table, contemplating it as if it held the secret to life. "She's holding on, but the reality is she's not going to recover from this."

Hesitating, she bit her lip, then reached out her hand, covering his. "I'm so sorry, Ian. Please let me know if there is anything I can do."

He regarded their hands. "Thank you, but unless you've got a miracle up your sleeve, there's nothing anyone can do."

A pall fell over the table, then Kendra arrived with their orders.

"Holy cow!" Millie blurted, as Kendra placed the mile-high burger down in front of her.

Ian's mouth lifted in a half grin, "Literally."

"I don't know how to eat that."

"One bite at a time," he instructed as he hefted the burger to his mouth.

---

After paying the bill and helping Millie on with her coat, Ian was reluctant for the night to end. The only thing he had to look forward to was the RFP with its *War and Peace* version of instructions.

"Hey, can you keep a secret?" Ian asked.

"I work in the home of a best-selling romance author, and as you know, overhear all manner of things, of course I can keep a secret."

"Right. Well, I'm working on a surprise for Darcy. Josh asked me to build a crib."

Millie turned to him, a look of wonder on her face. "Really?"

"Yep. Almost finished. Just needs another coat of varnish. Would you like to see it?"

Eyes beaming, she nodded.

A short time later, Ian drove into the loft's garage space and shut off the engine.

"You live in this huge building all alone?"

"For now. There are plans in the works to convert the upper floors into apartments." He showed Millie to the heavy oak door he'd found at an architectural salvage store and opening it, tried to see the space through Millie's eyes. Did it appear cold and unwelcoming?

"Wow," Millie said. "This is so spacious."

He directed her to the western corner of the building where he'd set up his residence. "This gives me space for everything all in one place." He pointed out his office, living area, kitchen, and finally his shop. Flipping on a light, Ian indicated the crib.

Millie looked up at him and then walked over to it, reaching out to touch it. "Can I?"

"Sure. The varnish is dry."

"It's beautiful. And you built this yourself?"

"Yes. Some people crochet to relax, I build and restore furniture," he said with a shrug.

After inspecting the crib, she wandered over to a burled walnut dining table. "And this?" Her hand skimmed the stripped surface of the table.

"I'm refinishing it. Found it in a renovation I completed last year. The new owner didn't want it. It'll be beautiful once I'm done."

"You're very talented."

"Thanks. Can I get you something to drink?"

"You wouldn't happen to have any tea would you?"

"I think I can scrounge up a bag or two." Allowing her to precede him into the living area, he said, "Take off your coat. Make yourself comfortable." Another first, he'd never had a woman in his loft before. Course he hadn't lived there for very long.

As he took out the makings for tea, Millie peeled off her coat and laid it over an armchair in the 'library' and then wandered the living space. Stopping in front of the desk, she picked up the RFP instructions and began reading them. "This is a different RFP."

"Yes. It's for a seventeenth century English manor outside of Oxford that was recently purchased by a hotel chain. They're converting it into an exclusive inn."

"Sounds like a lengthy project."

"Eighteen to twenty-four months."

"Oh." She bit her lip as a furrow creased her brow. "Extensive," she said. "Have you heard anything after you submitted the RFI?"

"No."

"How's this one coming, then?" She set the instructions back on the desk.

"Fine," he lied. He didn't have a teakettle, so he brought water to a boil in a pot then filled two mugs. Carrying them over to his desk, he handed one to Millie.

Wrapping her hands around the mug, she blew on the contents, drawing his eyes to her pursed lips.

*Damn.* He wanted to taste those lips again. He wanted to take those infernal pins from her hair and fist his hands in it as he kissed his way down her throat. Feeling her eyes on him, he looked up into her flushed face.

She cleared her throat and glanced back down at the packet. "I can help you with this."

He approached her, careful not to startle her, and set his mug on the desk, before taking hers and setting it next to his. Placing his hands on her shoulders he stepped into her, relishing the hitch in her breath. So much for 'just a burger.'

"There's only one thing I want from you right now." He tipped his head, and gently sucked her lower lip between his teeth. She quivered against him, then her hands found their way into his hair. "And it's got nothing to do with paperwork."

# CHAPTER NINETEEN

She sighed as Ian's hands slid down her ribs to settle at her hips. This couldn't be happening. First he calls her up, then he takes her to dinner. Now, here she was, in his loft, his lips pressed to hers. Again.

His fingers worked their way to the hem of her sweater, breaking their kiss, and lifting it up and over her head, before tossing it aside. She shivered as cool air hit her skin. Cupping her breasts, he grazed his thumbs over her already-hard nipples. She groaned. Bending, his mouth took over where his thumbs left off, suckling her through her bra. Legs quivering, she swayed into him.

"God, Millie. You have no idea how beautiful you are."

She squeezed her eyes shut. "You don't have to say that," she whispered.

He drew back, and she could feel his eyes on her face. "I know I don't. I want to. Because it's true." His fingers skimmed her jaw, gliding up, they tangled in her hair, pulling on the pins until they fell, tinkling as they hit the hardwood floor. Next, he removed her glasses, setting them on the desk.

Emboldened by his words, she reached up and began unbuttoning his shirt. He released her so she could slide the shirt down his arms, his eyes never leaving her face. Next, she pulled his T-shirt off, dropping it to the floor. He was beautifully made. "Can I touch you?"

He closed his eyes. "Good God, Millie. Yes."

Slowly, she skimmed her hands down his torso, fascinated by the way his muscles twitched beneath her hand. Leaning in, she pressed her mouth to his breastbone, feeling the deep rumble in his chest as he moaned. He smelled like soap and Ian. Grazing her nose across his chest, her hands grew brave, sliding down and around to cup his butt, drawing him against her. They both hissed when his erection met her stomach.

The average human has two yards of skin, and she wanted to kiss every inch of his two yards. Kissing her way across his chest, she stopped at his nipple.

"Millie, you're torturing me," he growled.

"I am?"

"You've no idea." His hands found the waistband of her skirt and tugged downward, taking her tights and panties along for the ride. Holding on to his shoulders as she stepped out of her clothes, she almost took a header when on the trip back up, he grazed her thighs with his teeth.

Backing her up against an interior wall, he reached around and unhooked her bra, palming each breast as he freed it. She couldn't wait any longer. Struggling with his fly, she finally freed him, grasping him in her hand.

"Okay, enough of that," he ground out. Dropping his jeans and boxer briefs to the floor, he palmed her butt cheeks. "Wrap your legs around my waist. That's it." He sandwiched her between the wall and him. She didn't know which surface was harder. The wall at her back, or his bare chest at her front.

*Oh, my first experience with suspended congress!*

"Millie." His voiced sounded tight. "You were a virgin, so I know you're safe. Do you trust me when I say I've been tested recently and I'm clean?"

She nodded.

"And tell me you're on birth control."

"Yes." A girl had to be prepared.

"Thank you, Jesus." He entered her in one long, slow, motion. Throwing her head back, she reveled in the feel of him, especially *sans* condom. The fullness, the delicious friction. She hadn't imagined it. Sex with Ian was just as earth shattering this time as the previous three times.

He nipped at her collarbone, grazing her with his teeth and tongue as he withdrew and entered her again, then again, picking up the pace with each thrust of his hips. She gripped his shoulders with the frenzy of a woman on fire. He engulfed her. Her senses were surrounded by him. His smell, his skin, his mouth, his sounds. At that moment, he made up her entire world. And her entire world spiraled away from where their bodies joined. The tension built until she thought she might shatter into a million pieces.

"Sweet Millie," he groaned, and she followed him into the cosmos.

Pressing kisses to her shoulder, he waited until their breathing returned to normal. Still palming her bottom, he stepped out of his jeans, struggling a little to maintain his balance, then carried her, still buried deep, up the stairs to his bedroom.

Barely catching a glimpse of a battered old wardrobe, she clung to him. Dropping down to his knees, he laid her on the bed and climbed in beside her.

"You okay?"

She nodded, the barely contained smile tugging at her lips. "More than."

"Good." He kissed her nose.

The light from downstairs cast enough light for her to see Ian's naked body in all its glory. And it was a beauty. Muscled arms, firm pecs, flat stomach, hard chest. She let her fingers do the walking down a thin trail of hair to find another tattoo, the one she'd seen their first night together. A quote that ran horizontally across his belly just above his navel, but it appeared to be backward. She tilted her head. "What does this say, and why is it backward?"

"It says, 'Fear Kills More Dreams than Failure Ever Will,' and it's backward so that when I look in the mirror I can read it."

That. That was why Ian was special to her. Everything he did had meaning.

And at that moment, she added something else to her Get a Life List.

"Where did you get your tattoos?" Her hand glided across the quote, making his stomach muscles quiver.

"Why?"

"I want one."

He propped his head in his hand and gazed down at her. "You want a tattoo," Ian said in confusion.

Millie lifted her chin. "Yes."

"Why?"

"Because. You have one," she whispered.

"I also have a penis. Do you want one of those too?"

"Only if it's yours," she said, and he laughed. "So . . . where did you get your tattoo?"

He huffed out a breath. "A tattoo parlor in Brownsville."

"Brownsville?" The Brooklyn neighborhood had long been one of the most dangerous in New York City.

"Yeah. No place for a woman alone." The finality of his tone indicated he thought the conversation was over.

"What's the name of it, the tattoo parlor?"

He hesitated and finally said, "Dangerous Ink."

Millie nodded. "Sounds apropos."

"You're not going there," he said, an edge to his voice.

"Why not? You did. And I like your tattoos." She brushed her hand along the tattoo on his forearm.

"You have a death wish or something?"

"No. I just want a tattoo."

Ian sighed. "If you're serious, I'll take you, but you're not going alone."

"Fine." Pleased, she rolled over and sat up. "So, will there be a round two?"

"Babe"—he snagged her around her waist and pulled her down on top of him—"there will be a round *three.*"

———

"I should go," Millie said on a sigh.

Ian contemplated the woman he'd just made love to for the third time. Her arm and leg were flung across his body, her head resting on his shoulder, her hair a wild tangle around her. He didn't want her to leave.

He swept his hand along her back down past her hips to her bottom then up again. "Stay."

Raising her head, she looked at him. "Really?"

"Yes. Really." The more he thought about it the better he liked the idea. "We'll go to breakfast at a diner not far from here. Best French toast in Brooklyn." Another idea sprang to mind. "Then, if you're up for it, I'm checking in on Ruby. Since it's Christmas Eve, I'm sure she would love the company."

"I'd like that. What does she like? Can I bring her something?"

"If you want. Being a retired librarian, she loves books, of course. Especially the classics."

"I have a first edition Edith Wharton I could bring if we could stop by my apartment."

He smiled. "Sure." He tucked her head beneath his chin and pressed his lips to her hair. "After we see Ruby, if you haven't come to your senses by then, we can go get that tattoo."

"Oh," she said, with a touch of reticence in her voice "They're open on Christmas Eve?"

He lifted a brow. "'Til seven. I'm not sure they even recognize Christmas Eve."

A few beats passed, then she asked, "Does it hurt?"

"Like hell."

"Oh."

He smiled into her hair. "You can always change your mind."

"No. I've added it to my list, now I have to check it off."

"What list?"

———

Millie cringed. "It's nothing." Why had she let that slip out? Oxytocin overdose, no doubt.

"Well, if the list is so important that once you add something to it, you have to check it off, it's not nothing," he said, his voice soft in the dimly lit room.

She threaded her fingers through the dusting of hair on his chest, making circles. Apparently, being bold wasn't something you checked off once. It was a lifestyle change. "Do you remember the day you hauled me from the street?"

"Of course I do. It's not often I get to rescue a damsel in distress."

She snorted. "I've given you plenty more opportunities since then."

"True that. It's practically a full-time job."

She plucked a hair.

"Ow!" He grabbed her hand and rubbed his chest.

"I decided that day that I needed a change."

"What kind of change?" He entwined his finger with hers.

How could she explain it? "One that would make me less invisible, more . . . alive."

"So you made a list." His voice rumbled in his chest beneath her ear. She nodded, surprised that he didn't laugh or think her silly.

"And what's on this list?"

"Oh, you know, have sex—"

"Check. Times five."

"Six, but who's counting?" She grinned. "Ride death machine."

He snorted. "Check."

"Get drunk."

"I don't know why that would be on your list, but check."

"It was on my list because I'd never done it. Just like sex." She shrugged.

"Well, don't make a habit of it. Getting drunk, I mean."

"No chance of that. The next morning I felt like I'd died and someone forgot to bury me."

He chuckled. "Good. Alcohol is bad for you. How much did you have anyway?"

"Um"—she hesitated, embarrassed by her response—"a glass."

"Of whiskey? Vodka? Gin?"

"Wine."

He snorted again. "Seriously?"

She lifted her head and glared at him. "Don't laugh. I'm a lightweight, what can I say?"

He continued to chuckle.

"You mean to tell me, you've never been drunk?"

"No."

His terse response piqued her curiosity. Then she recalled both times they'd had dinner, he'd only had water and root beer. "You don't drink."

"No."

"Why not?"

"I thought two alcoholics in the family was enough." He shifted, then began stroking her hair.

"Your parents?"

"My mother and stepfather."

"Oh. My parents don't drink. Too busy chasing Thomas Hardy."

"*As in Jude the Obscure and Far from the Madding Crowd Thomas Hardy?*"

Not all surprised that he would know that, Millie continued, "Yes. They've spent their entire academic career trying to prove an unsigned, untitled, and unfinished manuscript is Hardy's."

"And have they? Proved it?"

"According to my mother, yes." His gentle strokes were lulling her to sleep.

"That's pretty incredible."

"I suppose," she murmured.

"You don't think so?"

"No. It's great. It's just . . . It's been everything to them. To the exclusion of all else." Why was she telling him this?

"All else including you?"

God how that hurt. She didn't hate her parents. The logical side of her brain knew they didn't *intentionally* neglect her. They just got lost in their own world. And forgot. But that didn't mean that her emotional side didn't resent it. She'd never cared for Thomas Hardy for that reason. "Yes."

"I'd have traded places with you if it meant my stepfather ignored me. No. Check that. I wouldn't want you to take my place."

Rising up on her elbow, she studied his handsome face, covered with at least two days' stubble, his expression grim. "Why? What did he do?"

"He was a strict disciplinarian. Especially when he'd been drinking."

"He abused you?"

"Not according to him. In the World According to Hank, at first I needed to be taught a lesson for everything from a bad grade to getting into—and often losing—a fight. Then, apparently, I needed to be taught a lesson for my very existence."

"What about your mother? Didn't she defend you?"

"My mother was usually too drunk to notice."

"Oh, Ian." Tears stung her eyes, and she admonished herself for thinking her childhood had been bad. She pressed a kiss to his chest, and his hand settled on her hair. "Is that what killed your mother? Alcohol?"

"Yeah. Cirrhosis."

They lay quietly for a few heartbeats, then Millie said, "So, Ruby."

"So, Ruby." His hand grazed along her arm. "Now, back

to this list. What else is on it?" he asked, clearly seeking to change the subject.

"Get tattoo."

"Anything else?"

"Not at the moment," she said, not mentioning the novel. "But it's a living document."

"What about eating ice cream in bed? Ever done that?"

She giggled. "No."

"Babe, you haven't lived until you've eaten Rocky Road in bed."

"Then I'd better add it to the list."

He rose in all his naked glory, wide shoulders, narrow hips, firm butt, and headed downstairs. "Now, let's check it off the list."

She watched in appreciation as he padded barefoot out of the room. How she wished she could be that uninhibited. That comfortable in her own skin. She didn't think that was something you could put on a list and just check it off. It, too, would be a lifestyle change.

———

Oh what a night. Oh what a morning! Millie had no idea that two people could have sex so many times and still want more. A giggle bubbled to the surface. She'd read about the nocturnal penile tumescence phenomenon, also known as the morning salute, but of course she'd never witnessed it. Not only had she witnessed it, she'd put it to good use.

"What are you giggling about, woman?" Ian stepped up behind her, wrapped his hands around her waist, nuzzling her ear.

They'd each had a piece of toast to tide them over until

breakfast–all that sex really worked up an appetite–and she stood sipping her tea.

"Just thinking about last night. This morning . . ."

"Mmm. Good thoughts, then."

"More than good."

He nuzzled her neck again, brushing her hair aside.

"I think I just heard bells."

"Hmm." He nipped at her ear. "That's a first."

"Ian? Ian."

"What?" He pressed kisses along her neck.

"I think it's your phone."

"Right." Releasing her, he bound up the stairs two at a time.

The ringing stopped, and Millie heard Ian answer the phone. "Hi, Ruby."

Feeling a little hot and bothered all over again, Millie took a deep, calming breath. She needed to refocus her attention or they'd never make it out of the house today.

She wandered over to the desk and picked up the RFP. The questions were pretty straightforward. With all the right information at her fingertips, she could knock this out by day's end.

As she set her mug on the desk, she bumped into the corner and Ian's computer woke up. "Tsk, tsk. No password protection," she muttered. On the screen was a document that appeared to be his draft response.

"I'm jumping in the shower," Ian called down. "I told Ruby we'd be there before noon."

"Sounds good," she said, already preoccupied with the document. From the spelling and grammatical errors, it appeared that he'd dictated the document using voice to text software. There were homonym misspellings you might expect from that type of software. Spying a carelessly tossed aside headset on the desk confirmed her suspicions.

Pulling out the black mesh office chair, she sat down and began editing the document. He'd only drafted responses to the first two questions. Making quick work of that, she minimized the document and opened Ian's Internet browser, doing a Google search for his company's website.

"Why put off 'til tomorrow what can be done today?" she murmured to herself. The fact that she'd be helping him leave her wasn't lost on her.

Using information she found there, she drafted answers to the next three questions. Ian's portfolio was impressive. She didn't realize the level of his expertise in historic preservation and renovation, or the number of famous buildings he'd had a hand in preserving.

She was so engrossed in her work that she didn't hear him come down the stairs.

"What the hell are you doing?"

# CHAPTER TWENTY

Millie jumped up from the desk with a start. "I, uh, I'm working on the RFP."

Ian strode over to the desk. "Why would you do that? Is nothing beyond your snooping?" Feelings of shame and fear rose to the surface, taunted by painful memories of teachers looking over his shoulder as he labored over crafting his alphabet and copying sentences onto the lined pages of his notebooks. He wondered what Millie had thought of his messy draft.

"I'm sorry, I was just trying to help." She picked up her mug and moved toward the kitchen.

"I don't need your help. If I did, I'd ask for it. Goddammit, Millie." He turned away, dragged his fingers through his hair. "I'm not trading sex for your assistance."

"I'm not asking you to." She stopped and pointed to the computer screen. "Seems to me that this job is pretty important and with everything else you've got going on, I can help you with this."

God, it was so tempting to turn this over to someone

else. But could he accept her help and still hide his disability?

Millie was wicked smart. Not just well read. He'd put her skills of logic up against the world's finest philosophers and scientists. Why would someone with her brains want to be with him?

And with her deductive reasoning skills, it wouldn't take her long to figure out the truth. He should just tell her. Speak the truth.

But the words embedded themselves in his throat and wouldn't let go.

Her warm arms came around his torso, her hands finding their way to his chest, as she pressed her firm breasts into his back, and his anger fled. "You know my offer still stands."

"I thought we'd already put that offer to bed, literally."

She giggled. "Yes. But I'm talking about my offer to help. No strings attached."

"I'll think about it."

"Ian, let me help you."

Closing his eyes against the lure of that husky voice, he grasped her hands as they headed south. "I've apparently made a nymphomaniac out of you."

He felt her nod against his back. "You have."

Releasing her hands, he surrendered.

———

"I'll just grab the book and we can go," Millie said as she unlocked the door to her apartment.

Ian hesitated, then followed her in. He remembered little about her apartment the first time he was there. He'd been more focused on Millie and her sweet body.

The studio apartment boasted a tiny, but newly furnished kitchen right off the front door. Just beyond that, the bed, covered in a white comforter, stood along an exposed brick wall, a built-in bookcase loaded with books served as both the headboard and end tables. Against the far wall a long narrow table held more books and a stack of papers. Finishing out the room was a small armoire against the wall to the left and a loveseat at the foot of the bed. No visible TV. Tidy, but with just enough clutter to look lived-in.

"The book should be on this shelf," Millie muttered to herself.

Strolling across the confined space, Ian perused the books on the table. Seeing the *Kama Sutra* and *The Joy of Sex*, Ian picked up one in each hand and turned to Millie. "Reading up on the subject?"

Millie pivoted, gasping when she realized what he was holding up. Her face blanched the color of her comforter, then slowly, like mercury rising in a thermometer, turned scarlet.

Spinning, her back to him, she covered her face, shoulders hunched. *Dammit. He hadn't meant to humiliate her.* Laying the books on the table, he approached her and, placing his hands on her shoulders, said, "Millie. Babe. Don't be embarrassed. I like that you're curious. Inquisitive. It's sexy. And if last night was any indication, it's been time well spent."

He reached around, pried her hands from her face, and wrapped her arms around her waist along with his. He nuzzled her ear, enjoying her indrawn breath. "Got any favorites? Any positions you'd like to try?"

"Really?" she asked, her smoky voice barely above a whisper.

His hands glided up her ribcage stopping just beneath her breasts. "Make a list. We'll check them off one-by-one."

"When can we start?" The words came out in little pants as he sucked her ear lobe into his mouth.

"Now works for me," he murmured against her lips.

———

Carrying two small bags of groceries, Millie followed Ian into the apartment. She couldn't wipe the grin off her face. First, she'd seduced him. Not only into having hot wall sex again, but also into letting her help him. Then, after what had been Ian's humiliating discovery, he'd quickly turned that mortification into unadulterated arousal. They'd checked not one but two positions of her newly created Kama Sutra list: The Perch and The Snail.

"Ruby! It's Ian. And I've brought a friend."

"Ian?" a feeble voice called from the depths of the apartment.

"Kitchen's through there," Ian said, indicating the door to the right. "I'll just go set the Christmas tree in the living room." Ian had purchased a mini cypress tree decorated with tiny red and gold ornaments for Ruby. His thoughtfulness touched Millie deeply.

She entered an old-fashioned kitchen, harvest-gold appliances, linoleum flooring, and Formica countertops. Opening the fridge, she put away the eggs, butter, cheese, and milk. Unsure what to do with the bread and the canned goods, she left them on the counter and went in search of Ian.

He was bent over a frail woman in a recliner, pulling a floral blanket up over her chest. "You warm enough?"

"Yes. Don't fuss." Ruby caught a glance of Millie. "Who's this?"

Ian turned with a smile and lifted his hand to Millie. "This is a friend of mine, Millie Stephens. Millie, this is Ruby Sinclair."

*Friend.* She didn't know what else she expected him to call her. She wasn't really his girlfriend. The cliché friends with benefits, maybe? She didn't know how she felt about that label either.

"Hi. Ian has told me so much about you."

"Too bad I can't say the same." Ruby gave Ian a sharp look.

"Have you eaten?" Ian asked, clearly unfazed by Ruby's admonishment.

"I had some crackers earlier."

"Crackers." He released a heavy sigh. "How does an omelet sound?"

"Fine."

"Good. I'll leave you and Millie to get acquainted. Millie loves books, and earned her degree in literature with a focus on the Middle Ages from Sarah Lawrence."

Millie's gaze shot to his face. He remembered that from their conversation that first night in the diner?

He smiled, then headed for the kitchen.

Millie took a seat on the sofa next to the recliner. "So, you were a librarian?"

"Yes. Forty-three years. New York Public Library System."

Public library? She figured she'd been the librarian at Ian's school. "How did you meet Ian?"

"He didn't tell you?" At Millie's head shake, she continued, "Not sure it's my place to tell it, but suffice to say, he used to spend a lot of time in the Sunset Park Library. And what do you do? How did you two meet?"

"I'm personal assistant to an author, and Ian's doing some work in her home." She drew her hair over her shoulder and out of her face. She'd worn it down and loose at Ian's request.

"An author, huh? Who's that?"

"Darcy Butler."

"Darcy Butler? I love her books!" Ruby coughed, a deep wracking cough that made Millie wince, then drew in a ragged breath and continued. "Funny. And steamy. I like steamy." Ruby waggled her eyebrows at Millie, making her laugh. "I haven't gotten my hands on her latest, *Life is a Cabernet.*"

"Oh, I can bring you a copy." Millie felt the heat in her face at her presumption. "Or have Ian bring it."

"You can bring it."

"I brought you something today." Millie reached into the depths of her coat pocket and retrieved the book. "It's Wharton's *The Age of Innocence.* First Edition."

Ruby's rheumy eyes widened. "First edition! No dear, I can't take that from you."

"Okay. A loan then."

Ruby reverently took the book from Millie's hands, opened it, and read the first page aloud. Then she closed her eyes, a smile ghosting across her gaunt face.

"Would you like me to read to you?" Millie asked.

She looked at Millie, her eyes alight. "Would you?"

"Of course." Millie took the book and opened it back up to the first page and continued where Ruby had left off.

———

Ian paused, the plated omelet in his hands, listening to that sultry voice reading *The Age of Innocence*. Only Millie could make the subtle dramatic irony of Wharton read like an erotic novel.

Ruby lay with her head back, eyes closed, a soft smile on her face. Ian's gut clenched. She looked so frail. So ephemeral. But she also looked happy. Transported.

Bringing Millie had been a good idea. Her beautiful old soul made her a perfect companion for Ruby. Reluctant to interrupt, he placed the plate in the oven on low to keep the omelet warm. He'd noticed a few cabinet doors that needed tightening, and a drawer that didn't close properly. He'd fix those things and check back later.

———

"That's good. That's really good. Yes. Perfect."

Ian peered over her shoulder as she typed up the response to the question concerning his previous experience with major historic renovations.

His breath tickled her neck, and she redoubled her efforts to concentrate on the task at hand.

She'd begun reading aloud as she typed, refining his dictated responses, polishing the words until they sparkled like a crystal chandelier.

Satisfied with that response, she rose from her seat. "I could use some tea. Do you want anything?" She'd been making herself at home, at least in his kitchen. And his bed. And she couldn't forget his shower. Those body sprayers fulfilled some heretofore unknown fantasies.

"No. I'm good."

Opening the cabinet where he'd stored the fresh boxes

of tea they'd picked up that day, it struck her that he'd bought those for her. What did that mean? That he expected her over more often?

*Well, of course he did, Silly Millie. You were helping him with the RFP. Why else?*

Putting the pot onto boil, she took out a bag of tea–a soothing chamomile–and thought about the last few hours. How Ian had taken care of Ruby. How he'd listened attentively as she'd read to her. How he'd refused to continue reading when she'd taken a break.

Something niggled at her. Suspicions danced around the edges of her mind. She took the pot off the stove, poured boiling water into her mug, then placed the pot back on the stove. While she waited for her tea to steep, she called out to Ian. "Read the next set of questions."

Nothing.

"Ian?"

"I, uh, I shut the computer down. We're done for the night."

"Oh. We only had a few more questions left."

He sauntered into the kitchen, lifted the mug to his mouth, and took a sip. "It's been a long day. I should get you home."

He'd just confirmed her suspicions.

# CHAPTER TWENTY-ONE

"So much for crossing the tattoo off your list today," Ian said as he escorted her up the sidewalk to her building. "Sorry about that."

"It's fine." They'd spent the remainder of the afternoon and part of the evening with Ruby. Millie had finished reading *The Age of Innocence*, and Ruby had eaten to Ian's satisfaction. "I had a really nice time. Last night"—heat crept into her face—"this morning. All day, really. And did I tell you, Ruby asked if I would come back and read to her?"

"That's great. Thank you. It means a lot to me." Ian's eyes burned into hers as he stepped into her.

"I enjoyed it." She shrugged.

Leaning in, he propped his hands on either side of the wall next to her head. Her heartbeat ratcheted up and her breathing grew shallow as her hands drifted to his chest of their own volition. "I enjoy you, Sweet Millie." His lips brushed hers once, twice, then went in for the kill. His tongue found hers, tangled with it, sucked it into his mouth and her knees nearly gave out. Grasping her face, he changed the angle, intensifying the heat and the arousal.

Breaking the kiss, his breath came out in raspy pants. Touching his forehead to hers, he said, "I should go."

"K." She tried to keep the disappointment out of her voice. He leaned in, kissed her once more. "What are you doing tomorrow?"

Besides spending Christmas alone? "Nothing. Darcy invited me over, but I think she and Josh should be together with her family."

"I ordered a full Christmas dinner, complete with turkey, dressing, and cranberry sauce, for Ruby and me. Come with me."

"Oh, but—"

"No buts. Ruby loved your company. And so did I."

"You did?" Millie's heart trembled as something bloomed in her chest. Hope? *He could be leaving in the spring*, her brain said. *Yes, but he's here now*, her body countered.

"Yes."

"What time?"

"I'll pick you up at noon. Does that work?"

"Yes."

Pulling her in one more time, he pressed a tender kiss to her mouth. "Goodnight, Millie."

"Goodnight, Ian."

"Work on that new list."

Oh my! With that goal in mind, Millie headed up to her apartment to spend some quality time with the *Kama Sutra*.

———

The remains of Christmas dinner dessert were scattered on the coffee table, holiday music playing softly in the background, as Ian handed Ruby a beautifully wrapped box.

"What's this?" she asked, eyeing the package. "I don't need anything."

"Indulge me and open it, anyway," Ian said as he sat in the chair he'd pulled up next to her recliner. After a delicious meal, they were gathered in Ruby's living room where she was more comfortable.

Millie set aside her slice of pumpkin pie curious to see what Ian had purchased for Ruby. She gazed at his handsome face, still shocked that she was spending Christmas day with him. When he'd picked her up at noon, he'd held a piece of mistletoe over their heads, then taken her mouth with his. God, she could fall hard and fast for this man.

With shaking hands, Ruby tore open the giftwrap, and lifting the lid, sighed, as her hand reverently glided across its contents. "Oh, Ian. You really shouldn't have."

"You're cold all the time, and I thought this would help. It's cashmere." He drew a large deep plum cashmere throw from the box and draped it over Ruby.

Millie had to look away as tears threatened. He never ceased to amaze her. His thoughtfulness and generosity filled her heart.

When her gaze returned to them, Ian was leaning over the chair while Ruby hugged him, her thin wrists visible beneath her sweater. "You're a good boy."

Ian straightened, his eyes suspiciously shiny, and Millie's heart fluttered in her chest. *Danger, Will Robinson,* read the thought bubble over her head.

"I have something for you too," Millie said, and drew

her gift from her coat pocket where it lay on the end of the sofa. Not nearly as nicely wrapped as Ian's, it was from the heart nevertheless.

"You two," Ruby admonished, but took the gift from Millie and opened it.

"I noticed that you're a fan of the Brontës. It's not a first edition, but it's still quite nice."

This time Ruby's eyes were the ones suspiciously shiny. "Thank you." She opened the book, an 1869 edition of *Jane Eyre*, and regarded at it as if she held the Gutenberg Bible. "You'll read from it later?"

"If you'd like." Feeling Ian's eyes on her, she lifted her gaze to his, and the look she saw there almost proved her undoing.

———

"The book you gave Ruby. That was yours, wasn't it?" Ian asked.

"Yes."

"Why would you do that?" he asked as he peeled off his coat.

"Because I knew it would bring her joy," she said simply as she hung her coat on the peg beside her door.

She turned to look at him, nerves dancing along her spine. She really wanted to be the initiator tonight. She wanted to show Ian how he'd touched her heart today at Ruby's. She just didn't know how. Or maybe she just didn't have the courage.

Inhaling, she walked up to him, slid her hands up his chest along his shoulders and around to his neck. Curling her fingers into his hair, she pulled his mouth down to hers.

The minute her lips met his, his hands found her waist, hauled her close, as his tongue swirled around hers. After a long searing kiss, Ian withdrew, gazing down into her eyes, a sparkle in his own. "What position would you like to check off tonight?"

"I was thinking maybe the reverse cowgirl."

"Yee-haa!" He twirled an air-lasso above his head. "Ride 'em, cowgirl." He reached for her again, towing her toward the bed.

His eyes heated and his jeans hugged a noticeable bulge. Not even in her deepest fantasies did she ever imagine a man like Ian would want her.

"First things first." At Millie's questioning look, he continued. "Strip."

"What?" The bottom dropped out of her stomach.

"Strip for me." He sat on the bed, hands dangling between his thighs.

"I, uh, I can't." She shook her head.

"Millie, I've had my hands and my mouth over every inch of your body, and you're still modest?"

Embarrassment spread through her veins like fire. At her continued silence, Ian held out his hand.

"Come here." She approached the bed, where he drew her between his thighs and gazed up at her. "You trust me?"

She nodded.

"Good." He began unbuttoning her sweater, peeled it from her shoulders, then made quick work of the camisole underneath. Next he got busy removing her shoes, followed by her pants, panties, and bra. "Take your hair down."

She pulled the pins from her bun and set them on the shelf by the bed. When she stood naked and vulnerable in front of him he pressed a tender kiss to her navel.

"When will you realize how beautiful you are?"

She just shook her head.

Grasping her wrist, he tugged her into the bathroom, flipped on the light and had her stand in front of the mirror. "Look at yourself. No. Don't turn away. And don't cover yourself." He placed his hands on her shoulders and held her there. Her face flamed.

But something about her nakedness against his fully clothed body shot heat and desire through her. The vision they made was primal. Elemental.

His hands skimmed up her cheeks, then into her hair, down her shoulders to her breasts, where he lifted them as if testing their weight. His hands continued their descent down her belly, sweeping over her hips to her backside, then back over her pubic area, dipping between her thighs. "Every single inch of you is beautiful. I should know. I've explored all of your beautiful inches. You're beautiful here." Ian pointed to her head. "You're beautiful here." He laid his hand over her heart. "And you're beautiful here." He caressed her face, kissed her shoulder.

At that moment, Millie Stephens lost her heart for the very first time. She reached her arms up, then skimmed her fingers up his neck as she gazed into his eyes in the mirror. "Make love to me, Ian."

———

Ian's hands rested on Millie's thighs, as his heart rate dropped out of the danger zone. Millie straddled him, her hair a dark cloud around her, her cheeks flushed, her lips parted. "Magnificent Millicent," he said, breathing hard.

She'd rode him near to oblivion, her passion taking over, eclipsing her modesty and her self-doubt. If only she could see what he saw, she'd come to see the truth of her beauty, inside and out.

The moment he'd entered her, his inner caveman growled, *Mine!* He'd been her first, and now he wanted to be her last. He didn't know how, but Millie had found a way into his heart. His soul felt complete in her presence.

But with a two-year job possible, he owed it to her—and to himself—to keep things light. Avoid the entanglement. Avoid the hurt.

He'd seen the way she looked at him. Like she could see her future. He closed his eyes. It might be too late to avoid the hurt, but he couldn't bring himself to rip the Band-Aid off and end it before they were in too deep.

"You okay?"

Her mouth turned up into a sexy, satisfied smile. "More than."

Grasping her shoulders, he pulled her down, nestled her head beneath his chin. Their hearts beat in double-time, as he stroked her back.

"Can I ask you a question?" He felt her stiffen.

"Yes," came her tentative reply.

"Why the brown?"

Silence dragged on, until he thought she wasn't going to answer, then he felt her shrug.

"I didn't fit in in school. I wanted to be invisible, and since the Goths had already claimed black as their color, I went with brown."

He understood not fitting in, but he wondered why someone as smart and pretty as Millie would want to be invisible. "And now?"

"I don't know. Maybe because it's easy. Or maybe because I've become comfortable with my invisibility."

"But, you don't want to be invisible anymore. You said

so yourself. Besides, I hate to burst your bubble, but you're not invisible. Especially not to me." He pressed a kiss to her hair.

He felt her shake her head, as if she didn't believe him. Before he could set her straight, she spoke up. "Ruby said you met at the public library where she worked."

"Nice deflection, Millicent." Smiling, he brushed her hair back from her face to see that delectable mouth lift at the corner. "Yes. I met her at the Sunset Park Public Library."

"Is she the one who introduced you to philosophy and music?"

"Yes. But she, and her husband Curtis, did so much more."

"How so?"

Ian was having a hard time concentrating with Millie's naked body nestled against his, her leg thrown across him, her hand stroking his chest. "Um, when I was seventeen, my stepfather kicked me out of the house."

Millie rose up on her elbow. "Why?"

"For finally standing up for myself. By then I was no longer a scrawny kid. Ruby's hearty meals had added bulk and a good three inches to my height, and working with Curtis at construction sites after school had added muscle.

"One day Hank came after me for not telling him about my job. Called me selfish and ungrateful." And a few other choice words he didn't want to repeat to Millie. "Told me I should have been paying my fair share of the expenses. He demanded the money I'd managed to squirrel away in the bank account Curtis had helped me open. I refused. And when Hank raised his hand to me, I stood my ground, stared him down."

Millie's brow creased. "What did he do?"

"He backed down. That's when I realized bullies don't pick on those who stand up for themselves. And that's why I told you tell those punks to go fuck themselves."

Millie snuggled into him again, her soft skin sliding against his. "You make it sound so easy." She sighed, her warm breath tickling his neck.

"I never said it was easy. Nothing worth having is ever easy."

He heard her even breathing and thought she'd gone to sleep. He wrapped both arms around her and held her close.

"Ruby really loves you," she murmured sleepily, burrowing deeper against his neck. "Thank you for introducing me to her."

What she'd done for Ruby touched him to the core. She'd brought so much pleasure to her these last two days.

And she'd never demanded anything more from him than this. She didn't get all pouty when he left or if he didn't call.

He closed his eyes, breathed her in. His sweet Millie. No. Not his. Never his.

Because she deserved . . . more.

Millie shifted, sighed, and settled again.

And there was the rub. He couldn't give her more.

# CHAPTER TWENTY-TWO

After Ian left the next morning, following some pretty amazing shower sex, which in her tiny shower was no small feat, Millie took advantage of the quiet to take stock.

As she tidied up her apartment, she held Ian's bed pillow to her face and breathed him in. His scent permeated her senses and bombarded her with memories of last night, this morning, but also yesterday at Ruby's.

His tenderness toward Ruby. His thoughtfulness for a woman not his mother.

She had no reason to think that Ian would, or could, ever be interested in a serious relationship with her. Of course, she never thought he'd want to have sex with her either, and here she was, smoothing back sheets that should have been nothing but ash after last night's scorching escapades.

Did she dare think now that anything was possible? That Ian might be falling for her, just as she had fallen for him?

Recalling his words as he held her naked in front of her

mirror, her face heated and her heart warmed. He'd said every inch of her was beautiful. Then he'd shown her.

And while she didn't have much experience, something happened last night. Something changed. It hadn't been about just sex anymore. The physical act had become . . . more. It had progressed from lust to love.

All her work on the Hawkins Hall RFP—a job that would take him away from her for two years. She had complete faith in his skills, and that he'd be more than qualified for the job. With her work on the RFP, it would be polished until it shined, leaving no doubt he'd be selected. And she would lose him.

But she'd never thought of him as hers. A guy like Ian wasn't truly anyone's.

———

The day of Darcy's baby shower Millie hurried down the sidewalk through a crisp, cold day, the sun doing little to warm the air. In her arms, she carried the cake she'd ordered for the shower, her contribution to the festivities.

The cake, in the shape of a book open in the middle, revealed Pooh himself, seated on one side of the book, a honeypot in his lap, and on the opposite page, the Honey Tree with all his friends gathered round—Piglet, Eeyore, Christopher Robin, Kanga, Roo, Rabbit, Owl, and of course, Tigger—a quote from A.A Milne inscribed in the icing.

Shivering from the cold, Millie unlocked the front door and headed for the kitchen, on a mission to hide the cake before Darcy could see it. Laura should be there any minute, and the caterers shortly thereafter.

While the shower itself wasn't a surprise, the theme was. They'd set up in the dining room, and to keep Darcy occupied until the guests arrived, Millie had enlisted Josh's help. Darcy couldn't resist a good holiday-themed movie, so Josh took her to a special showing of *It's a Wonderful Life* still playing at the IFC Center. By the time the movie was over, they'd have everything set.

Glancing at her watch, Millie shucked her winter wear and grabbed the stack of Winnie the Pooh plates and napkins and set about the table arrangements.

She knew Ian would be there toward the end of the shower with Josh's gift. Her stomach flipped over and she looked down at what she hoped was a nice dress. Brown with pale pink stripes, it fit her better than most of her others. Instead of her sensible SAS moccasins, she'd gone with a pair of ankle boots she'd found in the thrift store around the corner from her apartment. The two-inch heel made her feel tall, but they pinched her feet, and she knew by the end of the day she'd regret the decision to put fashion before comfort.

After overhearing Laura and Darcy talking about the current popularity of braids, she'd braided her hair before twisting it into her customary bun, which she thought gave her an air of sophistication. Would Ian notice?

Two nights ago, they'd stayed up until the wee hours of the morning, finishing the RFP, fine-tuning it before hitting 'Submit.' With a click of a mouse, she was letting him go.

———

An hour later, Darcy's mom and sister arrived, arms laden with gifts wrapped in sunny yellows and cool greens. So different from the recent bright reds and greens of Christmas.

"She back yet?" Vanessa, Darcy's mother, asked as she kissed Millie's cheek.

"No, but I expect her any minute. Laura's in the kitchen"—Millie heaved a sigh—"ordering the caterers around like a general at war."

"That's our Laura," Vanessa replied, with a laugh.

Anne, Darcy's sister, took the gifts to the antique break-front buffet in the dining room. "Looks great, Millie." She leaned over to get a better view at the cake. "I've always loved Winnie the Pooh," she said, her eyes wistful as her hand slid down to her flat belly.

Millie's eye narrowed. *Hmm.* It wasn't that long ago when Anne and her husband, Matt, were separated, until Josh had stepped in and mediated their differences. Now, if the dreamy expression on Anne's face was any indication, another child was on the way.

The doorbell interrupted her thoughts as more guests arrived.

A short time later, the shower was in full swing, and Darcy looked radiant sitting in the midst of all the baby gifts, Josh by her side, no sign of the injuries she'd sustained from her fall.

Gloria, sipping on her usual Bombay Sapphire Gin and tonic, Elise, Darcy's editor, her brother Brandon and his partner, David, Laura, Cindy, Vanessa, Anne, and a couple of author friends sat around, *oohing* and *ahhing* over the tiny bodysuits, jumpers, and sleeper sets. Darcy's mom had knitted a baby blanket as soft as rabbit's fur. Josh's mom couldn't make the trip to New York for the shower, but she already had an open-ended airline ticket for mid-April when her first grandchild was due.

Darcy opened a huge box, pulling out a Winnie the Pooh crib set. "Oh, Anne. It's precious, but I don't have a crib yet," she said as she eyed Josh, an expression of disappointment on her face.

Millie bit her lip and glanced over at Josh. His lawyer's face gave nothing away.

As if on cue, the doorbell rang, and Millie's heart gave a start. *Romeo and Juliet! That's Ian.* Millie patted her hair to make sure the braids were still in place.

"Who could that be?" Darcy asked as she scanned the room. "Everyone's here."

Josh jumped up. "I'll go see. Probably someone soliciting."

Millie could make out Ian's voice, and her hand glided down the front of her dress as her mouth went dry.

"Looks like we have another guest," Josh said as he rounded the corner into the living room. "And another gift."

Darcy glanced up in confusion, then Ian followed closely on Josh's heels, manhandling the beautiful crib he'd built, an expectant look on his face.

"Oh!" Darcy stood, her hands at her mouth, her eyes brimming with tears.

Josh took her hands, and kissed each one. "You were saying about the crib?"

"Oh, Josh!" She wrapped her arms around him and buried her face in his neck and sobbed.

"Hey. This was supposed to make you happy."

"It does," she blubbered. "So happy. Thank you."

"Ian designed it and built it."

This made her cry harder and Josh looked up at Darcy's mother, helpless.

"Baby hormones. She'll be fine in a minute," Vanessa said, her hands waving away his concern.

Ian set the crib down and his gaze found Millie's. Her

insides quivered when she remembered last weekend and all that glorious, adventurous sex.

He gave her a quiet smile.

Darcy stopped sobbing long enough to inspect the crib. The headboard had been carved with the Honey Tree, and beneath sat Pooh, and just like the cake, he had the honeypot in his lap. The footboard depicted all his friends. It had been the inspiration for the cake Millie had ordered.

Darcy ran her hands lovingly over the varnished wood, tears filling her eyes again. "Oh Ian, it's . . . it's beautiful."

Startling both Millie and Ian, Darcy threw her arms around his neck and hugged him. Looking uncomfortable, Ian shot a glance at Josh before wrapping his arms around Darcy and awkwardly patting her on the back. When she finally withdrew, Ian appeared relieved.

"Have some cake," Darcy said.

"I, uh, thank you, but I have to run. I'm due at Ruby's."

Darcy placed a hand on his arm, her voice warm. "How is she?"

"Holding her own." His voice was quiet, and his face pained.

"Let me know if I can do anything."

He nodded and caught Millie's attention over Darcy's head.

Feeling Gloria's eyes on her, Millie rose. "I'll cut some for you to take. Your friend Ruby might like it. You can tell me how much you want."

"Right." He nodded to the guests and followed her to the dining room.

———

I an watched as Millie picked up a plate and the knife and cut into the cake. She looked different. For one thing, her dress fit her better than the others he'd seen. For another, she'd done something different with her hair. He liked it. He preferred it down, swirling around her, but he liked what she'd done with it.

His hands ached to touch her. To strip off that dress and bury his face in her neck. God, what was he doing? She deserved so much more than what he could offer. She deserved what Darcy had. A nice home. A husband, children. A family.

"Is this enough?" Millie asked, not looking back at him.

He stepped closer and her fresh scent assaulted him. "Mmm-hmm." Glancing over his shoulder toward the living room to see if the coast was clear, he turned back and gave in, pressing his lips to her nape just below her hairline.

She gasped, then leaning back against him, tilted her head forward, giving him easy access.

He'd missed her. It had only been a few days, but it felt like a lifetime. Wrapping his arm around her waist, he held her against him, her sweet ass against his growing erection.

"Don't mind me, I'm just getting another piece of cake," Gloria said, her voice like P30 grit sandpaper on fresh-hewn wood.

Ian stepped back from Millie as if he'd just touched a live wire.

Millie spun around, two spots of color riding high on her cheeks.

"I, uh," Millie stammered, hands fluttering with nerves.

"Oh give it a rest, Millie," Gloria admonished, narrowing her eyes at Ian. Leaning in, a gleam in her eye, she whispered in Millie's ear, "Teaching you anything . . . interesting?"

Gasping, Millie stepped back, then fled in the direction of the kitchen.

Ian stood stock still, feeling a little like the time Ruby had caught him sneaking in at two in the morning.

Gloria calmly considered which slice of cake she wanted, put it on a paper plate, and grabbing a fork, shoveled a bite into her mouth. Around her mouthful of cake, she said, "Don't hurt her," poking her finger into his chest with each word, the fork coming dangerously close to skewering him.

Wincing, he rubbed his sternum. Woman had some sharp bony fingers.

She smacked him on the cheek. "*Capeesh?*"

God, what was she, mafia? At her glittering eyes, he nodded. "*Capeesh.*"

# CHAPTER TWENTY-THREE

The next evening, Ian knocked, then unlocked the door to Ruby's apartment. "Ruby?"

"Ian? Come on in. I have a visitor."

Wondering who else could be visiting, he walked into the living room to see Millie seated in a kitchen chair next to the hospital bed Hospice had delivered a few days before, a book in her lap.

Ruby's frail form sunk into the pillow and blankets, her oxygen canister by the bed—another new addition to the medical paraphernalia surrounding her. The cashmere throw covered her feet.

"Millie's reading to me. *The Letters of Abelard and Heloise.*" Ruby's soft smile soothed the ache in Ian's chest.

"Hi," she said in that throaty voice of hers. A blush tinged her cheeks, and he thought of Gloria's interruption yesterday. Millie had been nowhere to be found when he'd left Darcy's. He'd wanted to see if she was okay and tell her goodbye.

"Hi, yourself." He approached Ruby and kissed her gaunt face, before adjusting the nasal cannula that supplied her cancer-ridden body with oxygen, helping to alleviate some of her breathlessness. "Don't let me stop you."

"Oh. I, uh, I was about to take a little break. Here." She held the book out to Ian. "Why don't you pick up where I left off?"

Ian froze, unsure what to do.

"That's all right, dear. I'm a little tired anyway," Ruby supplied.

Millie nodded and laid the book on the chair before heading in the direction of the bathroom.

As soon as he heard the squeaky door close—he really needed to oil those hinges—Ruby pounced. "You haven't told her?"

"No. I can't." He closed his eyes, swamped by the same feelings from his youth. Fear. Self-loathing. Inadequacy. "Besides, what point would it serve? We both know I could be leaving by spring."

"She'd understand. That girl is enamored of you."

"No." He didn't know if he was saying no to telling Millie, or no to Millie being enamored of him. Probably both.

His terse response brought a frown to Ruby's brow. "Is it so hard to believe that someone could care about you? Love you, even, if they knew?"

He shook his head. "Don't."

"It's a reading disability, not leprosy! You really need to get over yourself." Her voice gentled, and she lifted a frail, shaky hand to his face. "Ian. We both know I'm not going to be around much longer."

He squeezed his eyes shut, leaning his cheek into her hand, unable to face that reality. Her hand slid from his face as if the force of gravity were too much.

"Listen to me, no matter what's happening, you have to go to England. You understand?"

Ian's heart sank. He knew exactly what she meant. Even if she was still alive, she wanted him to go . . . even if it meant never seeing her alive again.

He nodded and made to rise.

She took a shallow, raspy breath, "I'm not done." She gazed into his eyes, hers fogged from the pain medicine she now took around the clock. "I don't want to think of you alone after I go. Tell her. Give that girl a chance. She deserves it. You deserve it."

Silence followed except for the sound of Ruby's labored breathing, every breath a struggle.

"If you can't give her a chance, then do her a favor. Leave her alone. It's clear she's well on her way to falling in love with you."

Ian shook his head. That couldn't be true. Millie was far too smart for that. Far too levelheaded to fall for a guy like him. But what did he expect? He was her first. Girls, or in this case women, tended to fall for their first. Thinking of Gloria's words yesterday, and Ruby's today, he knew he had to put a stop to it. ASAP.

"What do I do?"

"It depends on whether you decide to follow your heart or your head. But either way, be honest. With her. With yourself." Ruby's eyes drifted shut as she released a gravelly sigh.

Ian watched the tortured rise and fall of her chest. Be honest with himself. That meant recognizing Ruby would be lucky to make it to spring. And he just couldn't face that stark reality. Not yet.

But, she'd been right about one thing. If he couldn't give

Millie what she deserved, it would be better to let her go. And since he couldn't give her that, his choice was made.

———

After a particularly shitastic day, Ian brushed off the snowflakes as he entered the loft, Caleb behind him grumbling about the cold and wet.

Ruby had been moved to an inpatient Hospice facility after the Hospice nurse who checked on her daily found her lying on the floor by her bed, and Ian had spent much of the day seeing her settled in. Up until that point, Ian had relied on his dyslexia not to read the handwriting on the wall. Now, it had become crystal clear. Ruby was dying and there wasn't a damn thing he could do about it.

Caleb wandered into the kitchen, where Ian could hear him mumbling about not having any beer. He came out with a bottle of water in his hands instead.

Thumbing through the stack of mail, he saw a letter from the owners of the Yardley Mansion. He stared at it as if it might be filled with Anthrax. That he'd received a letter rather than a phone call left him with a sinking feeling in his already basement-level gut.

Inhaling, he slid his finger beneath the tab and pulled the letter out. "Fuck." He didn't need to make sense of all the letters to know the outcome. Thanks, but no thanks.

"What is it?"

Ian handed the letter to Caleb, who read it out loud.

*Dear Mr. Brand,*

*Thank you for your interest in the Request for Proposal for the Yardley Mansion renovation project. We received many excellent responses. Unfortunately, the selection committee felt that your company, Brand Construction and Historical Renovations, LLC, lacks the robust infrastructure and qualifications necessary to complete a job of this magnitude.*

*We wish you much success in your future endeavors.*

"Well, hell." He tossed the letter onto Ian's desk, then paced away. "Lacks the infrastructure and qualifications? That's bullshit. You've handled bigger jobs than this. We should appeal," he said, his voice tense.

Ian didn't want to have this conversation. He'd had a rough day and the letter was just insult to injury. But if he was honest with himself like Ruby instructed, he wasn't surprised.

"Let me see the RFI." Caleb stood, one hand on his hip, the other holding the bottle of water.

Ian *really* didn't want to go there. "I'm not really sure where it is . . ."

Caleb strode over to Ian's desk. "Maybe in this file marked 'Yardley RFI?'" he asked, his expression dubious.

Damn, he'd forgotten that Robin, his bookkeeper, had come in today and worked, so his desk was as neat as a pin.

Memories of standing at his teacher's desk while she read his book report engulfed him, and he knew he couldn't let Caleb see the RFI. But before he could snatch the folder from his hand, Caleb turned his back and opened the folder.

"Dude. What is this? The draft? Where's the final?"

His stepfather stood over him, his report card in his hand, as he berated him for being stupid. *"You really are a dumb fuck, aren't you?"*

"That *is* the final," Ian said around a tightening in his throat.

"Come on, man. Stop fucking with me. Jillie's five-year-old nephew could have done a better job."

"Yeah, well next time get her nephew to do it." Ian scrubbed his hands through his hair. Anger. Frustration. Fear. Deflection. "Ruby is ill, dying. I've been juggling too many jobs . . ." *I need to break it off with Millie and I don't know how.* Not only that, he didn't want to.

"Still." Caleb waved the documents in Ian's face. "What are you? Dyslexic or something?"

Ian froze, his eyes on Caleb's. No. Fucking. Way.

Realization lit Caleb's eyes. "Oh shit. You are." He paced away from Ian, then pivoted to face him. "You're dyslexic. That explains so much," he said, almost to himself. "Using voice to text for everything. All those audiobooks. Ordering without looking at a menu." He paused, his brow furrowed. "How did you prepare for the contractor's exam? Ruby," he said, answering his own question.

Ian couldn't take the pity that filled Caleb's eyes. But that pity quickly changed to anger.

"And you never thought to tell me? Your best friend? Your colleague?" He shook his head. "Dammit, Ian. I could have helped. Hell, I could have done the paperwork *for* you. For us." Then anger turned to hurt. "I thought you trusted me. I've always had your back, and you couldn't even ask me for help. Couldn't even tell me you had dyslexia."

Before Ian could find his tongue, Caleb slapped the piss-poor excuse for an RFI against Ian's chest, then let go, the pages fluttering to the floor.

"What have you got to say for yourself?"

Okay. That was too close to the bone. Too close to Hank. And Ian clammed up. He didn't owe anyone an explanation. It was his business and if he lost out on a job, then so be it. It was the reason he went into business for himself. No one to tell him what to do. No one to take orders from. And he sure as shit wasn't going to start now.

Game over.

At his continued silence, Caleb released a heavy sigh. "You've got some soul-searching to do, my friend. You'd better start letting people in, or you're gonna find yourself all alone someday." Caleb strode to the door without looking back. And Ian just let him go.

———

Stepping *way* outside her comfort zone—like halfway around the world outside her comfort zone—Millie reached Ian's loft, a pint of Rocky Road in her gloved hand. If things went as planned, she'd check off the newest item on her list.

With no apparent doorbell or buzzer she was unsure how to announce herself. So she fisted her hand and banged on the metal door.

A few moments later, it flew open. "What the hell do you want now?"

She drew back in surprise.

"Millie!" He scrubbed his face with his hands. "I'm sorry. I thought you were someone else. What are you doing here?"

Rethinking her impulsiveness, she swallowed. "I, uh, I brought some Rocky Road." She displayed the pint of ice cream.

His only response was a frown.

"Maybe this is a bad time," she muttered. "I should go."

"Yes. No." He heaved a sigh. "Come in. It's freezing out there."

He preceded her to the living area and began picking up papers scattered across the floor. Slapping them on the desk, then he turned to her. "I'm not pleasant company tonight."

"Oh?" She glanced over at the desk. "Bad news?" She gasped. "Not . . . not Ruby?" she whispered.

"No."

She sagged with relief. "Then what? Maybe I can help."

He huffed out a mirthless laugh. "A little late for that," he muttered.

She sat the ice cream on the desk. "Ian. What is it?"

He picked up a piece of paper and handed it to her.

Reading it, her heart sank. "Oh, Ian." Why couldn't he admit that he had dyslexia? Why was he being so stubborn? Why wouldn't he confide in her?

"Don't. Don't look at me like that." His eyes glittered with frustration, as the tension poured off him in waves.

Setting the letter on the desk, she stepped into him and reached out to touch his chest. "I would have helped you, just like with the Hawkins Hall RFP."

His mouth hardened, and a muscle twitched in his cheek, and before she could make contact, he grabbed her wrists, stopping her. "Don't. Don't touch me," he said through tight lips.

Rejection, searing and bitter, eviscerated her. He released her, and she retreated as if slapped.

Ian wouldn't look at her, but the tick in his clenched jaw told her everything she needed to know. He didn't want anything to do with her anymore. He'd finally come to his senses.

She turned to go, but his voice stopped her. "Millie!"

"What, Ian? What is it?" she demanded, finding herself mad, a rare emotion for her.

He ran his hands down his face, then looked at her. "I think it's best if we don't see each other . . . for a while."

"A while? As in never again." Her legs went numb, as her heart thudded heavily in her chest.

"We never should have started this." His hands fisted at his sides. "I never should have let it get this far." He stared at a spot above her head. "It was wrong and I knew it."

*Wrong?* He thought it was *wrong.* She covered her mouth with a shaking hand. She wouldn't cry. Through all the rejection and ridicule she'd faced in her life she'd saved her tears for seclusion. Something she could take a little pride in. No one had ever seen her cry. And it wouldn't start now. She had to get out. Now.

"Goodbye, Ian," she managed past the suffocating tightness in her throat. She pivoted on her heel and walked to the door. The closer she got to the exit, the faster her pace, until she finally ran.

"Millie! Dammit! Millie!"

With tears streaking her cheeks, she kept running out into the freezing, wet night.

# CHAPTER TWENTY-FOUR

"Well, that went well," Ian said at the last echo of the slamming door. "Just like the rest of my day." He paced over to the desk. "Goddammit!" Picking up the stapler, he hurled it against the brick wall with such force, it exploded, sending staples tinkling to the floor like so many shards of glass.

Why did everyone think he needed help? What was he, helpless? No. "Goddammit!" They thought he was a dumb fuck. Just like Hank did.

He couldn't take their pity.

It was one thing for Caleb. It was another for Millie. She was so smart, so well-read. He didn't deserve her. She deserved a college professor, with fucking patches on his sleeve who would sit in their library at night and read Wordsworth or Kant to her. Someone who would stimulate her mind, not just her body.

Bile rose in his throat. He didn't want to think about this paragon of a man stimulating her body.

Bending over, hands to his knees, he huffed like a man who'd just run a marathon, his chest tight. Straightening, he pressed a hand over his heart thinking this was what a heart attack must feel like.

All along he'd worried about hurting Millie. It seemed he'd hurt himself, as well.

"Get it together, Brand." He strode into the kitchen, tugged open the fridge, and grabbing a bottle of water, chugged it so fast it gave him brain freeze. "Good." At least it would take his mind off the ache in his chest.

Standing in the kitchen, the broken stapler lying at his feet, he couldn't think of a worse day. He'd put his mentor in Hospice, argued with his best friend, and broken up with the only woman who'd managed to touch a place deep in his heart. A place he didn't know existed. Until her.

He told himself the relationship already had an expiration date. He'd just moved it up a bit.

"I did the right thing," he said to the empty loft. If that was true, why did the ache in his chest linger.

———

After leaving Ian's, Millie had run as far as she could before a stitch in her side stopped her. Tears froze on her cheeks. Or was it the sleet? She couldn't tell.

His words echoed in her head. *It was wrong and I knew it.*

*Stupid, stupid Millie.* How could she have ever thought he'd even want a serious relationship with her, much less love her? She'd learned long ago that anything too good to be true, usually was. Fairytales didn't come true for people like her.

Walking through the dark, cold night, she berated herself for her stupid Get a Life List. The only thing she'd accomplished from it was a broken heart. And for all that, she was still just Mousey Millie. Invisible.

Ian had made it quite clear that his interest in her was over. He'd finally come to his senses. Realized he could do so much better than her. How could she fault him for that?

Except she did.

Didn't she deserve a little sliver of happiness?

Standing on a street corner somewhere in Washington Heights the pain of rejection consumed her, making it impossible to breathe, as the tears flowed down her cheeks.

She could now add 'broken heart' to her list. And check it off.

———

The next few weeks, Millie saw little of Ian. The nursery and bathroom remodel was almost complete, and he'd been spending most of the days at a new job he'd started in Greenwich Village. She wondered if he'd heard anything on the Hawkins Hall job.

The searing pain of rejection had eased to a dull ache. Keeping busy helped. Darcy had two books coming out within three months of each other, making for a busy marketing and public relations schedule. She and Josh worried it might be too much with the baby due in April, but Darcy had recovered from her fall and looked radiant in her happiness.

Millie rang in the New Year as she usually did, alone with a good book, refusing Darcy's concerned invitation to spend it with her and Josh.

As she helped Darcy hang the baby clothes in the nursery closet, and listened while Darcy chattered away about where she planned to place the furniture, she recalled the day she'd seen Ian standing among the cabinet doors, his black T-shirt covered in dust, that tool belt slung low on his hips. He'd been something to behold.

Heaving a sigh that went unnoticed by Darcy, Millie reached closure of some sort. She'd always be grateful to Ian. He'd given her a beautiful initiation into sex, and for that he'd always hold a special place in her heart. Even if that heart was no longer whole.

———

As Ian prepared for work, he glanced out the window at the bright sunshine. They predicted warmer temperatures today, so his bike was the preferred mode of transportation. Maybe he'd take a ride up to the job in Westchester later, open up the bike, clear his head.

The past few weeks had sucked. He snorted as he shoved his wallet into his back jeans pocket. That was putting it mildly. Caleb wasn't talking to him and he'd been sleeping alone in a cold bed.

"Whose fault is that, Brand?"

He had to make things right with Caleb, as soon as he figured out how. And as for sleeping alone, well, he still believed he'd done the right thing with Millie. Even if his heart hurt like a son-of-a-bitch and his soul felt empty.

It had been a mistake bringing her to his loft. Everywhere he looked brought back memories of her. His shop, where she'd skimmed her hand along the unfinished dining room table, the wall beside the desk where he'd pinned her as he'd had mind-numbing sex with her, and, of course, his bed. *Sweet Jesus.* He had to stop this nonsense.

He'd be leaving for England in a few weeks, and he had a lot of loose ends to tie up before he left. He didn't need memories of Millie to interfere. She'd been the best he'd ever had, and likely would ever have. And damn if wasn't the icing on his shitastic cake.

Grabbing his leather jacket, he headed down the stairs and out to his garage. First up, the job in Greenwich Village, then on to the Xavier house in Midtown. If all went well, he'd take that ride up to Westchester, then back to spend the evening at Ruby's side.

While most people were ringing in the promise of a New Year, he'd been preparing for goodbye.

He knew it wouldn't be long. She spent more and more time sleeping, less awake and aware. The morphine had a lot to do with it, but the hard truth was her body was shutting down. She'd had little to eat the last four days, a sign that her body no longer needed the calories.

As much as he wanted her to stay, it was time to say goodbye. To let her know it was okay. She'd suffered enough. But that didn't make it any easier.

The last time she'd been awake, she'd taken his hand and asked after Millie. He couldn't tell her he'd broken up with her, so he'd lied and said that she'd been very busy. Ruby had closed her eyes, a soft smile on her face. "Marry that girl, Ian. She loves you."

An ice pick to the heart would have hurt less. Even now, he rubbed his hand across his chest.

He picked up his helmet, then set it back on the seat as his phone vibrated in his pocket. Probably the plumber from the Greenwich Village job. "Brand."

"Mr. Brand, this is Constance Bessler with Hospice. You need to come right away."

## CHAPTER TWENTY-FIVE

Millie had just shut off the lights when there was a knock at her door. Her heart jumped to her throat. Glancing at the time, she knew a knock at this hour could only mean trouble. Yet, it had to be a neighbor, because the building was secure.

She tiptoed to the door and peered through the peephole. Ian! Unlocking the door, she pulled it open and with one glimpse at his face, she knew. "Oh, Ian." Tears filled her eyes. "When?"

"This morning." His voice broke as he swiped a hand over his face. "I've been walking around the city, and I . . ."

Reaching out, she grabbed his hand and hauled him into the apartment, into her arms, shutting the door behind him. God, he was freezing!

She didn't know what to say. She'd had little experience with death and grief, so, she just held him. "I'm so sorry, Ian."

He pushed off her, looked everywhere but at her. "Me, too."

"You're cold. How about some tea?"

"Sure." He sank down onto the loveseat at the foot of her bed, his hands hanging limp between his thighs.

Having something to do helped her until she could figure out something to say. After filling the kettle, she set it on the burner, then opened her cupboard, selecting a soothing chamomile tea.

She shot a worried glance at him, but he just sat, staring into space. Her heart broke for him, and ached for the loss of Ruby. It didn't matter that he'd essentially abandoned Millie. His grief was written all over his face, revealed itself in the tension in his shoulders, in the haunted look in his eyes.

And he'd come to her.

While the tea steeped in the mugs, she walked over and sat next to him. "It should be ready soon."

He nodded.

"Do you want to talk about it?"

He shook his head, then reaching up, latched onto the back of her neck and hauled her mouth to his, his tongue penetrating her open lips. Nothing gentle about his kiss. He poured all his grief, frustration, anger, and fear into that kiss. And she absorbed it all as his hands roamed her body with an urgency that left her breathless.

"Millie." His mouth skimmed her jaw to her ear where he nipped and licked until she'd melted into a hot puddle of goo.

His hand cupped her breast and she moaned her approval, her traitorous body responding to his touch. She'd missed him. Missed this. She wouldn't think about his abandonment of her. His rejection. She just reveled in the feel of him, the taste and smell of him. His warmth. His passion. His all-encompassing need.

Dragging her into his lap, he continued his assault, as she ground her behind into his erection, eliciting a hiss from him. Switching tacks, he lifted her indicating he wanted her to straddle him. Raising her nightgown he gazed down at her, his eyes burning with lust and the desperate need for something life-affirming. Like sex. Making quick work of his fly, he lifted her once more, sliding her onto him. She threw back her head at the sensations surging through her as he filled her.

Their coupling bordered on animalistic. Fast, furious, as he drove into her, pouring that same caustic mix of emotions when he'd first kissed her into her willing body. Grasping his shoulders, she took every punishing thrust until she cried out with her release. He followed her over the edge, her name on his lips.

———

Ian's breathing slowly returned to normal and as it did so did his senses. *What the hell had he been thinking? To use Millie as if she were a sexual punching bag?*

Her hot breath came out in pants, warming his still-chilled skin, her arms limp by her side.

He'd just needed her. Needed her so damn bad it scared the hell out of him. He'd walked all over the city in the cold, feeling lost and lonely, adrift in the sea of people he encountered on the streets. In a city of eight and a half million people, he'd never felt so alone in his life.

He could have gone to Caleb's, but that's not where his feet took him. Or should he say his heart?

Millie stirred.

"You okay?" he asked, afraid of the answer.

"More than." She smiled against his neck then leaned

back cupping his face in her hands, her eyes shimmering with tears. "Are you?"

He didn't know what he was except ashamed. Ashamed for using Millie. And ill-equipped to know how to handle it.

Lifting her off him, he avoided her eyes. Zipping his fly, he rose, noticed the mugs of tea still steeping on the counter.

"I'm sorry, Millie. I shouldn't have . . ." Oh God, he was going to lose it soon. And once the torrent came it would be unstoppable. Like a dam bursting, all his emotions would swamp him in their intensity. "I have to go," he choked out.

"Ian?" Millie's voice held hurt and confusion. If she touched him, his resolve would crumble.

He reached the door just as she stepped behind him. Snatching it open he strode through, closing it. He never looked back as he charged down the stairs and out into the frigid night air.

———

Determined not to let the hurt and the confusion over her last encounter with Ian stop her, Millie entered the Sunset Park Public Library a week later looking for Ruby's memorial service. Seeing a sign with the meeting room and a directional arrow on it, she made her way through the friendly, familiar hush of a public library.

Entering the room, she was gratified, and not a little intimidated, to see it filled with standing room only. Ian stood at the front looking handsome, but clearly uncomfortable in a dark suit and gray tie. God, the only thing sexier than Ian in a suit was Ian out of a suit.

Her breath backed up into her lungs the second his eyes met hers. His brow creased in confusion, as she raised her hand in greeting.

Hesitating a moment, he finally made his way down the makeshift aisle created by the rows of chairs.

Her face grew hot as she remembered the last time they were together. The almost-punishing sex. Followed by yet another abandonment.

He stopped in front of her. "What are you doing here?" he asked in a voice just above a whisper.

She glanced around at the people in the room. "I came to pay my respects to Ruby"—she indicated the rest of the room—"like everyone else." When he didn't respond, she continued, "Clearly she touched a lot of people."

His gray eyes held pain and loss. "Yes."

"Have you heard anything on the Hawkins Hall job?" Millie asked, almost afraid of the answer.

"I'll be leaving in a few weeks." He looked at a spot behind her.

"Ian, that's, that's terrific." And she meant it, even as her heart broke a little more. As if that were even possible. "Congratulations."

"Thank you. You deserve most of the credit."

"No." Millie swallowed hard. "It's your skills and portfolio that impressed the selection committee."

His mouth formed a thin line. "Thanks, just the same."

So, this was it. Probably the last time she'd see Ian Brand. She seriously doubted he'd look her up again after two years.

"I-I was wondering, could I, that is, would you mind if I read something . . .?"

Something flickered across his face. Surprise? "She'd have liked that."

She relaxed a millimeter. "Just . . . whenever it fits the program."

He nodded, and she turned to stand in the back corner

as more people filed in. The more people who came, the more butterflies took flight in her stomach. Could she stand up in front of all those people, the center of attention, no matter how momentary it was?

She owed it to Ruby.

Ian stepped up to the podium and cleared his throat. He appeared nervous too, but she noted his lack of notes.

"Ladies and gentleman, thank you for coming today to celebrate the life of Ruby Van Buren Sinclair. I'm Ian Brand and at this time, I'd like to invite Meg Dryer, head librarian for Sunset Park, to say a few words about Ruby." Ian stepped back, his hands clasped in front of him looking for all the world like a lost little boy.

---

Ian stood as one person after another came up to the podium, all talking about how Ruby had sparked a love of reading in them or their children, or their grand-children. Ruby had been loved, respected, and admired. She'd touched countless lives, opened doors for so many, him included, and she would leave behind a void that very few people could fill. He rubbed his hand over the empti-ness in his chest, an emptiness left deeper by Ruby's death.

When he held her hand as she'd breathed her last breath, the grief had been a physical thing. A great snarling beast that tore open his chest, stealing his own breath, suffo-cating him. She'd left him. Alone.

His gaze drifted to the front row where Caleb and Jillie sat, and Caleb's words came back to him. *You'd better start letting people in, or you're gonna find yourself all alone someday.*

They'd yet to make amends, but it didn't matter. Caleb was there. He had always been there when Ian needed him.

He lifted his eyes to the painfully shy woman in brown who stood in the back of the room, wiping tears from her cheeks. No. Not alone. If he'd just reach out, she'd be there. He just needed the courage to do it.

When the last speaker finished, he returned to the podium. "Millie? Would you like to come up?"

At her nod, she glanced around the room at all the people, then slowly made her way down the aisle, all eyes following her progress. When she stepped up to the podium, she looked like she did the day that the delivery truck barreled toward her. She swallowed hard, stared out at the sea of faces, then cracked open the book in her hands. Tentative at first, her voice found its courage as she read from Emily Dickinson:

"'If I can stop one heart from breaking, I shall not live in vain:

    If I can ease one life the aching, Or cool one pain,

    Or help one fainting robin

    Unto his nest again,

    I shall not live in vain.'"

"I didn't know Ruby very long, but we shared a love of reading, especially the classics, and she welcomed me into her home and made me feel like family. And from what I've heard about her, she'd give a person the shirt off her back if she thought it would help." Millie sniffed and wiped away a tear. "I'll miss her."

Ian felt his chest swell with pride. Standing in front of a crowd, the center of attention, speaking from her heart, Millie Stephens was the bravest woman he knew.

———

Drawing in a deep, calming breath, Millie lifted her gaze to the mourners. She'd done it. She'd seen Ian again, she'd spoken before an audience, paid her respects to Ruby, and she'd survived.

Glancing back at Ian, she was shocked to see his eyes shining with unshed tears. She reached for him, but he shook his head, and the pain of rejection warred with the pain of grief. Closing her book, she walked back down the aisle, feeling his eyes on her.

"Thank you, Millie." His voice gruff with emotion, he stood with his hands in his pants pockets. Clearing his throat he began, "I've known Ruby since I was twelve years old when she took pity on a frightened kid with a chip on his shoulders. She and her late husband, Curtis, became the parents my own mother and stepfather couldn't be. Ruby guided me through my adolescence, with a little help from Curtis when I needed a kick in the pants, gave me a home until I could support myself, and helped me start my business.

In other words, they, *she*, made me the man I am today." He paused, lifted his eyes to the ceiling, then looked out at the mourners. "I'll miss her more than she will ever know."

Millie stifled a sob as tears ran down her cheeks. *Oh, Ian. I'm so, so very sorry.* The urge to comfort him overwhelmed her. But he didn't want her. The sooner she accepted that, the better off she'd be. Having done what she'd come to do, she left quietly, leaving Ian to face his grief. Alone.

# CHAPTER TWENTY-SIX

"Well, if it isn't Mousey Millie." The three thugs sidled up next to her. "How's it hanging?" They all snickered.

The ringleader looked around. "What, no hot date with motorcycle dude? How much did you pay him to go out with you, anyway?"

Millie put her head down and kept walking up the sidewalk to her building, reciting Descartes' Rule of Sign. *Tell them to go fuck themselves.* Ian's words rang in her head. No, that she wouldn't do. But she would stand up for herself this time.

Drawing in a deep breath, she stopped short, surprising the three as they outpaced her, then put on the brakes. They turned in unison, brows furrowed in confusion.

"Why is it, I never see any of *you* with dates?" She tilted her head, eyes moving from one shame-faced teen to another, ready to give them a comeuppance they'd not soon forget. She sucked in a breath as her gaze landed on the face of the youngest. He had a black eye and a busted lip. "Who did that?" She glared the other two. "Did you do that?"

They held their hands up palms out and shook their heads.

She stepped closer, hand raised, and the teen instinctively stepped back. She hesitated a moment, then moved in again, taking hold of his chin then lifting it so she could examine his eye. "Who did this?"

When he wouldn't answer, the ringleader did. "His dad." Millie spun to gawp at him in disbelief, then returned to her inspection of the boy's face. "What's your name?"

"Kenny," he muttered.

"Well, Kenny. Have you put any ice on that eye?"

He shook his head.

"Then let's go." She nodded toward her apartment building.

"You going to call child protection?" he asked, his voice shaking.

"No. I'm going to put some ice on that eye, and clean up that cut on your lip." At his continued reticence, she prodded, "Unless you're afraid."

Drawing himself up, he lifted his chin and looked at his partners in crime. "No. I'm not afraid of anything."

"All right, then." She held her hand out indicating he should precede her.

Casting another glance at his friends, he shrugged and walked ahead of her.

The other two thugs started to follow, but she stopped them. "You can wait here." She wanted to help Kenny, but she wasn't stupid. Inviting three punks up to her apartment was only inviting trouble. "He'll be back."

She followed Kenny's plodding footsteps up the three flights of stairs. "I'm in 3G, to the left."

Once in her apartment, she indicated the loveseat at the foot of the bed. "Sit. And don't touch anything."

Kenny surveyed the apartment as he took a seat. "This is pretty nice," he murmured.

Millie went into the bathroom then pulled out a bottle of peroxide and grabbed some Kleenex. A Band-Aid wouldn't stay on his lip, so she'd just have to settle for cleaning the cut. She then stepped over to the freezer and grabbed a bag of peas. Carrying her makeshift first-aid supplies, she set them on the loveseat next to Kenny.

He eyed her, his expression wary.

"This is going to sting, but you need to clean that cut." She poured some peroxide on the tissue than patted the wound, recalling when she'd tended Ian's injury.

Kenny sucked in a breath. "Fuck, lady! That hurts."

"Watch your mouth. And I told you it would hurt." She tilted his chin up, examined his eye again. He had some blood behind his conjunctive, but not much. "Here." She handed him the bag of frozen peas. "Hold this on your eye." She wondered if this is what Ian had been through. Whether his stepfather had blackened his eye, busted his lip. Closing her eyes against the pain of that image, she fought back her tears.

When Kenny took the bag, he asked, "Why are you being so nice to me?"

"You mean after you were so rude to me?" she pressed as she dabbed more peroxide on the cut.

He had the wherewithal to look shame-faced. "I guess."

"Maybe because no matter how mean you are to me, you don't deserve this," she whispered, thinking again of Ian and his stepfather. This was met with silence. Then to Millie's utter shock, a tear trickled from Kenny's good eye. It broke her heart, but she wasn't ready to let him off the hook.

She could understand why a kid who was abused by his

father would turn to bullying others. And she wondered why Ian hadn't become a bully. Ruby. That's why.

"Does your father do this often?" Millie asked, as she found herself stroking his hair.

Kenny shrugged.

Okay, so he wasn't ready to talk about it. "Where is your mother?"

He sniffled. "She left. Last year."

*It just gets worse.* And she thought her childhood was tough. "You listen to me, Kenny. If he ever does this to you again, you call me. I'll give you my phone number. You understand?"

He nodded, still holding the peas to his eye.

She gathered the used tissues and the peroxide to put them away.

"Millie?"

"Yes, Kenny?"

He lowered the bag, and stared down at his beat up tennis shoes. "I'm really sorry for making fun of you. I won't do it again."

She nodded, more to herself, since Kenny still stared at the ground. "Apology accepted."

———

A few days later, Millie knocked on Darcy's office door. Darcy glanced around. "Hi. What's up?"

Millie's feet felt rooted to the spot and she gazed down at the box in her hands. Could she do this? "Do you have a minute?"

"Sure."

"You once told me if there was anything I needed, I just had to ask."

"Yep." Darcy folded her hands over her ever-expanding belly.

Drawing in a deep, calming breath, Millie handed Darcy the box.

"What's this?" Darcy asked, her expression confused.

"It's a manuscript. My manuscript."

"Get out! I didn't know you wanted to write. Why didn't you tell me?"

Millie shrugged. "Fear. Guilt."

"Guilt? Why guilt?" Darcy drew back in surprise.

"Because writing my own story felt disloyal. A conflict of interest."

"Pfft." She waved her hand. "Don't be ridiculous. And you want me to read it?"

"If you don't mind."

Darcy hugged it to herself. "Mind? How cool is this? What's it about? No, wait don't tell me. Just tell me, is it a romance?"

Millie nodded.

"Contemporary or historical?"

"Historical."

"I can't wait to read it." Darcy's eyes glowed. "Good for you for finishing a book," she effused, filling Millie's heart with hope that if she couldn't find love, maybe she could find contentment. Within herself.

Darcy reached out and took Millie's hand. "You okay?" Her eyes filled with concern.

Millie nodded.

"Sometimes it helps to talk about it. You know, a little male-bashing can go a long way to soothing a broken heart."

Millie didn't want to bash Ian. He'd not only given her the experience she needed to write about sex, he'd also provided her with the emotional well to tap so she could write about broken hearts. No experience was ever wasted.

"Well, that, and a pint or two of Ben & Jerry's," Darcy continued.

Millie's heart warmed. So what if she loved Ian, and he didn't love her. She had a true friend in Darcy.

The doorbell rang, and Millie rose. "That'll be the plumber." Before she left the room, she turned back to see Darcy, the open box on her desk, lifting the title page out. "*The Rake's Redemption*. Ooh. Nice one. By Millicent Stephens."

Feeling infinitesimally lighter than she'd felt since Ian had dumped her, Millie hurried down the stairs to let the plumber in.

―――

As Ian approached Caleb's office, he took in the other desks scattered around the open space, people working on computers, talking on phones, or with one another. He hadn't been to Caleb's office in about three years, and clearly, lots had changed. More employees. Bigger space. Caleb had come a long way from the two-room office he and Jillie used to occupy in a shithole area of East Harlem.

Impressed, he followed the hallway past what was Jillie's office, a sign on the door announcing 'Office Manager.' Ian wondered if she'd continue to work for the business once the baby was born.

Across the hall behind a closed door marked 'Caleb Montgomery, CEO (Chief Electrical Officer),' Ian could hear snippets of this end of a conversation. Waiting until Caleb finished up, Ian loitered outside his office.

"Ian?"

He turned to see a tall, slender tomboyish woman, with cropped blond hair and warm green eyes, a slight roundness to what had once been a flat belly. "Jillie. Hi." He stepped in for a hug, thinking impending motherhood looked good on her.

"Haven't seen you since Ruby's service. You doing okay?"

"Yeah," he lied. He missed Ruby. He'd picked up the phone yesterday to give her a call and remembered, the pain unfurling in his chest like a leviathan. He missed Millie too. More than he could have thought possible. Another situation he needed to rectify. And soon.

His hands had been full to overflowing with Ruby's estate, going through her things, clearing out her apartment. The woman had stashed cash throughout the apartment. In drawers, books, even shoe boxes. He couldn't give away or discard anything without checking it first.

And then there had been the box full of love letters and cards from Curtis. At first he'd felt like he was prying, but then he got a glimpse into how much they loved one another. For a gruff old construction foreman, Curtis had had a romantic side.

Funny, Ian had thought he had no model when it came to healthy relationships. He'd been wrong and it had been right in front of him for almost twenty years. Ruby and Curtis.

"You here to see Caleb?"

"Yeah." Time to apologize.

She knocked on the door then opened it. "Hey, babe, got someone here to see you." Then she turned to Ian. "Come have dinner soon."

"Thanks, Jillie."

"If it makes you feel any better, Caleb's been mopey ever since your argument, so I hope you two kiss and make up."

"That's the plan."

She nodded and headed into her office.

Ian stuck his head in the door. "Got a minute?"

Caleb looked up from his computer, his expression wary. "Sure."

After taking a seat in a chair across from the desk, Ian surveyed the room. Photos ranged along a bookshelf, most with Jillie, others with Caleb and his in-laws, who became Caleb's surrogate parents when his were killed in a car accident a few years ago.

Ian's gaze stopped on a photo of him and Caleb, hardhats on their heads, arms around one another's shoulders, at some generic construction site before he or Caleb had started their own businesses. They were just two young punks, one full of hope, the other full of determination.

And now he sat across from the one full of hope, determined to mend the fences between them.

"I'm sor—"

"I'm sor—"

They both spoke at the same time. Confused, Ian scrubbed his forehead. "Why are you sorry? All you did was tell the truth."

"Maybe. But you didn't need or deserve my anger. Jesus. Ruby was so sick. You had your hands full, and I didn't do anything to help."

"I didn't ask you to."

"No. You didn't."

Caleb leaned back in his seat, his eyes holding Ian's. Waiting.

"You're right. I should have asked. Especially with the

RFI. I know you were counting on that job, and I let you down."

"I don't give a good goddamn about the job. You didn't trust me."

"Not true. I just didn't want you to know. I didn't want anyone to know."

Caleb studied him. "You're not stupid, Ian. In fact, you're one of the smartest men I know. But you do dumbass things sometimes. Don't do dumbass things anymore."

Ian felt the corner of his mouth tug upward and he eyed Caleb's clothes. "I won't do dumbass things anymore if you'll stop with this metrosexual thing."

"Since when is slacks and a shirt metrosexual?"

"Since always."

Caleb paused for a beat, then asked, "How'd you do it? How'd you get all those jobs?"

"Ruby," Ian said matter-of-factly.

Caleb nodded. "Ruby."

"I, uh, I got the England job."

Caleb's eyes widened, then a big grin split his face. "Dude!" He stood and raised his hands for a give me ten.

Ian rose, slapped his hands. Their fingers curled into one another's holding the clasp.

"That's awesome! Congratulations!" Caleb's brow furrowed. "How long is that job, again?"

"Could be two years." Ian knew where this was going. Two years without his best friend.

Caleb sank back into his seat, a shadow erasing the light in his eyes. Then, just like the sun on a partly cloudy day, the light returned. "Well, Jillie and I have always wanted to go to England." A moment later, another cloud crossed his features, as his brow furrowed. "How? Surely Ruby didn't write your RFP submission."

"No. Millie did."

"Millie? That woman in brown?"

"Yes." Ian waited for the explosion.

"You mean to tell me she knew about your dyslexia before I did?"

"No. She just offered to help."

Caleb considered this a moment. "Well, okay, then."

Jillie stuck her head in the door. "You two lovebirds kiss and make up yet?"

"We're good?" Ian asked.

"We're good."

"Good," Jillie interjected. "I'm starving. Let's grab a burger."

*Apologize to Caleb. Check.*

*Next, Millie.*

# CHAPTER TWENTY-SEVEN

M illie stepped out of the Rockaway Avenue subway station in Brownsville, her purse clutched tight against her body. Looking around to get her bearings, she felt like a guppy in a shark tank.

The tattoo parlor, Dangerous Ink, was on Pitkin Avenue, e few blocks away. Surely she could make it that far without incident.

Lifting her chin, she turned her feet north.

She'd done her research, and all the articles recommended an appointment, so she'd called the previous week to schedule an appointment. The last thing she wanted was to come to Brownsville only to find she couldn't get her tattoo.

Her session was with a guy named Blade–the name not terribly reassuring. Preferring a female artist, she'd been told their one female artist was on maternity leave. What? She couldn't picture an ink-covered tattoo artist with an infant.

Finding the business, she took a deep cleansing breath before opening the door. A friendly bell chimed, out of sync with the dark interior of the shop. Though the place smelled like a doctor's office, antiseptic and sterile. Nothing like what her active imagination would have ever dreamed up.

Images of tattoos papered the walls. Everything from flowers and butterflies, to knives and guns. Some were quite pornographic, while others featured a cross with Jesus' face floating above it.

She heard the buzz of a machine, hushed voices, along with the heavy metal music that erupted from the speakers. This had been a mistake. Just as she turned to leave, a deep voice halted her. "Can I help you?" Millie turned. He sounded like a school teacher but looked like a creature from a Mad Max movie. Every inch of visible skin revealed tattoos. Even his bald head exhibited a tattoo artist's craft.

He had piercings up both ears, one in his eyebrow, a ring through his nose, and from the looks of his tight-fitting shirt, nipple rings as well. Millie winced. With his barrel chest, tree-trunk arms, and thick neck he could have been a professional wrestler, a football player, or bouncer. Hit man came to mind as well.

"I," her voice squeaked. Clearing her throat, she started again. "I have an appointment with Blade."

"You must be Millie." The thick-chested man stuck out his hand. A snake slithered across the back of it and twined through his fingers.

Millie tentatively reached out to shake his hand.

"I'm Blade."

"Oh." *Gulp.* His hand was warm and firm, but gentle. The thought of baring her behind to him was daunting.

"Right this way," he indicated a hallway, as dimly lit as the rest of the shop. He opened a door and stepped into a room that could have been a doctor's exam room. Bright, meticulous, with cabinets, an upholstered chair, and an exam table covered with that crinkly paper the medical profession had a penchant for. "Have a seat." He indicated the upholstered chair. "Now, Millie, is this your first tattoo?"

"Yes." She coaxed herself to release the death grip she had on her purse.

"Ah, a tattoo virgin. I love those." The gleam in his eye almost proved her undoing. "So, tell me what you're thinking about."

Millie explained what she had in mind and handed him a slip of paper with the phrase she'd selected and the font she preferred.

"And where would you like this?"

She rose and pointed to the spot.

"A popular choice for first-timers." He turned to a sink and washed his hands. "Hop up on the table and lie on your stomach."

Millie did as she was asked as he pulled on a pair of latex gloves.

"Slide your pants and underpants down your hips."

Millie hesitated.

"Millie, you have to trust me. I'm like a doctor, I've seen it all."

Closing her eyes against the mortification, she unzipped her pants and shimmied them down, leaving as much of her bottom covered as possible. *Couldn't have picked my arm for the tattoo, could I?*

After Blade prepared the area, stenciled the artwork and had Millie stand in front of a mirror to proofread it, he got to work. "This might hurt just a bit."

Blade, as it turned out, was the master of under-statement.

———

After last week's birthday gift to herself–Millie winced at the memory–she had one more gift, which she'd recently added to her GALL List. In search of Laura and Darcy, she found them in the kitchen, where Laura was sharing some story about dinner with her parents. Millie didn't know whose parents were worse, hers or Laura's.

She waited patiently for Laura to finish her story, wondering if she should just forget it. Just as she lost her nerve, Darcy spoke up.

"Millie? Did you need me?"

Taking a deep breath, Millie blurted out before her brain could stop her mouth, "I want a makeover."

"Thank God!" Laura said and raised her hands as if in supplication to the fashion gods. "I've been waiting for this day since, well, since I met you."

"Millie, are you sure?" Darcy asked.

"Yes." She unclenched the fists at her sides.

"Cool." Darcy regarded Laura. "I get to be Clinton this time."

"No, you don't," Laura replied, arms crossed over her chest. "You're always Clinton."

"That's because I have his green eyes and sparkling wit."

Laura huffed in exasperation and dropped her hands by her side. "Fine. But I'm only letting you get your way because you're with child."

"You guys are scaring me," Millie said, backing out of the kitchen.

"Already?" Darcy said on a laugh.

"Oh, no you don't, sweetcakes." Laura latched on to

Millie's wrist. "Don't be a tease. You're not backing out now when I've got my hopes up."

"Saturday," Darcy said.

"Deal," Laura agreed. "We'll start early."

Darcy cringed.

"Better get used to it, sweetpea." Laura had yet to let go of her death-grip on Millie's wrist.

"What's with you and sweet nicknames?" Darcy asked as she pried Laura's fingers from Millie's arm.

Laura released her grip and shrugged. "Ad campaign for a new no-calorie sweetener. Trying out a few."

———

Saturday morning, bright and early, someone rang the buzzer for Millie's apartment. "Who is it?" Although she knew good and well who it was. Her tormentors.

"Let us in. It's time for your intervention," Laura's voice said through the intercom.

When Millie opened the door to them, she did so with some trepidation.

"Why are you at my apartment?" Millie asked in confusion. "I thought we were going"—she suppressed a shudder —"shopping."

"Do you not know how the *What Not to Wear* intervention starts?" Laura drew back in surprise.

"That's a television show, right? I don't have a TV."

"You don't have a TV." Laura stood there, momentarily silent, a pained look on her face. "Darcy, or should I say, Clinton, why don't you tell Millie how the intervention starts."

"We go through your clothes and get rid of anything that we think should go."

"Which in this case is everything," Laura added.

Millie drew back in horror. "What? You're going to throw out my clothes?"

"No." Darcy patted her hand. "We're not going to throw them out. We're going to give them to charity."

Laura snorted. "The charity, however, will take one look at them and throw them out."

Biting her lip, Millie opened the door wider for them. She thought she'd add a few things to her wardrobe, not start from scratch.

"How cute!" Darcy exclaimed as she caught her first glimpse of Millie's apartment. "Reminds me of my apartment in college." At Laura's expression, Darcy continued, "What? I loved that apartment."

"Clothes?" Laura asked, all business.

Millie pointed in the direction of her clothes cubby.

Laura froze, then pointed to the tiny storage area. "*That's* where you keep your clothes?" At Millie's nod, Laura asked, "*All* of them?"

"Yes."

"Well, this won't take long." Flinging open the door, Laura grabbed a handful of hangers and tossed the clothes on the bed. Darcy followed suit and before long every article of clothing Millie owned was lying in a heap on her bed.

"Are you color blind?" Laura asked, eyeing the pile of clothes.

"No. Why?"

"Everything you own is brown."

"I like brown." Millie shrugged. Because it helps me blend in, she thought with some chagrin. *Which I no longer want to do,* she reminded herself. "And since I don't have to worry about matching, it saves me time getting dressed in the morning," she finished lamely.

"Clearly." Laura picked up a chunky wool turtleneck sweater. "You use this for birth control?"

Millie snatched the sweater out of Laura's hand as the heat rose to her face. "I like it. It's warm."

"So is an electric blanket, but I wouldn't wear one." Laura snatched it back. "It's outta here."

A half hour later, everything lay on the floor, including Millie's white cotton granny panties, as Laura had called them, her white cotton bras, brown wool tights, and flannel nightgowns. She'd fought hard for the nightgowns, but to no avail.

"Well, let's bag this stuff up for the homeless shelter," Darcy said, as she bent over to pick up a pair of pants.

"Oh, no you don't," Laura said. "You're not doing all that bending. Josh would have my head." Laura waved her hand at the pile. "Millie, make yourself useful."

At Millie's look, Laura said, "Hey. You asked for our help, remember?"

Okay. She did. But now she was thinking of having her head examined. On a sigh, she went in search of some bags.

After bagging up the clothes, something occurred to her. "Wait. What am I supposed to wear tomorrow?" The torture, *er*, intervention schedule, had been extended by a day.

"Good point." Laura reached into the closest bag and took out a brown corduroy dress. "Here."

"Thanks," Millie muttered.

"Next stop, the optical shop for contact lenses." Laura directed.

"But—" Millie protested.

"No buts. Ever heard the phrase, 'Men don't make passes at girls who wear glasses?'"

Millie snorted, thinking of Ian. He'd made a pass. More than a pass. Much, much more.

Then moved on. And now he would be going to England.

Maybe Laura was right. But she'd rather give away her book collection than admit that to her.

———

Millie thought she'd hate contact lenses. That she wouldn't be able to tolerate them. She thought she'd be conscious of them every minute of the day, but she'd been wrong. She'd worn glasses for as long as she could remember, and although she felt naked without her glasses, she also felt liberated without them.

She gazed at her reflection in the optical shop mirror. She could see her *eyes*. Not just the brown frames surrounding them.

"Laura wasn't always Miss Perfect, you know," Darcy said, looking over Millie's shoulder in the mirror.

Laura snorted.

"And she's perfect now?" Millie quipped. Although it was true. Laura always resembled a magazine cover model. Perfect. Like now, as she too joined them at the mirror, rolling her eyes.

"When I first met Laura in kindergarten, she wore glasses."

"Really?" She cut her eyes to Laura's reflection. That surprised Millie. She couldn't imagine the ever-beautiful Laura wearing glasses.

"It wasn't until, what, sixth grade that you started

wearing contacts?" Darcy asked, tucking a stray lock of hair behind her ear.

"And I never went back."

"Who wants lunch?" Darcy rubbed her belly. "Peanut's starving."

After lunch at a trendy café in Tribeca, Darcy and Josh had plans, and Laura was meeting Nathan at her parents, so Millie returned to her apartment and the bags of clothes still standing by the door. Sorely tempted to pull some of her clothes out and put them away, she reminded herself why she was doing this.

Tomorrow, who knew what Darcy and Laura would pick out for her, especially Laura. But she'd asked for this, and she'd follow through. What did she have to lose? Eying the bags again, she thought, besides her invisibility.

# CHAPTER TWENTY-EIGHT

The next morning, Millie, Darcy, and Laura climbed out of a cab in front of a large department store.

"Let's start with the basics and keep it simple," Laura said, as she led the way to the women's department. "And the color brown is strictly prohibited." She pointed her finger at Millie.

Millie sighed, wondering again what had possessed her to initiate this torture.

After about an hour, loaded down with clothes, everything from pants and tops, to dresses and jeans, Millie entered the dressing room with some apprehension.

"Try the black wool slacks with the red cashmere sweater," Laura called through the door.

Millie eyed the pants, convinced they were several sizes too small. Stepping into them, she gasped when she realized they fit. Glancing at her image in the mirror, she appeared taller, and slimmer.

"What? What is it?" Darcy asked.

"Nothing." She ran her hand over the soft, luxurious cashmere sweater. It was far too nice for her.

"Stop dawdling," Laura admonished. "We've got a lot to accomplish today and no time to spare. That, and I worked us in at the Elizabeth Arden Spa for later this afternoon."

Millie's eyes flew to the door. *The Spa? Oh, God.* She swallowed.

"You did?" Darcy asked. "How'd you swing that?"

"I helped out the manager last year with a charity event she put on. She owed me."

Trying to put the afternoon's spa punish—er, *treat*ment, out of her mind, Millie put the sweater on and stepped out without a second glance in the mirror.

Darcy's hands flew to her mouth, and Millie wanted the floor to open up and swallow her. Just as she thought. She looked ridiculous.

Darcy overcame her shock. "Shut the front door!"

Laura stepped back, examined her like she would a bug under a microscope, walking in a circle around her. "You've got girls!"

"I've got what?"

She rolled her eyes on a heavy sigh. "Boobs. Tatas. Breasts. You've got breasts. Who knew! But something's missing. Wait here."

"Oh, Millie," Darcy said. "Shame on you."

Millie could feel the sting of tears behind her eyes.

"For hiding that gorgeous body all this time."

Millie's gaze snapped to Darcy's face. "What?"

"Look at you!" Darcy spun Millie around to face the mirror. "You rock!"

Millie examined the woman in the mirror and didn't recognize her. The slim-fitting pants accentuated a narrow waist and skimmed over gently curving hips. The red sweater fit her torso and showed off her breasts, or her 'girls,' as Laura had called them. She ran her hands down her ribs and along her hips.

Reaching up, Darcy took the pins from her hair. "I've wanted to do this for forever." She shook out Millie's hair and tossed it around her shoulders. "Wow. Red is definitely your special sauce."

"My special what?"

"You know, your color. It looks amazing on you."

"Try these," Laura said, as she shoved a pair of high-heeled ankle boots at her before really looking at her. "Whoa! Who knew you had so much beautiful hair?"

Millie eyed the shoes, which to her mind were sky high. "I can't wear those. I'll break my neck."

"Pfft. Yes, you can. We'll teach you. Now put them on," Laura ordered with a wave of her hand.

Millie acquiesced and stood watching Laura and Darcy.

"Well don't look at us, look at the mirror," Laura said, indicating that she should turn around.

Feeling as if she'd go over like a felled tree any minute, Millie cautiously teetered on the heels as she turned toward the mirror.

She didn't know what to say when she regarded her reflection.

"Boom!" Laura said.

———

Ian had made up his mind to meet Millie, to take back what he'd said. To apologize. He knew some groveling would be in order, and that was fine, too.

He'd been calling her the last two days but she wasn't answering and didn't have voice mail. Either she knew it was him calling and refused to answer, or she'd moved. He'd stand outside her apartment in the cold if that's what it took, but he'd talk to her one way or another.

Thoughts of her were making it very difficult to leave. He'd begun to have second thoughts about a long-distance relationship being doomed from the start. Maybe it could work. But even if it didn't, he wanted–no, he needed–to make amends.

For now, he grabbed his jacket, his backpack, and his keys to head over to meet with Josh about another surprise for Darcy.

———

After hours being buffed, polished, waxed, and scrubbed, her face exfoliated, steamed, and moisturized, and her hair slathered with goop, cut, color-rinsed, shampooed and blown out, Millie couldn't imagine a more exhausting day. Whoever said the spa was relaxing needed therapy.

"That was wonderful," Darcy said as they got dressed for the return trip home.

"Put on those black slacks, red sweater, and black ankle boots," Laura instructed as she plundered through the bags of clothes they'd purchased. And not a single item in brown. "And don't forget the red lace panties and bra."

Millie had spent a fair portion of her nest egg today. Now she was second-guessing the extravagance. What had she been thinking? And really, what difference would it make in her life? She'd always be Mousey Millie, butt of jokes, despite her attempts at invisibility.

Laura and Darcy had instructed the spa staff not to let her see the final product, so when she stepped out of the dressing room, she had no idea what to expect, except to see the same old Mousey Millie but with new clothes. The collective gasp from Laura and Darcy said it all. She looked ridiculous. Like the clown the Mean Girls had called her in high school.

"Oh, Millie." Darcy had tears in her eyes. "You look . . ."

*Here it comes.*

"Beautiful."

"What?"

"What is it with you and mirrors? You a vampire or something? Turn around. See for yourself," Laura instructed.

Millie stepped in front of the mirror. And couldn't believe what she saw. Her hair shined like satin, and had been cut in long, soft layers, creating an ocean of mink waves around her. Her eyes appeared . . . big, warm, and luminous. And her mouth. Her lips gleamed with a reddish tint. She fairly glowed.

She thought she'd resemble a clown with all the makeup, instead she looked like herself, only way better. She could still see Millie underneath it all. Millie, but prettier.

She opened her mouth to speak, but nothing came out. Words couldn't express what she felt at that moment.

"I know, girlfriend." Darcy leaned in, hugged her shoulders. "I know."

———

As Ian folded the drawings for a rocking chair—Josh's baby present for Darcy and one of his last loose ends—the front door opened, and Josh and Nathan snapped to attention like they'd just been caught cheating on their wives.

"Josh? The victorious have returned," Darcy called.

Josh nodded at Ian, and Ian tucked the drawings into his backpack.

Darcy rounded the corner, arms loaded with shopping bags, followed by Laura, the snarky one. Their men greeted them like they'd returned from a ten-day trip, rather than just a one-day shopping spree. Ian felt a tug of something akin to envy at the warm welcome.

"Ian? What are you doing here?" Darcy asked.

"Oh, estate stuff," Josh muttered.

"I'm so sorry about Ruby," Darcy continued. "You doing okay?"

"I'm getting there."

"I didn't think you were buying any more clothes until after the baby was born," Josh said, eyeing the bags.

"Oh, these aren't mine," Darcy explained.

"Well then, whose are they?" Nathan asked in confusion.

Laura turned to the door. "Millie?"

*Millie?* Ian felt like he'd just been kicked in the teeth. He hadn't expected to see her today.

There was a moment of silence, then a woman stepped into the doorway. And Ian almost swallowed his tongue.

Dressed in slim black pants, a red sweater that contrasted with rich chestnut brown hair flowing across her shoulders, and heels (heels!), Millie knocked his socks off. He knew, intimately, what a beautiful body she had, and a part of him liked being the only one who knew. But seeing her dressed in clothes that fit—clothes that weren't brown, well, he was speechless. And the red sweater made her skin glow and her hair shine.

Nathan and Josh had a similar reaction, only they voiced theirs.

"Holy shit!" Josh exclaimed.

"Sweet Jesus," Nathan muttered.

"I know, right?" Laura said, blowing on her nails and then polishing them against her jacket lapels. "My work here is done."

"Amazing, huh?" Darcy said as she pulled Millie further into the room.

Ian noticed the blush in her cheeks, the way she chewed on her lower lip. Uncomfortable with the attention. And he wondered why she'd done it? Had Laura and Darcy talked her into it? Did she think she *had* to do it? Did she think *that's* why he'd broken it off with her? The last thought triggered an ache in his chest. He hated the thought of Millie's insecurities getting the better of her.

"You look fantastic, Millie. This calls for a toast," Josh said as he headed toward the kitchen.

Nathan, Laura, and Darcy followed, leaving him alone with Millie. An awkward silence descended.

She gazed at him, clearly waiting for his reaction. If only he could untie the knot in his tongue to say something. Her hands went self-consciously to her hair, and doubt clouded her eyes before she cautiously turned to leave the room.

———

"Millie. Wait."

She froze, but didn't look back at him. What was he doing here? Just when she thought she could get through a day without a painful memory, here he stood, bringing all her emotions to the surface.

"Do you need a ride home? I drove my truck tonight."

"Millie! Ian! Come join us," Josh called from the kitchen.

Without answering, Millie tottered toward the back of the house, still getting used to the heels. She sensed more than saw Ian follow her. Why would he offer to take her home?

After a round of toasts, champagne for the non-child-bearing in the group, sparkling cider for Darcy, Millie relaxed a little. She'd been pleasantly surprised by Josh's and Nathan's reactions. But then again, they were nice guys. They'd tell her she looked nice if she'd worn a flour sack, if only for politeness' sake.

Ian's reaction, however, hurt. Nothing. His reaction had been to say nothing. She reminded herself that she hadn't done this for him. She'd done it for herself. And she wasn't going to apologize for it. And why should she care what he thought? Lifting her chin, she took another sip of her champagne, and caught him staring at her over the rim of his glass.

Laura offered to pour her another glass, then thought better of it. "Better not. As I recall, you're a cheap date. And you like to drunk dial . . . people," she finished at Millie's glare.

Ian polished off his glass and set it on the counter. "Well, thanks for the champagne, but I'd better head out. I'll take Millie and all her loot home. Millie, you ready?"

She frowned. She hadn't said she'd go with him. But then she didn't want to take the subway with all her bags. "Yes."

Darcy drew Millie in for a hug, shifting slightly sideways to make room for her belly. "You look beautiful. Now own it." Then Darcy held her at arm's length and gazed into her eyes as if to ask, 'Are you okay with Ian?'

Millie nodded.

Laura stepped up to her, gave her a once-over. "Damn! I do good work."

Nathan and Josh bussed her cheek. "You really do look amazing," Josh whispered in her ear.

Warmed by the kind words and champagne, Millie put on her new black wool and leather-trimmed coat and gathered up her bags.

"Here, let me help you." Ian took the bags from her hands and a jolt shot through her when they made contact. Clearly he'd felt it too, because his eyes flew to her face and lingered there.

*Gatsby and Daisy!*

He placed his hand at the small of her back and followed her out into the cold, clear night.

# CHAPTER TWENTY-NINE

I an flicked on the seat heaters and cranked up the heat, before heading toward 4th Street. Painfully aware that he'd yet to comment on Millie's transformation, he took her hand, felt her gaze in his direction before she pulled her hand away.

Right. Groveling first. But not while he had to concentrate on driving. She deserved his full attention while he begged for forgiveness.

A quiet thirty minutes later, he parked in front of her building.

"Well, thanks for the ride. I can take it from here." Millie reached for the door handle.

Ian grabbed her wrist. "Wait."

"For what, Ian? What am I waiting for?" Anger, frustration, and hurt colored her voice.

"This." He snagged her around the waist and hauled her across his lap.

She released a startled squeak but didn't budge. His motor revved at the hitch in her breathing. Inside the dark, now-warm cab, he cupped her face and felt himself go hard when she bit that plump bottom lip. Her nervous tell. Her eyes traveled to his mouth and held. Transfixed, he grazed a thumb over her lower lip, then followed it with his tongue.

A low throaty moan escaped and she melted into him, her mouth open to his. God, she was sweet. Sexy. Innocent. Willing. Pressing his lips to the corner of her mouth, he inhaled a new scent. Something light. Illusive. Floral. It suited her. He continued to rain kisses along her jaw to the sweet spot beneath her ear and felt her shiver.

He wanted her in the worst way. And not in the cab of his truck. But first things first. He drew back, waited for her to open her eyes. Eyes that no longer hid behind heavy brown-rimmed glasses. Eyes glazed with desire. "Millie. I'd like to come up."

Holding his gaze, she waited a beat as if deciding, then she asked, "What for?"

"Anything you'd like."

Withdrawing, she said, "I don't think that's a good idea."

"I need to talk to you. Please."

She captured her lip between her teeth again. "Fine." She poked him in the chest. "But only to talk."

---

The minute Millie closed the door to her apartment, Ian took the bags from her and dropped them to the floor. Noticing the other bags by the door he lifted a brow.

"My old clothes. They're going to charity."

He nodded, then surprised her when he pressed her against the door, all six-foot-two inches of him, his hands braced on either side of her head, caging her in. Her pulse kicked up a notch or two hundred.

"Before I tell you how amazing you look, I need to know

why. Is this something you let Laura and Darcy talk you into?"

"You think I look amazing?" Millie whispered, her chest too tight to do anything more.

"Jesus, Millie! Who wouldn't think that? But I need to know why."

"I can't think when you're pressed up against me like that." She placed her hands against his chest and he backed away. Pacing over to her windows, she pulled the blinds closed. Still not looking at him, she asked, "Why do you think you deserve to know?"

"You're right. I probably don't. But, please tell me you didn't do this for anyone but yourself."

"I wanted this. I added it to my list, and I asked Darcy and Laura to help me."

"Okay. But why?" Ian pressed.

"I'm tired of living in the shadows. Of being invisible."

"You weren't invisible to me," he said, his voice soft, touching her in places she didn't want to be touched. Not now. Not by him.

She spun to face him and nearly did a face-plant in her heels. "Really, Ian? Because that night in your loft, when you said we were *wrong*, it sure felt like I was invisible."

"I didn't mean *we* were wrong. I meant . . . God, Millie, I don't know what I meant." He approached her and she held her ground. Placing his hands on her shoulders, the heat of him filled her senses. "I was angry. Frustrated. It had been one hell of a day." He paused, gazing into her eyes. "Millie, you're the one thing in my life these last two months that's been right. Until I fucked it up."

"I don't understand." She tamped down the glimmer of hope his words sparked in her.

"I got scared. I've never felt this way about a woman. I

didn't know what to do. How to handle it. I thought I was doing the right thing, but I pushed you away when I should have been holding you close, and I hurt you terribly. Can you forgive me?"

His face solemn, he gazed into her eyes, as they filled and her vision blurred. Blinking, she felt a tear slip down her cheek. He lifted his hands to her face, brushing the tear away with his thumb, waiting patiently for her answer.

She considered his apology. She knew she couldn't take that kind of rejection again. She wouldn't. This was the new and improved Millie. The strong and bold Millie. "Before I answer, I need to know when you're leaving."

"In two weeks." A pain looked skittered across his face and then disappeared.

She nodded. "Okay." She needed to prepare herself. "I forgive you."

He released a breath and tugged her into his embrace. "Thank you." He brushed his lips to her temple. "And you really do look amazing, but then I thought you were beautiful before."

Millie withdrew and gazed up into his eyes. *Throw caution to the wind,* her body told her. *But he's leaving,* her brain reminded her. *He's already broken your heart,* her traitorous body argued, *what more could he do?* Her body won that argument. "Is this the part where we have make-up sex?"

"I thought you'd never ask."

"Go sit down." She pointed to the loveseat.

He lifted a brow, but did as he was told.

Taking a deep breath, she presented her back to him and lifting the hem of the sweater, peeled it off, turning with what she hoped was a flirtatious smile, and tossed it in his direction.

He caught it in one hand, an expression of surprise and lust on his face.

Kicking off her shoes, hoping to avoid going over like a felled tree, she shimmied out of her pants next and glanced over the shoulder to see his mouth hanging open.

"Sweet Jesus."

Spinning to stand before his hot gaze in nothing but the red lace panties and bra Laura made her buy, she felt anything but invisible. She felt . . . emboldened.

———

"**C**ome here, woman." Ho-ly hell, but she looked hot! The red lace cups barely concealed her breasts, and the panties! She may as well have had nothing on. But he wasn't complaining. Hell no.

He spread his legs and drew her in-between, pressing his face between her breasts, breathing her in. Gripping her hips, he spun her around.

"What's this?" Ian's hand swept up her curving backside to her sacrum. Tattooed in script was:

*A WELL-READ WOMAN IS A DANGEROUS CREATURE.*

"The tattoo I told you I wanted."

"Tell me you didn't go to Dangerous Ink," he growled.

"Okay, I won't tell you. But I did."

"Jesus, Millie. Why?" He pulled her around to face him again.

"Because I wanted a tattoo and you weren't around."

Ian closed his eyes against the pain. "Okay. It's done. Don't go back there again."

"No chance of that. One tattoo is enough for me. I couldn't sleep on my back for a week after I got it." She shrugged. "But I have no regrets." She twisted to admire her own backside. "I love it."

His hand brushed across the ink. "Me, too. It suits you. And it's sexy. You're sexy, Millie." Clasping her neck, he took her mouth, tasting her, drinking her in like a man who'd just crossed the Sahara. God, how he'd missed her.

Tongues tangled and teased, hands roamed and groped, both making up for lost time.

When they'd both been reduced to panting, writhing maniacs, he rose from the loveseat and took her hand. Her hair was wild from his fingers, her lips wet and swollen, her eyes glazed with desire. "I'm going to make sweet, hot love to you, Millie Stephens, but before I do, any requests?"

Biting her lip, she thought for a moment, then grinned. "How about the Kneel?"

"Sweet Jesus."

———

"There's something about me you don't know," Ian said, his voice tight. They lay face-to-face, limbs entwined, sated for the moment, although he didn't think he'd ever get enough of her. What would he do without her in England?

*You're leaving, asshat, remember?*

Even so, she'd forgiven him, and she deserved to know the truth about him. All of it.

"If you're a hundred-year old-vampire, I don't want to know," Millie quipped.

He laughed, then took a deep breath. "No, I have a juvie record."

She drew back, a look of surprise on her face. "Okay. Didn't expect that. So . . . what? Vandalism? Criminal mischief?"

"Assault and battery."

"Oh." Millie was silent a moment. "What happened?"

"I was seventeen when I was working on a construction job in the Upper Eastside. I'd just finished my lunch break when I saw a couple walking down the street. They were well-dressed, in their element. They started arguing, and when the man tried to grab the woman's arm, she yanked it away from him. He grabbed her and shoved her into an alleyway. She almost fell, but managed to right herself.

"I walked over and peered into the alley. He had her up against the wall, and let's just say she didn't appear to be enjoying his rough treatment. When he slapped her across the face, I'd seen enough. I grabbed the guy's shoulder to get him away from her and he turned and swung at me. I ducked, but then I hit him in the chin with an uppercut. He staggered back into the wall, hitting his head."

"Oh, God," Millie whispered.

"She screamed and went to *his* aid. Go figure." Ian paused, remembering the frustration. And fear. "He pressed charges, saying I'd attacked him and his girlfriend when they'd ducked into the alley for a little grope session. Even said I'd slapped his girlfriend when she'd refused to perform a sex act on me. Turned out he had the money and the lawyers to press the case."

"But what about the woman? Didn't she testify against him?"

Ian leveled her with a look. "What do you think?"

Millie sighed. "She took his side."

"Good guess."

"So what happened?"

"Curtis hired a lawyer and I pled to a lesser charge."

Millie gasped. "You pled guilty?"

"With their money-backed word against that of a seventeen-year-old construction worker, the lawyer thought it best. I served six months' probation, did another six months community service. And the lawyer had my record sealed, otherwise, I could forget my chances for a contractor's license. So your initial impression of me as a thug was right."

Millie drew back. "Gloria."

He nodded.

"Cheese and crackers. Gloria spoke out of turn," she muttered.

Ian snorted. "Cheese and crackers?"

"What? You've never heard that before?"

He laughed. "No." He stared at Millie, a smile on his face.

"What?"

"You're adorable." He kissed her nose, and she blushed. Even with the 'new and improved' Millie, he hoped she never lost the tendency to blush. Then he grew serious again. "I just thought you should know your first impression was correct."

"Ian, you did what you thought was right by defending that woman, even as ungrateful as she proved to be. I wouldn't call that a thug. I'd call that a hero. Just like all those times you saved me. And Darcy."

"I'm no hero," he murmured, uncomfortable with that label.

"I'd bet Ruby would beg to differ."

"Ruby had no illusions as to what I was." One down. One more confession to go. He wanted Millie to know who he was through and through.

"There's one more thing."

"You're not a serial killer, are you?"

Ian snorted. "No. But I am dyslexic." There. He'd said it. Out loud.

"I know."

He pulled back, thinking he hadn't heard her correctly. "Wait. What?"

"I know you're dyslexic."

"Did Ruby tell you?"

"No. She didn't have to." She studied his face.

"Then how?"

"I suspected." She lifted a shoulder. "You listen to audiobooks, yet you also had the books in your backpack. The two times we went to a restaurant, you didn't order from the menu. You use text to voice on your phone, and you have Dragon Speak software for your computer."

He lifted a questioning brow.

She shrugged. "I saw the software box on your shelf. But it wasn't until I asked you to read the questions from the RFP and that day at Ruby's that I knew for sure."

"Well, I'll be damned," he muttered. She'd known all this time. "And what do you think about that?"

"What do I think about you being dyslexic?" She held his gaze, licked her lips. "I'm sure it wasn't easy growing up dyslexic, especially in school. Being . . . different is tough at any age, but especially in middle and high school. It couldn't have been easy for you."

"But?"

"But, Ian, look at you." She cupped his face. "You're a successful businessman. You do beautiful work, you genuinely love and care about what you do. You should be proud."

"You still haven't answered my question. What do you think about my dyslexia?"

She sat up and looked down at him, her hair falling like

a curtain around them. "Do you honestly believe I would think less of you because of it?"

"It's just that you're so smart—"

She pressed a finger to his lips. "Don't even go there. Your reading disorder has nothing to do with your intelligence. Our discussions of Kant and Descartes, or music and poetry, have been some of the most stimulating conversations I've had in a very long time."

He sucked her finger into his mouth. Watched her eyes go from the heat of anger to the simmer of desire.

She tugged her finger free. "Don't. I'm not finished. Just because you're intelligent doesn't mean you aren't dumb."

Sounded a lot like Caleb's lecture.

"You didn't get selected for the RFP. Not because you aren't capable of doing the work, but clearly you're not capable of asking for help."

Own up to it. "Yes."

"Oh, Ian. I would have helped you."

He wouldn't get angry and defensive over the offer of help. Her offer, and his acceptance, of her help was the single factor that landed him the Hawkins Hall job. But, he couldn't help but remind her. "For sex."

She turned a lovely shade of pink. "Oh. Well. That."

"If I'd known sex with you would be so mind blowing, I would have jumped at the deal."

"You think sex with me is . . . mind-blowing?"

"I think sex with you is seismic. But I think making love to you is earth-shattering." He lifted his hand to cup her face. "Here, let me refresh your memory." Claiming her mouth with his, his heart felt lighter, yet more full than he'd ever thought possible.

Skimming his hand along her backside, he remembered

her tattoo. "So, you checked the tattoo off your list. What else is left?"

Millie considered telling him the latest item on her GALL, but chickened out. She went with another secret item instead. "Well, I already checked another item off my list. I finished writing a novel."

Ian stared open-mouthed so long, she squirmed in discomfort.

"Seriously?"

She responded with a tentative nod.

"That's . . . that's amazing!" He hauled her in, giving her a big hug, then kissed her with an audible smack. "What's it about?"

Feeling a little shy, she delivered her elevator pitch.

"I don't even know what to say, except congratulations. I'm so proud of you."

A flush of pleasure heated her cheeks. Then he proceeded to show her just how proud of her he was.

# CHAPTER THIRTY

The next morning, Ian's pressed a kiss to her mouth. "I've got to run. I have a to-do list that would give you a run for your money." She smiled at his joke, but her heart throbbed slow and heavy in her chest.

They'd avoided the elephant in the room for the remainder of the night. He didn't beg her to wait for him, or better yet, to come to England with him. And she didn't ask. But they'd created memories she would hold close to her heart forever. And she'd enjoy his company until he left, but she'd made up her mind about one thing. She couldn't say goodbye to him again.

"I'll call you later," he said as he opened the door.

"Ian?" He looked back at her. "Do me a favor?"

"Anything."

"Don't tell me what day you're leaving. Just go." Tears blurred her vision.

"Millie—"

"Promise me." A tear spilled over and ran down her cheek.

Ian nodded and quietly closed the door behind him.

———

A few days later, Ian sat outside a coffee shop, an Italian roast in his hand, waiting for Caleb. He couldn't get the vision of Millie asking him to leave without saying goodbye out of his head. He'd promised her. But it was a promise he could no longer keep. Things had changed. *He'd* changed.

The last few days had been busy, but the nights had been spent with Millie. She'd given him everything, but he could see the hurt and confusion in her eyes. Hurt and confusion he hoped to erase.

A chair scraped behind Ian and he turned to see Caleb swing the chair up to the table and plop down.

"So, what's this favor?"

Ian had called Caleb the night before asking him to meet up. Now that Caleb was here, he didn't know where to start. "Since you have experience in the area, I need you to help me pick out an engagement ring."

Caleb sat back in his chair. "I'm sorry, I don't think I heard you right. Did you just say engagement ring?"

"That's what I said."

"For who?"

"For me. Well, for me to give to Millie, you know, when I ask her to marry me."

A look of utter confusion settled on Caleb's face. "Millie? You mean the woman dressed in all brown that I met at the Park Slope job? The one who helped you with the Hawkins Hall RFP?"

"Yes."

The furrow in his brow deepened. "So, she needs a green card, health insurance, what?" He sat forward. "Is she knocked up? Tell me you're not the baby-daddy."

Ian's blood pressure rose at the implications of Caleb's disbelief. Taking a deep calming breath, he admitted he couldn't blame him. Caleb knew nothing about his relationship with Millie. Another guilty secret he'd kept from his friend. "No, on all three accounts." Where to start. "I'm in love with her."

Caleb sat back again, as his breath left in a rush. He scrubbed his hand over his face, then regarded Ian. "Since when?"

Good question. Maybe since the day she'd stood awkwardly outside the bedroom at Darcy's in her full-body brown and thanked him for saving her life. "A while."

"Explain, please." He grabbed Ian's coffee cup, took a swig, then made a face. "Blech. How do you drink that shit black?"

Ian told his best friend the whole story as Caleb sat silent and in shock for the entire half hour. Ian finished with, "I want to spend the rest of my life with her."

Caleb eyed Ian as if he'd morphed into the Stay Puft Marshmallow Man. "Well, smack my ass and call me Sally."

———

Forty minutes later, Ian and Caleb climbed the subway stairs to the busy street above.

"Tell me again why we're going to a law office in the Financial District to buy an engagement ring?" Caleb asked as he closed the zipper on his jacket against the biting wind. "You getting a prenup to protect the vast fortune you've amassed?"

"Funny." Hanging a right, they walked stride for stride. "You remember Josh from the Park Slope job?"

"Yeah. The lawyer."

"He's got a contact in the jewelry business, and he's meeting us at Josh's office."

After an hour of poring over rings, Caleb, heaved a heavy sigh. "Dude, it didn't take this long to build Rome. Pick something before she's too old to marry you."

Ian clapped his hands on his thighs. "I'm sorry to have wasted your time, Mr. Workman." It wasn't the money—well, within reason anyway—it was that everything he'd seen had been too . . . fancy for Millie. She needed something pretty, not flashy. Something a respectable size, not the Hope Diamond.

"I do have something I acquired from an estate last week, but I haven't had a chance to appraise it yet. A vintage Victorian, platinum setting, one carat, with a matching band." As he spoke, he opened a drawer in the bottom of the jewel case and lifted a pair of rings from the slotted blue velvet and laid them in the black velvet viewing tray.

Delicate filigree formed a beautiful setting for a one-carat round diamond. The same filigree encircled the band, highlighting six smaller diamonds.

Ian lifted the rings, and they winked in the sunlight streaming through the window. "Perfect."

———

Darcy had insisted on throwing Millie a birthday party. Since Millie wasn't exactly a party girl, she couldn't say she was thrilled.

"You only turn thirty once. Besides, it will give you a chance to show off your new look," Darcy had said.

So Millie stood, clothes strewn about the bed, trying to

decide what to wear. Hoping to get lucky later, she'd already chosen a black lace bra and matching panties.

Putting Ian's impending departure out of her mind, she selected a little black dress, or LBD, as Laura had called it. Slipping the simple, swingy dress over her head, she had to give Laura credit—much as it pained her—but she really knew her style. The dress whispered down Millie's body, stopping just above the knee.

Clean, simple lines, a scoop neck, and long sleeves worked well for Millie. Nothing to fidget with. Nothing she could get wrong. Walking over to the cubby, which frankly was no longer big enough, she stepped into a pair a black pumps with a reasonable heel. Kitten, her fashion guru had called them.

Checking her appearance in the bathroom mirror, she liked what she saw. She'd finger-dried her hair so that it hung in soft waves down her back. She'd even managed a little mascara, blush, and lip gloss. Not as 'made up' as she'd been after her spa torture, but pretty.

*Pretty*. Now there was a word she never expected to apply to herself. While she'd never be beautiful, notwithstanding Ian's effusive comments to the contrary, pretty worked. Mousey Millie was no more.

She dashed down the stairs and out the door to see Ian standing beside his truck, arms crossed over his broad chest, looking so sexy she could hardly believe she'd spent every night that week in his bed. He wore black slacks and a light blue shirt. Other than Ruby's memorial service, she'd never seen him so dressed up. His casual stance quickly turned defensive.

"Hey, Millie! Lookin' good."

She spun to see Kenny, Cole, and Jesse standing on the corner, skateboards in their arms. "Hi, guys! Thanks!"

She approached Ian, took one look at his face, and asked, "What?"

He beamed, shook his head, and said, "You never cease to amaze me."

She drew back in surprise. "Why?"

"You've come so far, and I've enjoyed watching you grow, step out of yourself. You took charge of your life. You accomplished so many things on your list. You obviously not only tamed those punks, but you clearly earned their respect." He kissed her on the mouth. "I'm so proud of you."

———

"What's with Laura and Josh?" Ian asked as he wrapped his arm around Millie's waist and handed her a glass of champagne. "Don't they get along?"

When they'd greeted one another, they'd called each other villain names Ian had remembered from his comic book days when the pictures helped him figure out the scenes.

Taking a sip of the champagne, she said, "Thus has it always been, and thus shall it ever be."

Darcy approached, ending the topic of conversation. "Millie, you look amazing!"

True that. When she'd walked out of her building to meet him, he'd practically swallowed his tongue. The dress she wore swung at her hips, showing off her shapely legs, and fitting the delicate curves of her body. And that hair. He'd wanted to fist his hands in it and drag her mouth to his. Later, he'd promised himself. And if everything went as planned they'd have something else to celebrate besides Millie's birthday.

Then there was how she'd handled herself with those

punks. His heart nearly burst with pride. On the way over, she'd explained how she'd befriended the three erstwhile bullies. Millie had blossomed right in front of his eyes. And she dazzled.

Darcy took Millie over to a woman he believed was Darcy's mother. Silver gypsy hair hung down her back, and the long skirt she wore couldn't hide a youthful body.

"So, what happened to Millie the Brown?" Caleb clapped him on his back, his gaze on Millie's back. "You've been holding out on me. Again."

Ian's face broke into a big smile. A dopey one he'd be willing to bet. One similar to the one he'd often seen on Caleb's face when he talked about Jillie. "Yeah. But here's the thing. She's even more beautiful on the inside."

"Spoken like a man in love," Caleb replied just before taking a pull from his beer. "When's the big 'event?'" Caleb managed to make air quotes with his fingers without spilling a drop of his beer.

"When the time is right."

"Well, don't leave us hanging, dude." He wandered off, in search of Jillie, no doubt.

The brownstone was filled with Darcy's family. Laughter and good-natured ribbing seemed the rule of the day. Must have been something growing up in such a close-knit family. He'd take special care to ensure that he and Millie would have that kind of relationship with their kids.

*Getting ahead of yourself there, Brand.* She hasn't said yes, yet. And, come to think of it, he didn't even know if she loved him.

Laura and her husband Nathan stood talking to Darcy's father, and Josh held a little girl in his arms while another one clung to his leg, as he spoke to Darcy's brother. Wouldn't be long before Josh held his own child in his arms.

Millie's parents weren't there. Not that she'd been surprised. They were in England doing research on their latest obsession, a letter they'd unearthed in a private collection that had recently been donated to the Bodleain Library.

His eyes drifted back to Millie and followed her as she headed toward her office. There was no time like the present to start his new life with the woman he loved.

———

M illie needed a moment. The champagne had gone to her head, and the press of people became too much. Her office provided a little peace.

"I'll take that," Ian said as he slipped the half-empty glass from her hand and set it on the desk. "Come with me." Taking her hand he led her into the hallway and up the stairs.

"Where are we going?"

"You look like you could use some quiet."

When they reached the top of the stairs, he pulled her into the nursery and pushed the door to before enveloping her in an embrace.

"Ian?"

"Shh. Let's enjoy the solitude a moment."

She took a deep, calming breath and relaxed into his hard chest, enjoying the feel of his arms around her. His heart beat a steady rhythm beneath her ear, and the stress of all the unaccustomed attention melted away.

"Ian, I have one more thing on my list."

"Oh yeah? What's that?"

Pushing back, she looked into his eyes. She'd miss those gray eyes, the way they sparkled when he smiled, the heat in them after he'd just kissed her senseless, and the contentment after a mutually satisfying round of lovemaking.

She took a deep breath and gazed into his eyes. "Tell Ian I love him."

His eyes went warm and wide, as he stood silent.

Well, that went over like a lead balloon. And that same balloon settled in the pit of her stomach.

He withdrew, his hands on her shoulders.

Confused, she added, "It's okay if you . . . don't." She shook her head, tears filling her throat. "Ian? What?" She had a funny feeling in her stomach, like butterflies were riding a roller coaster.

Ian sank to his knee, her hands in his, as he gazed up into her face. "I love you, too, Millie. Marry me. Discuss Kant and Descartes with me for the rest of our lives. Come to England with me. Have my babies." He squeezed her hands. "Grow old with me."

*Emma and Knightley!*

Releasing her right hand, he reached into his pocket. "If you'll have me, this is for you." He opened the lid of a black velvet box and her free hand flew to her mouth, as tears filled her eyes. "I—" She couldn't breathe. *Oh God, please don't let me faint and miss this moment.* "Oh, Ian," she gasped. "I don't know what to say."

"I believe the customary response is, yes."

They both turned to see Gloria standing outside the door, her usual gin and tonic lifted in a toast.

Millie returned her gaze to Ian's. "Yes. Yes."

Winter had finally loosened its icy grip on the northeast, and while it wasn't yet officially spring by the calendar, someone forgot to tell that to the daffodils and crocuses, the tulips and the hyacinths.

Darcy fluffed the spring green chiffon of her matron of honor's gown before picking up her bouquet. "Are you ready? We've got to get this show on the road before I have to feed Emma again." Following in her mother's footsteps, Darcy had named her little girl Emma, after her favorite Austen character. Josh went along, already wrapped around the baby's finger.

Millie had angst over the decision to go to England, abandoning Darcy. But Darcy wouldn't hear it. She'd decided to take a year off and devote herself to Emma.

Earlier that morning Millie had added 'live in England' and 'stalk the Bodleian Library' to her list. She'd also scratched out 'Find contentment' and replaced it with 'Find happiness.' Then she'd checked that off her list as well.

Millie pressed a hand to her stomach to calm the butterflies. The fear had nothing to do with marrying Ian, and everything to do with walking down the aisle, the center of attention.

It would be a small quiet ceremony with just friends and family in Darcy's tidy backyard, but even so.

"You'll be fine. You look radiant!"

It took some wrangling, but Millie had finally talked Laura and Darcy out of the formal wedding gown and into something more sedate. Something she'd be less likely to trip over.

The ivory organza dress had a sheer bodice overlaying a satin slip, and long sheer sleeves, a jewel neckline, and full skirt. Underneath, the satin shimmered. No veil, no train. In a compromise with Laura, she wore ivory satin kitten heels with just a touch of beading across the toe.

Darcy had piled her hair on top of her head, letting tendrils brush her face and neck. The only jewelry, a pair of pearl earrings from Darcy—her something new—a pearl choker from Laura—her something borrowed and old. For her something blue, she wore a traditional blue garter on her left leg.

Josh waited downstairs to walk her down the aisle. Her parents couldn't break themselves away from an international conference on Thomas Hardy, where they were presenting their findings.

But their absence no longer had the hurtful affect it used to. She had her chosen family, and with a little luck, she and Ian would start their own.

"Let's go, ladies," Laura said as she stuck her head in the door. "Time's a-wasting." She eyed them both critically, then nodded. "Couldn't have done better myself."

Darcy handed her a bouquet of white roses tied with spring green ribbon, and Millie descended the stairs on wobbly legs.

Millie's one regret was that Ruby wasn't there to see Ian marry. She'd impacted their lives even after her death, leaving her entire estate to Ian, along with a life insurance policy, and in a surprising twist, her extensive book collection to Millie.

Ruby and her late husband had lived a modest lifestyle and managed to put away a substantial nest egg. The money would be invested and used to grow Ian's business, including the build-out of the remaining floors in the old warehouse where she now lived with Ian. Those apartments would provide a steady income for them and Caleb and Jillie.

Millie had received a request for a rewrite from Darcy's publisher, and Gloria had agreed to take her on as a client. In the meantime, she'd still happily worked as Darcy's personal assistant, albeit as a virtual assistant.

As she approached the French doors that opened onto the backyard, her gaze found Ian, standing in a simple black suit and blue tie, Caleb at his side as best man, and the butterflies that had plagued her all morning suddenly settled.

Caleb tapped Ian on the shoulder and directed his attention to the door where his bride now stood. The emotions racing through him nearly overwhelmed him.

Millie looked breathtaking. Radiant. Happy. She deserved it, and by God so did he. They'd both broken free of their old inhibitions to find happiness.

His bride-to-be filled his heart, challenged his mind, and replenished his soul. He could see the future–their future–when he looked into her beautiful brown eyes. A man couldn't ask for more than that.

Gloria sat in a ray of sunshine watching Millie and Ian as they exchanged vows. To Millie's left, stood Darcy.

Seated in front of Gloria sat Josh, holding their baby girl, who slumbered, oblivious to the quiet spectacle around her. Next to her Laura and Nathan clasped hands, cutting glances at one another, no doubt wondering when they would get their hands on one another again.

She did good work.

Three fairytales come true. Three happily-ever-afters. Whoever said dreams don't come true didn't know Jack. And they certainly didn't know Gloria.

On that cool, but sunny late-April day, Millie gazed into Ian's gray eyes, listening to him vow to love, honor and cherish her as long as they both shall live, and she checked off another item on her list: Marry the man I love.

# DREAMS OF PERFECTION
## EXCERPT FROM BOOK 1 OF THE DREAMS COME TRUE SERIES

Darcy Butler sat across the table from her blind date in a trendy new SoHo restaurant contemplating the fact that he was no Blake Garrett. Blake was . . . perfect. But why wouldn't he be? After all, she'd created him.

Listening with half an ear, she nodded at something he said. Her date was handsome, polite, successful, charming even. He had good taste in food, wine, and from the looks of his expensive suit, clothes as well. But the comparisons continued, and she found him lacking at every turn. Robert, or Russell, or something that started with an 'R' asked her a question.

She could hear her mother's well-deserved admonishment. He's buying you dinner. The least you can do is remember his name.

Focus, Darcy.

"What do you like to do with your free time?" He gazed into her eyes, clearly trying to make a connection.

"I love going to Yankees' games," she said, excited that the season started that week.

"Baseball? Really?"

"Yeah, do you like baseball?" Her excitement rose at the prospect of finding a fellow baseball lover. Provided, of course, his loyalties didn't run in the wrong direction.

"No. I find baseball boring. Too much standing around. I prefer boxing or hockey, something with a little action."

Okay—first—baseball boring? Her excitement fell in proportion to the rise in her blood pressure. Second, boxing? Hockey? Where guys beat the crap out of each other? Did she want to date a man with a proclivity for violence?

*All right, all right. Down, girl.* Maybe she could educate him on the subtleties of baseball, the beauty of a breaking ball, the rarity of a no-hitter, the excitement of a bottom-of-the-ninth-down-by-three-full-count-with-two-outs-and-bases-loaded game. Help him see the light.

"Do you like boxing or hockey?" he continued.

"No. Sorry. I don't."

The clatter of silverware against china, the clink of glasses, and the low hum of conversation from other diners did nothing to diminish the uncomfortable silence that descended. "So"—he cleared his throat—"Laura tells me you're a writer. What do you write, fiction, non-fiction? Murder mysteries? I love a good murder mystery."

He signaled to the waiter for another gin and tonic. His third so far, but who's counting.

"No, I write romance." Was that an eye roll?

"Seriously?" he asked, his highball glass poised halfway to his mouth.

That was definitely an eyebrow lift, and not the wow-that-intrigues-me sort of lift, but the you-can't-be-serious sort of lift. "Yes, really. I'm a New York Times and USA Today best-selling romance author," she said, with no small amount of pride in her voice. "In fact, my latest book, The Doctor's Dilemma, will be out in a few months."

"That's, um, great."

"You seem surprised, and not pleasantly." She tilted her head.

"Well, I mean," he stammered, "Laura said you had a B.A. in Creative Writing from Columbia, and, well, using it to write books about half-naked men and heaving bosoms seems . . . a waste." He made no further attempt to hide the disdain in his voice.

Her blood pressure soared, not to mention her temper. She set down her glass of Chardonnay so she could make her point without the risk of throwing the wine in his face, and propping her elbows on the table, leaned forward.

"Romance is serious business. Did you know that romantic fiction has the largest share of the U.S. consumer market? That romantic fiction generated over one billion, that's billion with a 'b,' dollars in sales last year? That almost seventy-five million people read at least one romantic novel a year? And that includes men."

He held up his hands in surrender. "Okay, okay. I get it. It's a money thing."

"No, it's not a money thing," she replied with a dash of snark. "I happen to love what I do. And so do my fans. All three hundred thousand of them." Wow, I really need to get a grip. She'd caught the unwelcome attention of neighboring diners.

Mr. R.—and 'R' didn't stand for 'Right'—glanced around as if seeking the closest exit. His phone rang—one of those sultry sax tones—and from the look on his face, he welcomed the interruption. Excusing himself from the table, he stepped outside to take the call.

Darcy snatched up her phone and texted Laura, the instigator of this blind-date-gone-wrong.

HE HATES BASEBALL. HOW COULD U?

Momentarily her phone buzzed.

How am I supposed to know he hates baseball? And who cares? He's cute! And rich.

Darcy dropped her phone into her purse as Mr. R. approached the table.

"I'm sorry, I've got to go. My sister's in labor. Twins." He gave Darcy a lame smile.

She couldn't tell if he was lying or not, but if he was, he got an 'A' for creativity. Either way, she didn't care. The evening couldn't end soon enough as far as she was concerned. "Well, congratulations."

Darcy stood as he tossed a hundred dollar bill down on the table. "This should take care of it. I'm really sorry. Good luck with your new book." And with that, he left.

Well, another one bites the dust. She sat back down with a sigh, before signaling the waiter. "I'll have a Grey Goose Cosmo, and the Ahi tuna salad, with the dressing on the side. Oh, and the melting chocolate cake for dessert." Since Mr. R. was buying, she might as well eat.

Rebecca Heflin is a bestselling, award-winning author who has dreamed of writing romantic fiction since she was fifteen and her older sister sneaked a copy of Kathleen Woodiwiss' Shanna to her and told her to read it.

Never quite sure what she wanted to be when she grew up, Rebecca didn't attend college until age 30, and earned her bachelor's in literature, before going on to complete her law degree.

Ever the late bloomer, Rebecca finally turned her attention to fulfilling her dream of writing, and published her first novel at age 48. When not passionately pursuing her dream, Rebecca is busy with her day-job at a major state university.

She and her husband are also co-founders of a non-profit organization, which raises money to help cancer patients and their families.

Rebecca's pen name is an abbreviated version of her great-great grandmother's name: Sarah Anne Rebecca Heflin

Apple Smith. Whew! And you wonder why she shortened it.

Rebecca writes women's fiction and contemporary romance, and she is a member of Romance Writers of America (RWA), Florida Romance Writers, RWA Contemporary Romance, and Florida Writers Association. Rebecca and her mountain-climbing husband live at sea level in sunny Florida.

Sign up for Rebecca's monthly newsletter, Rebecca's Readers, for all the latest news on upcoming releases, appearances, and contests.

www.ingramcontent.com/pod-product-compliance
Lightning Source LLC
Chambersburg PA
CBHW070624100726
47907CB00007B/1858